THE SHAMAN'S BLESSING

BY PATRICIA BARNETT

The Shaman's Blessing
Copyright © 2025 Pat Barnett

This is a work of fiction. Names, characters, places, and incidents are either the product of the author's imagination or used fictitiously. Any resemblance to actual persons, living or dead, events, or locales is purely coincidental.

This second edition incorporates revisions from the original version independently published in 2017.

First published in Great Britain in 2025
ISBN: 978-1-0684310-2-9
British Library Cataloguing in Publication Data.
A catalogue record for this book is available from the British Library.

Edited and designed by Dr Simon Robinson

Typeset in Eagle Lake, and Lora
Printed and bound by IngramSpark

For more information visit: www.wordbotherers.com

WORDBOTHERERS PRESS
SCARBOROUGH
MMXXV

'It has begun'—Fiedra

Purple Mountains
Plains
Forest of Whispers
Plains
Plains
Clan Settlement

SACRED GROVES
FISHING VILLAGE
GREAT LAKE
MYSTIC CAIRNS
SLUMS

Chapter One

lt was the *tinkle of tiny bells* wafting across the vastness of the plain that first alerted the youth. He swallowed down the fear grasping his throat and wiped the palms of his hands down his buckskin pants. It was his turn to guard the entrance to the settlement—and apart from the children and their minders inside the gathering house, he was alone.

On the plain's horizon, dust appeared to gather and swirl like sand devils around the skirts of the approaching women. Involuntarily, his mind warned: *Marsh Wives*, before reason assured him they could not possibly be of harm—besides, there were only two —and one was a small child.

As the females neared the gates, the youth could see the child was lame, making the rhythm of the bells around *her* ankles sound off-beat—creating discord with the perfect chimes of the old woman who accompanied her.

Invitingly, he opened a gate ready and waited for them to pass.

As the females moved by he could see that the layers of rags covering the old woman hid her true shape, and the high-pitched tinkle of her bells caused confusion in his mind. He had heard stories of Marsh Wives—told to him in hushed

voices by older cousins—and warned by sisters and aunts—never to allow one to embrace him for young men lost their innocence to these witches. He had heard that on the flowering of a fertility plant called the Mooncap, they rolled over the prickly petals to puncture their naked bodies with its erotic musky perfume.

Yet when the old woman spoke, her voice held music—not unlike that of the bells hidden in her skirts—music that belied the wrinkles on her face.

'We have travelled far, my lovely, and are in need of sweet water to drink and to bathe away the dust of the plains.'

The young man swallowed again and tried to sharpen his wits. He coughed and wiped another layer of sweat down his thin, deer-hide trousers. The woman's deep purple eyes bore into his soul—waiting for him to speak.

'Do not be troubled my lovely, we will find what we came for.' Keeping her eyes on his, she indicated with a sideways nod towards the central building—a huge circular construction with a reed-thatched roof. 'Be calm my lovely, I presume we will find Urdeth, the wife of your chief in that Roundhouse.'

In a trance, he watched them almost glide past; his ears ringing and tinkling—her voice echoing against his skull—like the sound of water trickling onto deep pools inside a huge cavern.

The sun was high, casting shadows around the feet of the strangers—both barefooted—both tinkling their bewitching melodies with every step. He caught glimpses of the old lady's ankles—and glints of the tiny bells that covered the silver bracelets around her legs.

The little girl turned her head back towards him and her smile broke the spell he was under. He smiled back—unaware he was now under *her* spell. She held her head high, and continued towards the Roundhouse, but now it was *her* lopsided, offbeat jingle that filled the hot, midday air.

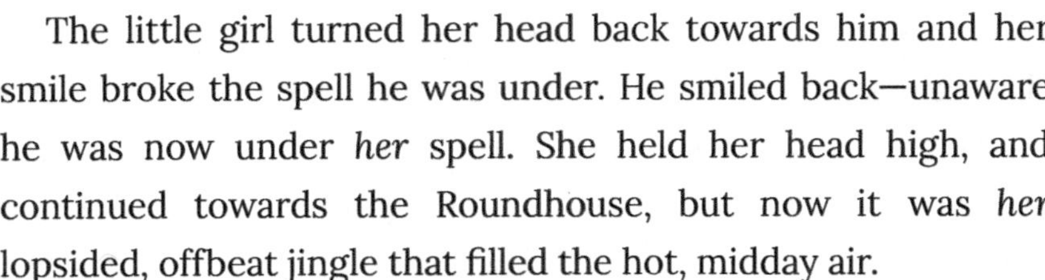

Inside the cool of the building, children ran and played games, some singing repetitive songs, whilst others drew pictures in the dust.

The tinkle of hidden bells paused their play, prompting them to look to the brightness of the Roundhouse's entrance, and to the silhouettes of an old woman and a little girl who they guessed to be no more than three summers old.

'Welcome,' Urdeth greeted whilst rising from the dirt floor, 'come into the shade and sit down. I will have the children fetch water—please, this way.' The Chief's wife gestured to a cluster of simple benches placed by the open hearth of an unlit fire.

Perak, daughter to Urdeth and also three summers old, emerged from the games she had been playing and ran towards the new child. She took hold of her hand, urging her to go with her. Before the old lady let the lame child free, she whispered assurances to trust the little girl. Wide-eyed and puzzled by the remark, she stared at the face of the crone for several heartbeats. Before long, a bluish-black blur moved across the corner of her eye and landed in the rafters of the

cone-shaped roof. Reassured, she gave the old lady a nod and allowed herself to be led to a courtyard at the rear of the building, where a sparkling stream fell like a miniature waterfall onto rocks to form a cluster of shallow, soothing pools.

'The water tastes good. Drink your fill. I am called Perak.'

The little girl chattered non-stop whilst the newcomer washed away the dust and drank scooped handfuls of water. Perak sat on a boulder dangling her feet into one of the pools and, when her new friend had quenched her thirst, she moved up to make room, 'Come, sit by me, the water is cool, what do they call you?'

'I am Fiedra.'

When they returned to the Roundhouse, Perak sensed something was wrong, she kept hold of Fiedra's hand and steered her to where her cousins sat cross-legged on the cool ground. 'What happened?' She asked Kira, an older girl with responsibility for keeping the children safe during their play.

'Your mama sent the old woman away,' She whispered, 'I think she is afraid of her.'

Perak bristled, 'Mama isn't afraid of anyone.'

'I tell you, the old lady was scaring her.'

Perak turned to Fiedra, 'Why should your grandmother wish to scare my mama?'

Fiedra turned her eyes up to the huge roof, scanning the beams supporting the thatch—searching for something. A raven ruffled its blue-black feathers—drawing her attention. She smiled and breathed easier. 'My companion,' She told Kira at last, 'isn't my grandmother; she is a Marsh Guide—a wise woman of the plateaus and the deserts. She navigates them and was given the task of bringing me here—so that I can be nurtured by the wife of your chief, Urdeth.'

Perak clapped her hands together, 'I knew it—we are to become friends. We will be the best of friends.'

Kira looked past the childish eyes of Perak to study those of the newcomer. There she saw the eyes of a girl who was physically similar in age to Perak, yet mentally older and a lot less trusting. Kira sensed this lame child had witnessed many things, none of which contained much fun.

Urdeth grabbed their attention when she stormed back into the gathering house. She was incandescent with rage, striding back and forth, hissing words, cursing the air beyond the entrance, making signs towards the plains and using language unknown to Kira.

The moment Urdeth strode past the group of children and into the courtyard, Kira got to her feet. 'Come, little ones,' she urged. 'You too,' she said as she grabbed Fiedra by the arm. 'Quickly now, it is time we played elsewhere.'

Chapter Two

The noise came from the direction of the mountains and was bounced through the crisp autumnal air down the valley and through the forest that lay on the edge of the Clan's settlement. It halted the children in their play—a mournful, terrible howl.

Wolves.

Mothers who were moments before gathering the last of the summer fruits looked back to where they had left their offspring—their collective sighs of relief audible when they caught sight of older siblings gathering the little ones close.

'She-wolf,' Urdeth, wife of their leader, whispered, 'something has taken or hurt her cub.'

'Wolves howl for other reasons, Urdeth; how can you be sure it is a she?'

Urdeth's eyes scanned the distant hills, their colour reflecting similar shades of amethyst. She held her head to one side, listening to sounds the others could not hear. 'I tell you, the howl is full of pain for a lost little one.' The fruit pickers heard the agony in Urdeth's words. They did not question the empathy their leader's wife felt for the she-wolf's loss. Losing a

child was Urdeth's burden, a loss she bore well—as well as any mother could, that was.

In silence, but adding haste, they continued to fill baskets, gathering the fruit they would need for the traditional arduous journey that lay ahead. This was the last of the pickings, the earlier fruit having been stowed in jars of honey, preserving it for later when the dark spell of winter would be at its worst.

Two boys came upon the party carrying the carcass of a fine beast. They bowed their heads to Urdeth, 'See what we caught, mother?' Urdeth dropped her berries into the nearby basket and examined the boy's kill with the eye of a worthy appraiser.

'A prize like this will make jealous enemies,' she warned.

'Not when they taste it.'

'Maybe not, but be cautious how you relate the chase, boasting is for fools.' In acknowledgement to her wise words, they lowered their eyes and continued along the beaten path.

'You are harsh with them, Urdeth.'

'I know, but these two boys are all I have left of the six sons I gave life to.'

'You have Perak.'

'Yes, but the curse was not put on Perak.'

She watched her boys go, the pole on their shoulders sagging under the weight of the kill. Her sudden scream caused crows to rise squawking from the treetops. Urdeth called for her boys to halt and ran to catch them up. 'Where did you get that?' she yelled, her trembling finger pointing to the grey fur tail decorating the pole's end.

'It was given to us—a token of our hunting skill.'

'Take it off.'

'But, Mother.'

'But nothing—take it off—fling it as far away from here as you can! Do you hear me?' Air filled her lungs. 'That tail,' she hissed, 'belongs to a cub whose mother is crying for revenge. Do you not think I have buried enough sons? Now—do as I bid.'

Skaldric, Chief of the Settlement and Urdeth's husband, threw the leather strap across the largest items of his cargo and tied them fast against the sides of the cart. Between the gaps he packed fleeces, the contents of the vats too precious to lose during the hard ride. Skaldric's spiced boar and heady mead was much prized by wealthy traders, and gained most notoriety in the lands that lay far across the salt seas.

'Why the haste this year?' asked Perak, Skaldric's daughter of fourteen summers.

'Because the elders say we must. They say this winter is predicted to come quickly and they fear we will perish on the plains.' He wiped his calloused hands down the rough hide of his trousers and placed them around her maiden waist. 'Besides,' he teased before hoisting her onto the cart and tossing the next strap for her to catch, 'they say, there are strong signs that the Shaman is on his way.'

Perak's eyes lit up, their colour matching that of her mother's and of the mountains beyond the forest. She looped

the strap through the cart's side and flung back the remainder. 'Will he give us a blessing?'

Catching it, Skaldric laughed, 'I may be Chieftain of our peoples, but that does not qualify me to predict what the Shaman will or will not do.' He secured another vat, unravelled a new rope and passed it to the girl. 'A mere man such as me quakes at the thought of questioning the elders, though some of the reasoning that comes from their lips raises the hairs on my arms.'

'Like our leaving early?'

'No, I understand their concern. They have lived through many more winters than anyone, if they say the snows will come early, I believe them.'

'But how do the elders know?'

'How does your mother know the language of the beasts?'

It was Perak's turn to laugh and for one beat of his heart, he felt sorrow for the future, knowing what lay ahead—knowing he must give her to another clan, just as his clan would take a daughter to be the bride of one of his sons when they came of age. His heart ached more so knowing his only daughter was to be married to someone who lived across the sea, and far into the west. Her smile faded, 'What is the matter, Dada?'

'Nothing, my daughter.'

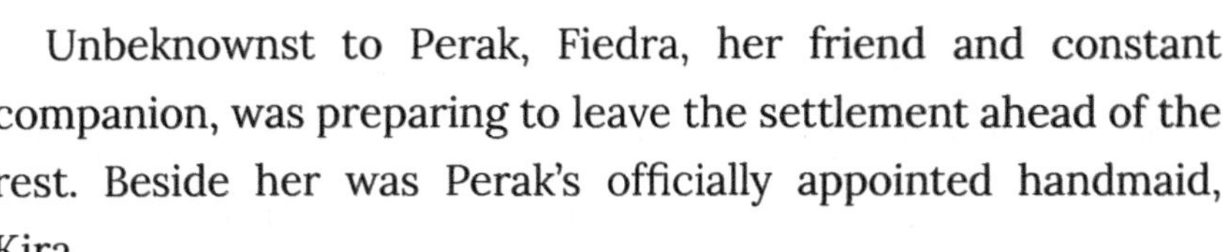

Unbeknownst to Perak, Fiedra, her friend and constant companion, was preparing to leave the settlement ahead of the rest. Beside her was Perak's officially appointed handmaid, Kira.

'Is that all you intend to take?'

Fiedra pulled the blanket's corner to meet up with the other and tied both ends with a defiant tug. 'I came here with nothing.'

'But look,' said Kira, holding a headscarf in the air, its beaded tassels hanging heavy and swaying. 'This was your fourteenth birthday present, given to you by Zak's wife—surely you must take it with you?'

Fiedra tried to hide the scorn she felt. 'Kira, don't you understand? Don't you realise the trek alone will be hard enough for me?' She hitched up the hem of her skirt to reveal bare feet—one foot no more than a stump. 'I must keep the weight to the minimum. If you like the scarf so much, you may have it—together with any other clothing I leave behind.'

They fell silent as Fiedra continued to wrap her scant necessities into the blanket. 'I forget your deformity. Please forgive me.'

'There's nothing to forgive. Anyway, I like it when my withered leg is forgotten—it makes me feel normal.'

'Must you leave like this? Can't you wait and travel with the rest of us?'

'Now that Perak is to be betrothed, there is nothing to keep me here.'

'Where will you live?'

'I'll seek out an old uncle—he will find work for me.'

'But what of us, your kinfolk?'

'Kira, you know I'm not really akin to you. Believe me when I say I am truly grateful for raising me when Urdeth refused. But sooner or later I will be forced to marry someone I don't want. You and I don't have parents who will barter a good deal for us —but we *will* be matched with someone—someone horrible, I fear.' She looked down to her bare feet. 'What's the chance of me snaring a Prince of the Westlands, eh?'

She pulled on her soft hide boots, gave the tearful woman a hug and hobbled through the settlement's stockade to follow the tracks made by all manner of people over centuries of tradition. From the roof of the settlement's meeting house, a raven took to the air and flew in the direction of the lone figure, where it hovered and circled before coming to rest on the bundle of meagre belongings tied across her back.

Five days later the rest of the clan were making final preparations to their packing. Released from their normal duties, the young men took to honing their weapons and learning the art of warriorship. Urdeth's boys fought hard— shaming some who were many winters older than they. Shaming some who held it in their hearts to be glad the Chief's sons may never live to rule the Clan. Some who believed it was a sign—an omen for change.

Though he wished no further harm to come to the sons of the chief, Zak was a man hungry for change. Almost nineteen winters old and wedded to the daughter of a noble family and father to a boy born one winter and six moons ago, Zak was ambitious.

During the meal given on the eve of their leaving, he rose to his feet, and stood with his back to the fire: his muscular frame silhouetted against its glow. He turned to those gathered. 'I ask for permission to speak my mind.'

The elders, who were seated cross-legged on their pile of furs, conferred for several long heartbeats before allowing the young man's request. Mowdah, the highest ranking elder spoke for them, 'We grant you permission to address the assembly—Zak, son of Sarash.'

'I thank you.' Zak turned his attention to those members of the clan who sat with their kinfolk in little clusters. 'I wish to question the need to leave our homestead and make this perilous journey every year.'

Hushed tones carried around the gathered assembly, intakes of breath by those shocked by such a bold, impertinent question. Zak held up one hand, 'Please, hear me out. I know the tradition is to find brides and husbands for our children. I know we must trade our goods for those we cannot make ourselves, I know all of the reasons why tradition says we must, but why in winter? Why can't we make our homestead strong enough to withstand the dark months? That way we can invite the other clans to visit us during, say, the equinoxes and trade under better climes, under our *own* skies?'

The roundhouse fell silent save for the crackle of wood burning brightly in the great hearth. Sparks rose like mischievous sprites and circled around the vent in the roof. Mowdah the elder inclined his head sideways to hear the words of his fellow wise men. Limbs stiff with age, and needing others to assist him, he rose to his feet. All the clan's people watched in silence as their eldest and most revered wise man mustered his dignity to address them.

'These words have reached our ears before, Zak, son of Sarash. You forget the old men here were once young, like you. They remember the time of Leetah's reign and know well enough what perils lie in the folly of questioning the wisdom of the trek.'

Leetah was the grandfather of Skaldric, a mighty leader in those days and great swordsman who fought ferocious bears that came in search of stored provisions during one particularly cruel winter. Legend tells of the bears' teeth and claws killing many of the clan's kinsmen during those raids.

'We elders were amongst those who witnessed the bones of our people stripped clean of their flesh and strewn across our lands by hungry wolves and scavenging boars.'

The crowded assembly made the sign warding off the evil eye. Most in the meetinghouse now wished Zak had kept his thoughts to himself. Memories emblazoned in the minds of everyone present were suddenly brought to the fore. Horrific stories told down the generations lest the young should forget, but warned never to be spoken of lightly, in case the evil one should listen and return to taunt them.

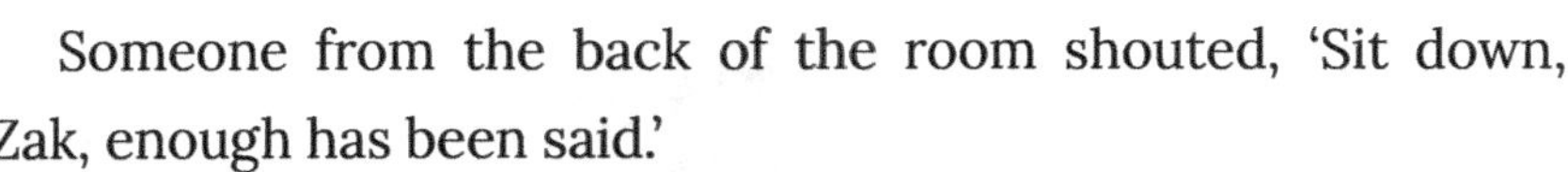

Someone from the back of the room shouted, 'Sit down, Zak, enough has been said.'

'I will sit down and I will hold my peace. But, when we return, I wish to address the assembly again, will the elders grant me that?'

'Why do you persist with your passion for change? Have we not survived by obeying the laws of our ancestors? Have we not seen others mock the wisdom of the elders only to vanish, be wiped out? Where, for instance are the great swordsmen who ruled over Silver Falls? Why did the mighty hunters of the Red Gorge disappear? No one knows; except that, for the sake of change, they refused to join us by the lake. They were skilful warriors like yourself Zak, son of Sarash, yet no match for a pack of hungry wolves.'

So Zak decided to bide his time. He returned to sit with his cousins and their wives and sleeping children, but he would never give up his passion. His dream burned within him. His mind ran with visions of building a stockade strong enough to keep out a hoard of savage beasts, one with walls thick enough to withstand gales: one with roofs able to take the weight of snow. He knew his words were too fancy for the minds of simple folk. He realised they feared the consequences of sitting out the winter. He knew the scent of animals held in barns would bring hungry predators to their door, starving boars that would soon find a taste for human flesh. Zak knew all of that, yet come the Equinox, he would address the assembly again.

The following day, the clan's remaining animals were herded together and taken ahead of the loaded carts across the plains. They would be shepherded by their keepers and led to feed on the coarse grasses, and the children of the keepers would play merry tunes to lighten their journey. The path they rode was slow with oxen tugging their provisions and goods to be bartered for, and it was marked along the way by the burial sites of those who failed to make previous journeys and many more who failed to return.

For it was an evil that had been learnt about their destination but can never be uttered; a dreaded fear that the sprawling townships alongside the lake's edge played host to more things than weary travellers - an awful sickness that lurked near the outlets, brought, it was said, by the ships that travelled the network of rivers to anchor by its decaying wharf. But the Clan took comfort in the wisdom of their leader, Skaldric. It was he who persuaded the elders to allow his people to leave the lakeside before the thaw—thus, he was convinced, was the reason most of his people had been prevented from falling sick.

It took the moon's full cycle to reach their goal. And when the blue water glistened across the horizon, joy filled the hearts of the Clan.

Lush green land spread up the hillside towards them and already their animals could be seen grazing with relish. And as they neared the lake, the town below them came into view with huts squatting together, sending pillars of smoke into the cool, still air. Down by the water's edge stood the lodging houses, solid in their structure, and in marked contrast was the wharf, with its ill-kept timbers. Tied up were three foreign ships; their brightly painted hulls reflecting in the deep blue of the water. Men could be seen moving around the ships, transporting containers to and from reindeer-drawn wagons.

Set apart from the bustle of the water's edge, stood the lake's Roundhouse, the Great Hall built to accommodate the visiting Clans who, like Skaldric's people, needed to flee their own winter.

This was the time of reuniting with kinsfolk. There would be great feasts to look forward to, with each family determined to outdo the other; each filling platters with lashings of delicacies brought from all the lands that surrounded the lake and beyond.

As the travellers settled in their allotted quarters, talk of the Shaman grew louder, and more positive with each telling. There were signs, they said, omens to be read in the starlit skies that proved he was on his way, and, they said he could possibly reach them by the eve of the Midwinter Feast.

The children talked of no one else. They willingly helped to shake or lay down the skins ready for bedtime, or carry kindle and logs to fill the stores. They did this so that space could be made in the darkening daytime to forage in the woods for the glossy evergreens and climb the trees for sacred berries vital to be made into garlands in commemoration of the Midwinter Solstice. They watched the elders weave boughs of dark green leaves entwining red and white berries on them before fixing the sprays to adorn the lintel above the great entrance to the

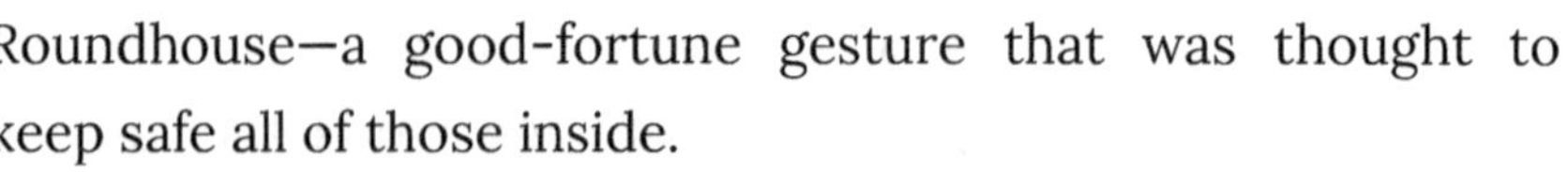

Roundhouse—a good-fortune gesture that was thought to keep safe all of those inside.

On the eve of the Solstice, musicians struck up notes familiar to everyone's ears; songs—whose lyrics told of times long ago when mighty kings rode with the gods to fight evil face to face, and of magical creatures now long gone who walked the Earth, breathing fire and terrorising everything in their wake: now made into glorious choruses that depicted triumph over adversity.

Skaldric opened one of his precious vats, instructing his clan to fill jugs enough to share the heady liquid amongst the gathering. When each goblet was full; he stood tall and raised a toast, thus opening the first of the many great feasts that lay ahead.

'May the longest night always be spent with merry men and our bellies remain full until spring.'

With a resounding cheer, the feasting began. They drank the gift from the bees, ate the sweetmeats offered, but above the laughter, the singing, and the music, they kept one ear for the greatest blessing wished for: the sound of bells, a sure sign that the Shaman's sleigh was drawing near.

Chapter Three

Perak took her place by Urdeth's side and looked eagerly around the crowded Roundhouse but still, there was no sign of Fiedra. She brushed aside her hurt to concentrate her mind on what was ahead, that of her intended betrothal. She fingered the new braids in her hair, careful to allow her wild locks from springing free.

Her hand froze when she sensed her mother's heart suddenly quicken. Sharpening her wits, she tuned automatically into her mother's mind and held her breath; biding several heartbeats, sharing the struggle her mother's body underwent before the quickening was brought under control.

Perak ceased playing with her hair, taking hold of her mother's hand instead. Immediately her mind's eye saw what her mother felt. The Shaman was trapped in a snowstorm, forcing him to find shelter. She turned her eyes towards her mother, and as always, she knew they were the only people in the Roundhouse who shared that knowledge. Urdeth patted her daughter's hand.

His many winters are weakening him, but he brings a blessing, said the voice inside Perak's head. But another voice, barely perceived said, *a blessing that concerns you.*

The hearty laughter of Perak's father took her attention. He was sitting amongst other clan leaders; his distinctive jovial character relaxing her confused mind, bringing a smile to her lips. Also sitting with the men was Zak—whose wife was daughter to one of the chieftains entertaining Skaldric. Zak appeared to be amused by the merriment of Skaldric's wit, but when he locked his eyes onto Perak's, she lowered her lids, embarrassed at the fire in his gaze. *He is not for you,* said the voice in her head. She turned to face her mother who was engaged in conversation with the wife of an elder and not looking in her direction.

At that moment the doors to the great hall opened, blowing flurries of snow into the room where they whirled for tiny moments, before melting in the warm air. Three travellers and a hound entered, and before losing no time, they pushed the wintry weather behind the sturdy doors. Mowdah and other elders rose to greet them, bidding them to shed their icy cloaks and warm themselves by the fire. Food was brought with Skaldric leaving his merry companions to order fresh jugs of mead to fill more goblets.

'Did you catch sight of him?' Mowdah asked, seeking knowledge of the Shaman's whereabouts. The leader of the trio shook his head and around the hall, sighs of disappointment carried like waves over shingle. Perak raised her eyelids. Everyone in the Roundhouse watched the three warmly clad latecomers except for Zak, whose eyes had not left her. Her cheeks flushed over again but this time, she lifted her chin and held his gaze. For some lengthened heartbeats, the noise in the great hall faded away and it was not until Zak's amply bosomed wife took position between them, did Perak look away. She turned to her mother who was now in conversation with her father, their attention focused on one of the newcomers. Perak followed their gaze and saw him. Involuntarily, her eyes flicked back to Zak, his wife pulling on his arm to follow her, his gaze no longer on Perak but now fixed with iciness onto the youngest member of the three.

'Come,' Urdeth whispered, 'it is time you met your intended husband.'

'But Mama, I am too young. Other girls aren't betrothed until after sixteen summers have passed.'

'Other girls are not the daughters of a chief.' Urdeth stroked a curl of hair from Perak's cheek and tucked it behind an ear. 'Besides, you are mature enough, the hot blood warming your face is not all heat from the fire.' Perak turned her attention back to the new arrivals where her father was introducing them to the chiefs of the other clans. Her mother brushed another escaped hair with the back of her fingers. 'Their land is to the West, across the salt sea on the other side of the mountains, they have journeyed far to be with us.'

'Are they heathens? Do their kinsfolk not gather for the Solstice?'

'Do not look so shocked. Yes—of course they honour the seasons. Their Midwinter Feast is celebrated in the west—they have made a sacrifice to join us.'

Perak faced her mother. 'They live a long way from here?'

'Yes.'

'Are you saying I must go with them, leave all I have known?'

Urdeth took hold of Perak by the shoulders, felt the strong bones beneath her smooth skin. 'You can never leave me. We are entwined in spirit with as much strength as my hold on your shoulders is now. I will never leave you.' Perak felt her mother's pain, the welling sorrow of the occasion rising, ready to break the strong woman's resolve. She knew then how like her she must be, for what did it matter whether she took a husband from one of the clans around the lake, or from one further away? All her senses at that moment told her the mother-daughter bond existing between them could never be broken, not even through distance, not even through death.

'How old is my intended husband?' Perak's eyes rested on the young man who chatted with ease as Skaldric introduced him to male members of her family. He stood tall—his teeth white against his sun-tanned skin, hair similar in colour to that of her own brothers: white blonde. Sensing her gaze he looked across the room to her, his eyes deep blue, like the surface of the lake.

'Well, well, we had his older brother in mind for you Perak, but I'm sure we could negotiate for him instead, both are handsome men are they not?' Perak took her eyes from the younger man to rest them on the man standing by his side. He too was blessed with good physique but was serious in manner, he listened to her father intently, nodded gravely answering only with short words. He too sensed her eyes and shot a curt glance her way, making her blush throughout her whole body. 'Ah,' her mother whispered, 'our original plan was right after all.'

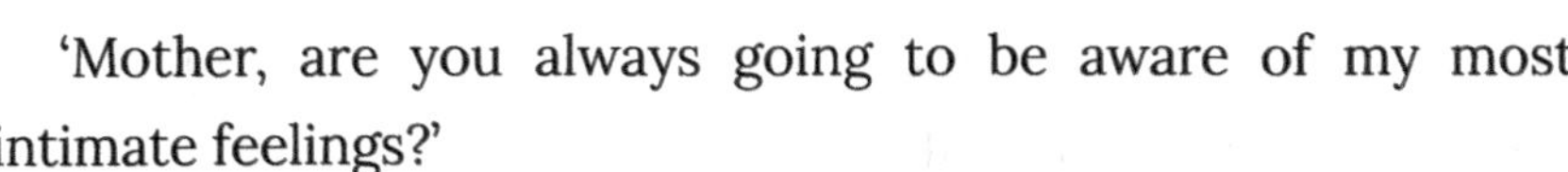

'Mother, are you always going to be aware of my most intimate feelings?'

The crackle of a log falling onto glowing embers mingled with soft noises around the great hall. From the shadows came the sound of rhythmic breathing where families slept, content their stomachs were full and that the furs covering their babes were soft and dry. Set away from them, and nearer to the great doors, the whispered voices of the Chiefs and Elders could be barely heard above the wind whistling against the timbers outside. These great men had many topics to discuss, but their dry throats were quenched by Skaldric's soothing liquor, momentarily easing their burdens of State.

The wolfhound rose from her position by the Roundhouse's entrance and gave a low growl, alerting her master that someone unknown to the loyal canine was approaching. Skaldric stood ready to help Mowdah to his feet. He whispered, 'Come, the hound smells the Shaman's reindeer. We must bid him welcome.' Deftly the leaders of the Clans placed fresh logs on the embers whilst food kept aside for the Spiritual leader was made ready. These were easy tasks done in hushed tones, so as to not rouse those huddled asleep around the hall: and allowed the Holy man some meagre respite before the inevitable adoration he would receive when they awoke.

Skaldric sent young men from his clan, together with other trusted youths to unharness the Shaman's sleigh and lead the deer to graze on the lush mosses that grew by the water's

edge. Others carried the Shaman's possessions and stacked them safely inside the hall.

Those awake assembled to greet their leader; their hearts lifting when he stopped briefly to pay homage to the greenery above the lintel before crossing beneath it. The Shaman's face caught the light of the flames when he pushed back the red-deer hood of his snow-covered cloak: before him Chiefs and Elders knelt—offering whispered greetings to the Holy man.

'See how they fawn,' Zak sneered to his brother. 'Is he not a man like many?'

Cadic grabbed Zak's arm. 'Your foul words slide off your tongue too easily, my brother, one day, someone will grab it tight and cut it out.' Zak shrugged his arm free, drained the last of the mead from his cup and turned away. He was tired of his kinsmen and their weak snivelling, and now that the honey wine ran in his veins, he grew restless for the day of change. He turned his face from the scene by the entrance to scan the hall, searching the shadows to find the place where the violet-eyed Perak slept; his eyes locking onto where she lay. He breathed a ragged breath, chest swelling with desire, lusting for what he could never have - *unless*, his alcohol-induced mind told him - *unless*.

By his side, Cadic rose to his feet and stooped to whisper in Zak's ear. 'Only fools are blind to the words of wise men. And more the fool who eyes another's woman.' He warned before leaving the company of his clan to join those by the door.

The Shaman grimaced as he fumbled to unbuckle the leather strap that held the deerskin coat tight around his body. A youth ran to assist, whilst another placed a warm goblet into

the icy, travel-weary hands. Soon the cloak was taken to dry and replaced by one fashioned of soft, white fur. With boots exchanged for warm, fur-lined slippers, the Shaman was led to the place of honour: a throne of a chair softened with fleeces and finely woven blankets crafted by the women of the Clans. It was there that they left the Holy man to nibble the sweetmeats and dainties prepared in his honour. They spoke in quiet voices, answering his questions, bringing him up to date with all that had happened since the night of his last visit.

Younger men came and went, sliding through back doors unnoticed, keeping the log piles topped up, bringing in buckets of ice, ready to thaw for drinking.

Having rested a while and eaten his fill, the Shaman rose from the chair, bidding a couple of youths to bring forth the bundles carried in from the sleigh and stacked by the door. With care, he unfastened the thongs wrapped around the top of one sack and pulled the neck wide. Whispering instructions to the young men, he returned to his chair and to the company of the Elders and Chiefs where he raised his goblet in salute. 'May the light lengthen from this day forward, may green shoots bring harvests of plenty, and may all your children live to see you die.'

Amongst the gathering of Chiefs and Elders in earshot of the blessing were those whose children lay beneath the Earth: yet their hearts bled with sorrow for Skaldric, a good man stricken by much loss. They whispered their 'ayes' in acknowledgement of the litany until the Shaman held his goblet towards the hoard of sleeping followers, his eyes catching sight of the young men sent amongst them. 'I raise my goblet to the children here, for without them, our people

have no future.' More hushed 'ayes' of agreement were barely heard and goblets were raised to lips; sips taken. When the Shaman raised another toast, they made to follow. 'We must continue to guide the path on which our children tread; but hark my words: if they speak of change, give them a platform: else their voices will be uttered in dark halls where tis known they do manifest into anarchy.'

The Elders sat upright, their mouths tight; goblets poised to drink the toast suddenly became frozen: held fast in age-rigid hands. Chiefs glanced at their sons and to those of their kinsfolk; knowing there were rumours of discontent amongst some of the young. The Shaman was waiting. He held his cup to his lips, holding sway for those with goblets ready, to join him in the toast.

Skaldric took the lead by giving a solemn nod before drinking. Other Chiefs followed, but the Elders' mouths remained dry, turning more thin and icy: allowing none of the mead to pass.

For those watching—those who would survive that particularly deadly winter by the lakeside, it was remembered that change for all the people would come, whether it be good or evil, it would be forced upon them.

Chapter Four

'I haven't seen Fiedra since we arrived,' said Perak to her mother.

'Apparently, she has an old uncle who needs her.'

'I know that. Kira told me. But why hasn't she come here to see me?'

'I've told you all I know. Now hold your peace and let that be an end to it.' Urdeth dragged the comb through her daughter's tangled hair. 'When will these locks ever be tamed?'

Perak did not flinch. 'Is it because she is not high born?'

'These childish thoughts must be put aside. You are to be betrothed, and our Clan cannot be shamed. You know that. Why I ever allowed you to mix with her, I'll never know. Now hold still, the Shaman will rise soon and we must be ready to hear his words.'

They were in the back of the anteroom, a place away from the eyes of men, a sanctuary where women of high birth could bathe and groom. Despite the flames licking the cauldron of warmed water, the room was draughty making goose pimples form over Perak's pale skin. An involuntary shiver ran through her, more in anxiety of meeting the man she was deemed to marry, than the movement of air.

'What is he like?'

'Who? The Shaman?'

'Don't tease, mama, I speak of Kaylak.'

Her mother parted a segment of Perak's hair, divided it into three and began to make a plait. 'He is a thoughtful and studious man. Both brothers, it is said, have knowledge of many things; the younger is also learned in the art of healing the sick.' She threaded silver beads through the plait before dividing another section of wild curls that were reluctant to be tamed. Perak sat still, wanting to hear more. Her mother continued, 'Your father says he is a good man.' This wasn't what Perak wanted to hear. She knew her father would vet all the suitors in line for her hand.

'How old is he?'

'Do you think him old?'

'Older than I thought.'

'He is one and twenty winters.' Urdeth noted her daughter's intake of breath but concealed it by letting out a false laugh, 'Goodness me,' she chided, 'what is the world coming to? He is perfect. A man beyond eighteen winters has dispensed with boorish games. You should think yourself fortunate to be considered a prize for such a fine man.' Another tug to Perak's roots and her mother continued with the grooming.

'Prize?' Perak winced. 'Am I considered a prize?'

'Most certainly—and it is most auspicious that the nuptials will be blessed by the Shaman himself.' She wasn't meant to let that news slip, but Urdeth reasoned Perak would have read it

from her mother's mind before long. 'You must be presented in the best light possible.'

'Then let me have Fiedra.'

'That's precisely why you can't have Fiedra. How on Earth can that scraggy waif help your cause?'

'She plaits my hair as good as you.' This was a dangerous remark to make knowing her mother took particular care over Perak's grooming. 'Well, nearly as good,' She added. The tension in her mother's fingers relaxed and another scoop of rebellious curls were divided and conquered. 'Oh mama, Fiedra has watched you comb my hair since we were little—it is bad enough I be parted from you and dada *and* sent to live across the salt sea. But to be parted from my dearest friend—is—unbearable.'

'I feel your pain, my daughter, but if you are to be accepted by Kaylak's people, then Fiedra must be hidden from their eyes.' With aching sorrow, Perak knew that would be the answer. Accepting her fate, she sat in silence whilst her mother threaded silver ribbons and linked each plait, one entwined with another down her back; her thoughts no longer on meeting her future husband, but filled with deepening sadness for those she must leave behind.

Chapter Five

The assembly woke in different sections of the large hall, with women taking wide-eyed children to the latrines before shaking the furs to freshen them for nighttime. In truth it was dark and would remain so until late morning, but the children woke early to find a miniature reindeer or sleigh or doll carved from antler bone held tight in their hands: a gift from the Shaman, mysterious as it was welcome. Their squeals of delight woke other, older children—grown too serious for such toys; yet they too found trinkets amongst their bedding, combs for the girls and meat-knives for the boys. All carved from the same magical bone given freely by the red-furred deer that roamed the fabled forests of legend.

Zak watched his wife suckle their child, whose eyes stared at the reindeer clutched in his podgy hand. 'They're trinkets,' he said with scorn, 'meant to blind us and nothing more.'

'Why do you fret over harmless toys?' His wife covered her breast and tried to interest the child in the other. 'Whether the gifts be given to blind us or not, I think it's a wonderful gesture.' The boy's appetite was more for play than milk. She gave up and pulled her woven shawl across her chest, placing the babe onto the floor.

'He grows well.'

She took the observation as a compliment and smiled. 'Very soon he will be completely weaned.' She sighed, 'Time we had another, hey, my husband.' Stretching forward, she reached out to stroke Zak's knee, moving her hand to caress his inner thigh. A snigger from one of her clansmen caught Zak's ears, breaking the intimate moment shared between man and wife. Zak turned away, his distaste for his in-laws matching that of his own kin. He scanned the hall, seeking the company of those who shared his vision of a better future.

Away and south of the sprawling township, a row of humble dwellings stood by the side of the lake. Between their reed-thatched roofs, smoke and steam poured from vents, filling the surrounding air with the stench of boiled fish. Fiedra carried empty pails to the lake's edge, stooping to fill them before returning to her uncle's shack. In the dim light of mid-morning, she lost her balance, spilling water down her tunic, its iciness taking her breath.

'Here,' sung a voice from out of the mist, 'allow me to help.'

Fiedra hadn't heard the man approach. Before she was able to reply, he took one of the pails in one hand, holding her elbow with the other, steadying her over the slippery edge.

'Please, I'm alright. I can take the bucket now.'

'I'm looking for the glue maker, perhaps you know him?'

'He is my uncle.'

'Good. Then we can walk together. My name is Yorevyn.' Fiedra tried to keep up, falling into her escort's long strides. 'You will tell me,' his melodic accent chimed, 'if I go too fast for you?' She let out an earthy laugh. 'Why do you mock me?' He asked, his manner sincere.

'Oh 'tis naught but silly-maiden humour. Forgive me—I forgot my manners.' In the murky light, she caught a glimpse of his twisted smile. He took hold of her elbow once more and they continued towards the shacks, his pace slower now.

Under the cover of her hood, Fiedra took sly glances at her escort. His clothing and style of beard told her many things, but it was the manner in which he spoke she warmed to; it had a lilt to it, a sound she'd heard before, but long ago, hidden in the depths of memory.

Kaylak pinched a bite-size morsel of salted fish from the platter and held it to his nose before tasting it. 'You like it?'

'Mmm,' he nodded. Savouring the taste before swallowing, he reached for another sample, 'Lakeside dried fish is highly talked of in the West, but never have I tasted it. It is very good.'

Satisfied, Skaldric offered a different platter, 'Tell me what you think of this. I intend to barter many casks of mead for it.'

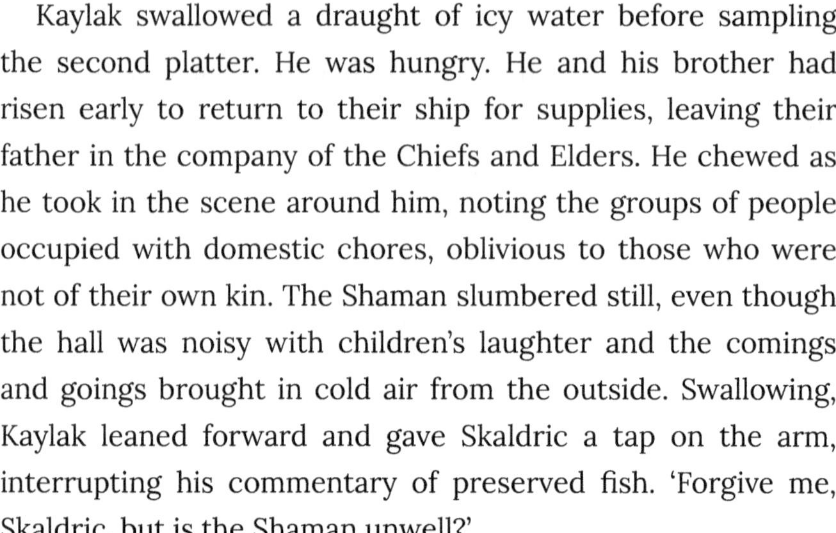

Kaylak swallowed a draught of icy water before sampling the second platter. He was hungry. He and his brother had risen early to return to their ship for supplies, leaving their father in the company of the Chiefs and Elders. He chewed as he took in the scene around him, noting the groups of people occupied with domestic chores, oblivious to those who were not of their own kin. The Shaman slumbered still, even though the hall was noisy with children's laughter and the comings and goings brought in cold air from the outside. Swallowing, Kaylak leaned forward and gave Skaldric a tap on the arm, interrupting his commentary of preserved fish. 'Forgive me, Skaldric, but is the Shaman unwell?'

Skaldric placed the dish to one side, rose from the floor and walked to where the Holy man lay atop of furs, cured especially in his honour. Others in the hall stopped what they were doing and followed, concern etched in the folds of their foreheads. The Shaman's familiar features, honed sharp and craggy from a lifetime in the open air, appeared smooth; his skin no longer the colour of ox-hide but as pale as that of the beard that lay motionless on his chest.

Methiu, father of Kaylak, stopped mid-sentence when his son interrupted a many told saga to whisper in his ear. Without hesitation the spritely warrior left the hall taking the she-hound with him. Kaylak returned to Skaldric's side. 'My father will fetch tonics from our ship, tinctures known to wake a deep sleeper.'

The wave of concern rippled across the hall. Even the children sensed unease by returning to the laps of their mothers, thumbs in mouths: playthings clenched tight in fists. Water was drizzled onto the Shaman's parched lips. Some

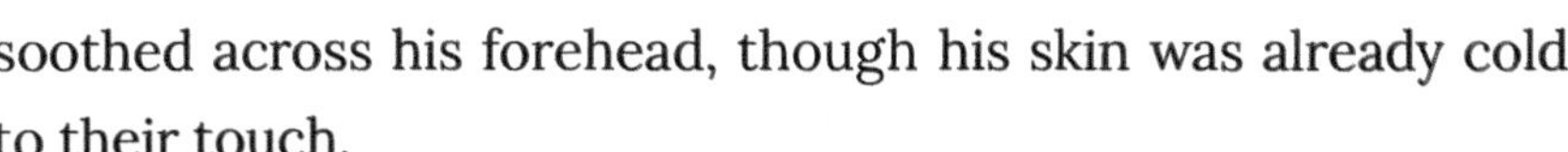

soothed across his forehead, though his skin was already cold to their touch.

From outside, Elvad, younger brother of Kaylak, rushed to examine the Shaman. Giving way, the Elders allowed him access, watching closely as the young man laid fingers on the Holy man's neck and throat. 'There is hope,' he told them. 'He breathes, though his breath is shallow.' With confidence others lacked, Elvad eased the Shaman's upper body from the furs, grabbed a woven blanket and placed it under the ancient's head before opening the front of the old man's robe. 'Have your people stand back,' Elvad pleaded, 'allow the great man some space.'

'And since when has a foreigner told an Elder what to do?'

Elvad looked to the voice, 'Forgive me. I meant no offence to your Elder.'

'And none was taken,' assured Mowdah. 'Go back to your family Zak, son of Sarash; your radical views are not needed here.'

'Maybe not—but the time is nearer than you think.'

Chapter Six

Perak's mother stopped mid-tightening of her daughter's waist-sash. 'Something's happening to the Shaman.'

Perak spun round, her sash falling to the straw-covered floor. 'I feel it too, Mama. Should we do something?'

'No,' Urdeth bent to pick up the embroidered band, plucked off strands of yellow grass before replacing it around the girl's tiny waist. Perak turned to allow her mother to fasten the delicate laces up her back. 'The Shaman knows his time has come. He is ready for the long rest.' Her mother's words bothered Perak. Immediately she felt ashamed, her anxiety stemmed from selfishness rather than genuine grief for the Holy man. She brushed the selfish thought aside. Tried to settle her disquiet. 'A new Shaman will be chosen,' Her mother whispered in her ear. Again Perak felt the guilt rise inside her. 'It's alright, my love, remember 'tis only I that shares your thoughts.'

'I didn't mean to disrespect the Shaman.'

'I know you didn't,' Urdeth pulled tight the sash's ribbons. 'You were confused, told one moment you would receive the Shaman's blessing, the next learning he gasps for air.' The

ribbon was tied with a bow. 'There—my child is almost to become a bride—soon to be a woman.

Perak fell forward when her mother's hand pushed gently from behind. She twirled around feeling the finely woven skirt of her ceremonial dress fill with air as the hem lifted from the floor, 'I feel I could fly in such a gown.'

Her mother's eyes glowed with pride and love for her only daughter. Catching Perak's flaying hands; she took up the step and both danced in a circle, one shedding off years during the carefree movement, the other piling on maturity by as many heartbeats, 'Don't worry, my child, you will get your blessing.'

'Mama, I am already blessed, yet I cannot come to terms with you reading my thoughts.'

'I don't read your thoughts. I pick up your emotions, that's all.'

'Sometimes though, especially since we arrived here, I've felt another is picking up on my emotions, placing thoughts inside my head.'

'Don't be silly, it's just—well, it's just that you are especially energised at this time, after all, it isn't every day a girl of our clan is betrothed to a man as fine born as Kaylak. They say his father Methiu is like a King to his own people.'

'Then if he's so powerful, why should we worry what his folk will think of Fiedra?'

Urdeth rolled her eyes, 'You're being selfish again.'

Perak blushed, 'Not entirely Mama, unless it's selfish to fret what will happen to my friend.'

'She chose to go.'

'No—you and dada sent her away.'

'We didn't argue, or beg her to change her mind I admit, but we didn't send her away.'

Tears wetted Perak's eyes, filling above the brim and falling in big droplets over her flushed cheeks. 'Why would she do that to me?' She sobbed. Her mother gently wiped the tears away.

'Because she loves you.'

'But...'

'But nothing, she wanted what is best for you. Now come, we must attend to our duties. The Shaman grows weak—put your mind to matters spiritual, the great man may pass before the afternoon dark comes upon us.

Yorevyn guided Fiedra across the ruts of frozen scree, his hand gentle on her elbow, his pace keeping steady with hers. She concentrated on what he was saying, his voice rhythmic, flowing up and down with cadences she felt was mystical and hypnotic, even though the topic of his entire conversation was glue.

He paused, waiting for her to answer.

'I'm sorry, what did you say?'

'If your uncle can supply us, my ship can buy many vats from him.'

'Oh, I don't know, I've only just moved in with him, I'm sure he can supply a whole fleet with the stinkin....er sticky stuff if the price was right.'

Pleased with her words, Fiedra's escort took a long stride catching her by surprise, she slipped, water in the pale she carried spilling more iciness onto her boots. In one fluid moment, Yorevyn put his bucket onto the ground and steadied her fall. 'Come,' He took her bucket and placed it by the side of the other. 'You need to get warm. Point the way, I'll carry the water.'

Fiedra stooped to take the handle, 'No—it is not the custom for a high-born man to labour on a glue-maker's niece.'

'Oh, please, I am not *that* highborn. But as you brought it up, we have a king needs as much good glue as I can barter for. So do as you're told and point the way.'

Letting go of the rope handle Fiedra shook icy droplets from the hem of her cloak and pointed to the cluster of hovels darkly silhouetted against the deep grey sky and purple rocks bordering the lake. 'My uncle lives in the one nearest to the water.' They walked in silence until the smell from her uncle's chimney-vent reached her nostrils. 'What does your king want with so much glue?'

'Glue is needed to fix spearheads to their shafts—we are training men to fight a great army.'

Fiedra had heard the youths of the settlement talk of a mighty army, one that had come to take treasures from people unable to fight back. 'Does this army come from the east?'

'Yes.'

'Cadic said they worship demons and hang people by their arms until their sockets fall out.'

'Aye and they call *us* barbaric.'

'Uh! We're no such thing.'

'Not you, us—my people.'

'Barbaric people do not help the niece of a glue-maker to carry water.'

Yorevyn showed his twisted smile. 'What's your name?'

'Fiedra.'

'I think, Fiedra, that you and I will become friends.'

In the dark, a hound rushed to them, jumping up to greet Yorevyn it knocked Fiedra to the ground. Taken by surprise by the sudden appearance of the huge animal, she let out a fearful scream. Further along the shore someone called—the words foreign to her ears but known to the hound. Immediately the beast ran from the scene. Yorevyn shouted back, his words matching those of the man with the beast. 'The hound meant you no harm,' he said as he turned to help Fiedra who lay sprawled on the shingle, her head covered by her arms. 'She ran to greet me.'

'She?'

'Yes—she belongs to the king. She loves all who are loyal to him.'

Fiedra stifled a sob. 'She knocked me over,' she whimpered as she lifted her head from the frosty ground and wiped her face with the fur lining of her hood.

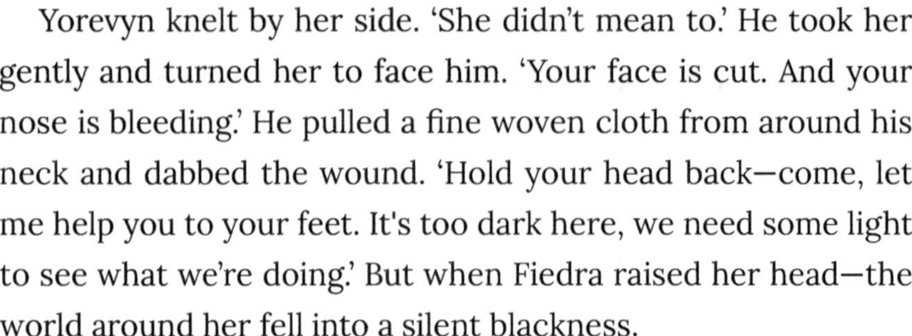

Yorevyn knelt by her side. 'She didn't mean to.' He took her gently and turned her to face him. 'Your face is cut. And your nose is bleeding.' He pulled a fine woven cloth from around his neck and dabbed the wound. 'Hold your head back—come, let me help you to your feet. It's too dark here, we need some light to see what we're doing.' But when Fiedra raised her head—the world around her fell into a silent blackness.

Chapter Seven

Methiu, father of both Kayak and Elvad, entered the Roundhouse carrying a leather casket. He began to open it as he crossed the floor to where the Shaman slept. 'I came as swiftly as I could.'

'You did well, my father. He breathes but not as robust as you do.'

Methiu laughed, aware of how rapid his breathing came, 'Keeping up with Meg makes the lungs work—tell me, my son, are we being unkind to use potions on a man who simply needs to rest?'

'Who can say?' Elvad took a wad of sheep's wool and poured a drop from a tiny stone jar. He replaced the wax stopper and put the jar safely into the casket.

Mowdah came to Methiu's side. 'What is it?'

'A potion brought back by our seafarers—it has properties to quicken those who've fallen into a deep sleep.'

'How can that be?'

'It isn't magic—it has a very pungent odour—see, my son merely waves the fleecy wad under the sleeper's nose.'

'And this will awaken him?'

'If the Shaman wishes to leave us, then it is his will. See he turns his head aside—the smell is repugnant. He stirs.'

Elvad took away the wad of wool, handed it to his father. All those present stood in silence as the old man's nose wrinkled and his mouth opened and closed. Mowdah bent to sniff the wad held in Methiu's hand. 'Uhh!' he recoiled, holding his hand to his nostrils. Someone in the Roundhouse laughed, but it wasn't in mocking Mowdah's distress but in delight that the Shaman's eyes opened, and colour came back to his pallid skin. Elvad placed his arm under the blanket cushioning the Holy man's head and raised him into a sitting position.

'You slept well, Wise one.'

The old man turned his rheumy eyes towards the young man cradling him, 'I did,' He croaked, 'and my journey was a thirsty one.'

A rush of eager helpers ran to fill ewers; others gathered soft furs to place around the ancient shoulders. Elvad took the offered cushions and gathered them under his patient's back, allowing him to rest unaided before he joined the company of his father and Mowdah, the elder.

'How can you scoff at men with knowledge such as this?'

'I scoff at their hidden motive.'

'What hidden motive? You talk in riddles Zak. These men have joined our gathering for the Midwinter feast. One of them is betrothed to one of our lasses, you know who I mean, the one you can't keep your eyes off.' Cadic held his brother's stare, 'you are blind if you think only I have noticed.'

'They want more than a bride—I know it.'

'They want to trade—what's wrong with that?'

'More than trade—they want to rule us. The one healing the preacher—he's trouble—I feel it.'

'You're the one who's trouble, Zak—maybe you should get him to perforate your skull? Find out what ails you of late?'

'Maybe you are right—and when he lifts the chisel I'll grab it and ram it down his throat.'

Cadic rose. 'You make our father's spirit restless.'

'Father made his own spirit restless by not standing up for our clan.'

'How dare you utter words against him—he died trying to save our sister from the Marsh Wives—or have you forgotten?'

'She wouldn't have ventured into the marshes if you'd've all listened to me.'

Cadic's laugh held no humour. 'If we all listened to you—then we'd all need the services of the trepan doctor.' He turned to leave the section where his people gathered; some held their faces towards Zak—their eyes filled with dismay. 'You shame our people with your vile tongue. These men you scoff at have travelled to lands so far away, their peoples have never set eyes on snow. Think of it Zak—what knowledge they

must've learned from such peoples—think what crops could be grown in a land without snow and ice.' But Cadic left Zak's side when he realised his brother's attention had wandered towards the anteroom where the females from all the clans were gathering to catch sight of Urdeth and her daughter.

Chapter Eight

'**Put** her over there—she'll be right by morning.'

'I want to see her right before I leave.'

'Why? What's she to you?'

'What kind of a question is that? She's fallen and hurt her face.'

'Look—she's clumsy—she's always falling over. Put her in the corner—I've got work to do - too busy to nursemaid a wench.' The skinny man narrowed his eyes, 'Look, if you've come here wanting me to pay for your blooded cloak....'

'It was my fault she fell over.'

'Nah—she's awkward—fit for nowt and that's the truth. She's a Marsh Wive's bastard, like I say, fit for nowt. Be away with your business—she'll be right by morning. Did she get the water?'

'She got your water.' Yorevyn placed Fiedra onto the pile of rags and left the hovel. He returned to find the glue-maker shaking Fiedra by the shoulders. Placing the buckets by the stove, Yorevyn grabbed the man from behind. 'Leave her be.' He pulled the man aside, lifted Fiedra's limp form and carried her away.

'She'll bring you nowt but trouble,' the glue-maker shouted, 'I'm warning you so when you've finished with her, don't be bringing her back to me - she's nowt but a bloody drain.'

Urdeth knelt and bowed her head before the Shaman. He raised a weak hand, 'Rise, Urdeth, daughter of Mira.'

'Joy fills our hearts to have you with us Lord.'

'Joy fills an old man's heart to be here.' A murmur rippled around the hall—it held high notes and sighs of thanksgiving, the Shaman looked up and smiled. 'What riches could compare with this? ' Before taking a sip from the offered goblet, his gnarled hand swept towards the crowd, 'Now, Urdeth my daughter, where is your child?

Perak stepped into view, 'I am here my Lord.'

'Come close.' Taking a deep breath and standing as tall as she could, Perak walked towards the Shaman. Aware of the eyes upon her, aware too that Kaylak stood by her father together with Elvad and Methiu and her younger brothers, whose chests were pushed out fit to burst. Perak knelt, taking hold of the Shaman's outstretched hand, the other he gestured to the men on his right. Kaylak stepped forward and knelt by Perak's side. 'You will weather the storms of marriage better than most. Your children will honour you as you have honoured your parents. They will live to see you die.' Urdeth's intake of breath was muffled by the gathering's collective sigh. To have such a blessing boded good fortune for the couple.

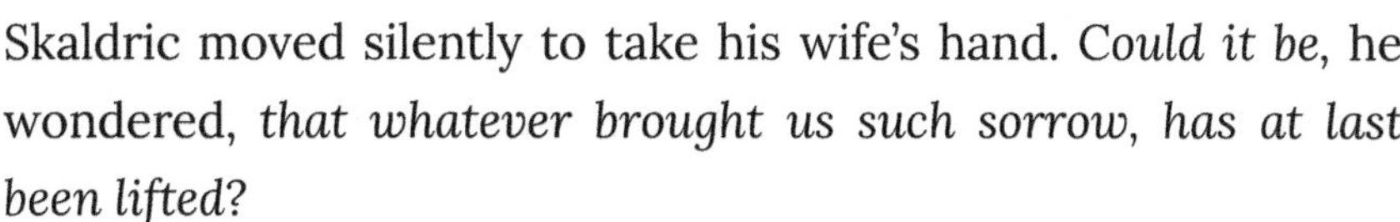

Skaldric moved silently to take his wife's hand. *Could it be,* he wondered, *that whatever brought us such sorrow, has at last been lifted?*

'Where's the casket?' Yorevyn blurted as he searched the ship's medicine chest.

'Methiu came for it.'

'Why?'

'His mission was urgent—I learnt long ago not to interrogate a King in a hurry. Are you ill?'

Yorevyn shook his head and smiled at the genial captain. When he closed the chest's lid—its weighty thud assured them both the contents remained watertight. 'Did Methiu take the casket to the ceremony?'

'Aye. Well, that's the direction he took—you say you are not ill yet you are covered in blood.'

'Meg knocked a snippet of a lass over—the blood is hers.'

'So?'

'She hasn't wakened.' The captain scratched his chin, his fingers disturbing layers of orange-red hair that curled like snakes around them. His eyes first roamed the deck, then the wharf before they settled on a bundle of rags nestled by the glowing braziers. Yorevyn followed his gaze, 'Her uncle makes glue.' Suddenly the captain's eyes flashed back to meet with

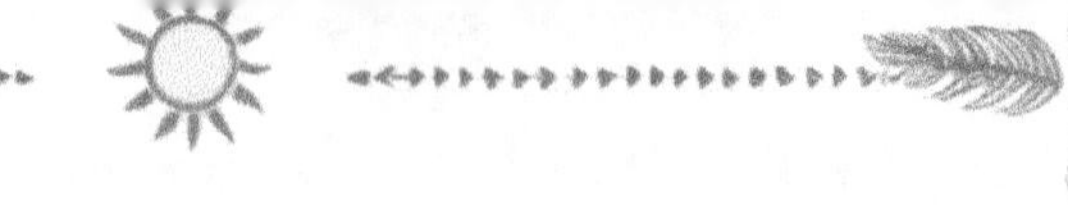

those of Yorevyn's. 'Yes, my friend, you heard me well enough—so you see how important it is to our fate that she recovers.'

'Bring her to the mess.'

Chapter Nine

Zak brooded outside the Roundhouse before wandering down the slope that led to the shore. Lazy-eyed, he scanned the horizon where a watery, distant sun barely rose above the mountains beyond the lake. Something caused a splash, making him lower his gaze to where the sky reflected in the central waters. For a few moments, it became the focus of his attention, in the foreground, an odd seabird ducked and dived, but further back, where the shadow of the hills darkened the water, something else dipped below the surface—something massive and slow and silent was moving with little effort. The wake it was causing travelled fast and ripped towards the wharf, breaking hard against the upright timbers. Bells on moored-up fishing boats began to tinkle and clang against their masts—the noise grew louder, like they were sounding an alarm.

In the murky light, Zak caught sight of Cadic walking towards one of the foreign ships that was tied to the wharf beyond the fishing village. Like a hound that smells a rat, Zak felt the hairs on his neck go rigid. Curious as to what business his brother might have with foreign seamen, he pulled his hood around his face and followed. The waves along the water's edge grew stronger and crashed onto the pebbles

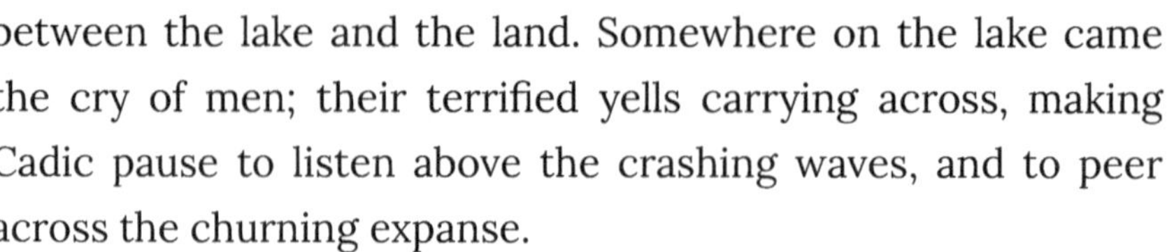

between the lake and the land. Somewhere on the lake came the cry of men; their terrified yells carrying across, making Cadic pause to listen above the crashing waves, and to peer across the churning expanse.

Zak also turned to the source of the yells but the creature remained below the water's line—he smiled, in awe of something invisible yet powerful enough to be felt on the shore and around the valley. His brother cupped his hands to his mouth, calling to the distressed fishermen before turning his voice to sound the alarm on land. Soon, those within earshot signalled him and the scene became active with men preparing a boat ready to take onto the lake.

Under other circumstances Zak would have joined in, even led such a heroic task, but times were changing for him. Scheming plots and suspicious thoughts held him close to the shadows, and hugged his disquiet like it was his only friend— like it was a trusted fellow conspirator.

His brother, who was once his best friend had turned against him—everything Zak talked about, his brother found fault with. Other members of the clan were taking sides, most of them agreeing with Cadic's views, opinions Zak felt were forced upon them by narrow minded elders too scared to strive for a better future. He stared across the lake and exhaled deeply—unwilling to admit to himself what the real cause for his isolation was. Perak.

In the dark grey day, he stood watching the men struggle against the lashing waves. They were fools to think they could fight against such odds. Fools: all of them. He turned his back on his kinsfolk, closing his ears to the screams of the

fishermen as they battled against the thrashing, swirling surface of the normally flat calm lake.

As he slunk further into the shadows, his feet squelched through a mire of slush, kicking up debris thrown from the hovels lining his path. Here and there a painful cough could be heard from those who dwelt within—people of too low in caste to be invited to the Shaman's Midwinter celebrations—people too wretched to care for their loss. People who existed, yet polite folk found it easier to pretend otherwise. People referred to as the Forgotten.

From out of nowhere a boy suddenly lurched and vomited over Zak's boots. Reflex lashed out and in the space of a heartbeat, the child was sent sprawling onto the filth. Repulsed by the stench of the vomit burning into the hide of his footwear, Zak ran past the motionless urchin, and headed further into the squalor of the shadows. Undigested mead began to rise from his gut and burn his throat causing him to gag. He ran on until he emerged at the north of the bay where he gulped lungfuls of crisp, cold air.

Fiedra's awakening caused the two men to fall back— stunned by the suddenness of it, the captain dropped the pot of precious unction he held and watched with horror as it slid under the bulkhead. She stared for a moment at Yorevyn before her eyes rolled to the top of her head and her body fell limp.

'Hold onto her.'

'I can't—it's the motion of the ship. Yeh gods, it's like being on the Salt seas.'

Members of the crew began to pile on board. 'What do *they* want?' Yorevyn asked as he strapped Fiedra to the sides of the bunk.

'How should I know? Maybe they've run out of ale.'

'Best if they don't see her. Go out—explain something, anything,' he pleaded with the captain, 'but don't tell 'em there's a girl in your bed.'

'By the gods.' The captain pulled handfuls of fiery red hair from his scalp, 'Don't you think I have enough to cope with in stormy seas, without evoking my crew's superstitions too?'

Yorevyn knew well enough about sailors' foibles, but where else could he have taken her? He stood up and patted the captain's shoulder. 'Tell them I was the one who brought her here—no, better still, there's so little flesh on her bones, they'd think she'd be nowt but a boy—an apprentice bought from the locals.'

'And what if she dies?'

'She won't die.'

'That cut to her head—no mere bruise—it goes deep.'

'The unction will heal it.'

'Arrgh,' cried the captain as he fell on hands and knees, fingers reaching under the partition, 'where did it slide to?'

Chapter Ten

Kaylak stood by the entrance of the antechamber and leant against a roof support. His cough alerted Kira. She spun round. 'I—er, I was.'

'You were brushing out the creases ready for your mistress, is that what you are trying to say?'

'Y-yes.' She smoothed the palm of her hand down the layers of silk before placing the gown across the open chest that dominated the room.

'Where is your mistress?' Kaylak asked without moving from the post.

'She is with her mama.'

'Good, then now you have *un-creased* her gown, will you tell your mistress and her mama that the Shaman is preparing to leave, and wishes to say goodbye.' He straightened up, turned and left.

Kira closed her eyes and took a deep breath. What was she thinking of? Holding such a valuable gown against her body— like it was hers? And the look on his face—he was laughing at her—not with his mouth but with his eyes. She had been mocked and it did not sit well with her. She slid off the bracelets and placed them back in the jewel-encrusted box

together with other gifts Perak had been given by her new family. Kira's long breath trembled as she reached towards the chest to give the gown another stroke, the silk feeling like nothing she had felt before. Just then, the heavy tapestry moved aside making a gap for Perak to enter followed by her mother. They both gave Kira a strange look, like they could read her inner thoughts, which Kira knew was ridiculous, but nevertheless, found unnerving.

'The Shaman is leaving us.'

'Yes,' said Urdeth, 'we know.'

'He, er he....'

'Wishes to say his farewells.'

'You heard,' Kira suddenly realised her hand rested on the silk gown, 'I—er, I've pressed out the creases for you, Perak.'

'The reindeer are restless to leave the area,' Kaylak whispered to Urdeth and Perak as they entered the crowded Roundhouse, 'something is churning the waters of the lake.'

'A storm?' asked Perak. 'Is it wise for the Shaman to leave in a storm?'

'My father wishes to travel with him, he will keep the Shaman safe.' Kaylak took hold of Perak's hand, 'You know the Shaman's time is near, my father will guide him to his resting place.'

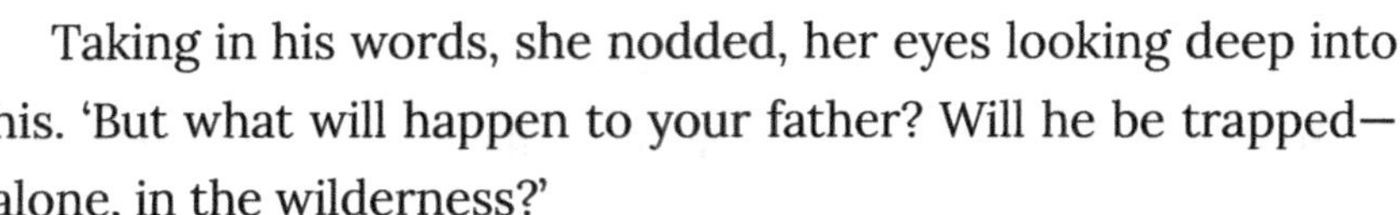

Taking in his words, she nodded, her eyes looking deep into his. 'But what will happen to your father? Will he be trapped—alone, in the wilderness?'

Kaylak squeezed her tiny hand and shook his head, 'My father has travelled across many wildernesses. He will be fine, and no doubt will make his way to a wharf and wait until one of our ships dock, then board it.'

'You make it sound like an adventure.'

'You have much to learn Perak, my beloved. Now, see, your father and the Elders beckon.'

'We've come to fetch our tackle, fishermen are caught in a whirlpool that's churning the lake.'

Yorevyn climbed onto the fore of the deck to see where the crew indicated, 'What's causing the whirlpool?'

'Dunno—we just heard the screams and ran to the wharf.'

'Take the cargo boat—I'll grab the captain.'

The crew took orders without question, the cargo boat stood empty, ready to be filled with the glue that Yorevyn was hoping to buy at a good price from Fiedra's uncle.

On the shore, Cadic was grabbed by the arm, 'What chance do we have against such a storm?'

He turned on the exhausted helper, grabbing him by the shoulders, 'We have to try.'

'And lose our lives in the attempt?'

Behind, Yorevyn's sturdy ship was mastering the waves, its crewmen pulling their oars to the rhythm of their coxswain's drum. It arrived at the maelstrom guided by the screams of the frantic men who struggled in the icy water clutching onto floating fragments of their fishing crafts. The coxswain split the crew, one half to keep the rowing steady whilst the other men reached out, ready to pull the terrified men aboard.

Cadic stared at each of the men. Defeat etched into their eyes. Exhausted and battle weary by waves unfamiliar to them. He looked at their battered boats, each one chopped by the surges and thrown back, like toys onto the shingle.

'See,' yelled a voice above the roar of the waves. 'See, over there, the cargo boat, it's slicing into the whirlpool like it was ...'

'They're not slicing into it—they're riding it,' said another. 'Can you see? They're using the whirlpool's power to speed the ride.' When Cadic stood up, water poured from under his hood —cold against his skin, washing away the sweat of his efforts.

'By the gods,' He stared across the lake, 'these people know no bounds.'

One of the men, unable to take his eyes off the drama said, 'I've heard they master the salt seas where mightier waves than this flare up all the time.'

Beyond the mountains, the sky gave off a pale glow much like moonlight, giving Cadic and the men a clearer view of the swirling waters, and of the cargo boat as it manoeuvred between the wrecked fishing boats and the drowning men.

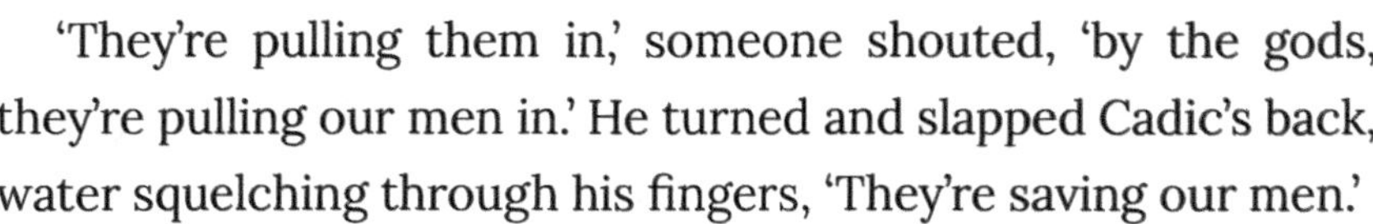

'They're pulling them in,' someone shouted, 'by the gods, they're pulling our men in.' He turned and slapped Cadic's back, water squelching through his fingers, 'They're saving our men.'

Away from the drama and to the north of the bay, Zak broke the icy crust with the heel of his boot. He knelt and scooped handfuls of water into his mouth. The tingle felt good. He scooped more and washed it over his face. Below him, the sound of water running fast on shingle drew his attention—*the monster.*

He had forgotten about the fishermen and their distress, forgotten about the phenomena of large waves churning the lake and the huge creature moving beneath its surface.

He stood and looked across the frosted mossy slopes and back towards the wharf where braziers gave off dots of flickering light. Other stuff, too distant or murky to focus on, no longer held his attention. He felt he didn't belong any more, especially, to his kinsmen. Again, he knelt by the stream, cupped hands and drank the clean water. It soothed the burning of the mead, pushed it down his gullet and into his stomach where it gurgled and churned like the lake behind him.

Chapter Eleven

The gathering in the Roundhouse had no sooner waved the sleigh carrying Methiu and the Shaman farewell, when they were receiving news bit by bit from those down by the shore. First, they heard the lake had turned rough, yet the wind was no stronger than usual. Then, men tried to save a party of fishermen, feared to be drowning but couldn't get into the water. Finally, news came that the fishermen had be saved, but by a foreign trading boat. The clans-folk merely shrugged their shoulders, praised the gods for a good outcome and continued with preparations for that evening's feast. Like all good-living people, they were content and at ease with their conscience after donating dry furs and extra food to the fishing village and arranging for more thanks to be given to the gods.

Fiedra sat bolt upright. She tried to move her legs but they were tied fast to the timber sides of the cot she lay in. Beneath her was a giant of a man sprawled across a wooden deck his face turned from her but his hair looked to be on fire.

'Am I held prisoner?'

The giant stopped searching for whatever lay beneath the partition and swung round, face as fiery red as his hair. 'By the gods—I thought you were a gonna.'

'Gonna?'

'Dead.'

The ship rolled, throwing Fiedra sideways, she grabbed hold of the straps, realising now, why they were there. 'He's lost,' She said, 'needs to reunite with his kinfolk.' She closed her eyes and fell back.

'Yeh—well that'll be the knock you've taken to your head. Doubtless you'll make no sense from now on. But....as Yorevyn, *we*, need your family's glue, dunna fret wee lass, you'll be looked after.'

'The object you seek is being played with by a cat. She is below us.'

The Captain looked up in time to watch Fiedra's eyes rolled back to the top of her head. He stared at the unconscious girl and scratched his head. 'How did the lass know we have a cat?'

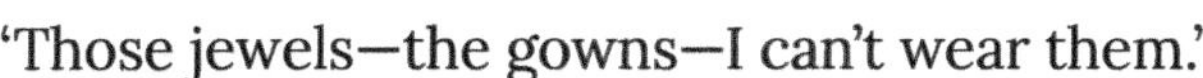

'Those jewels—the gowns—I can't wear them.'

'Why not?'

'I'm a girl who likes to help her father spice a boar, smoke a deer, or roast water fowl, clothes like these.' Perak stroked the silk of her gown, 'aren't practical.'

Kaylak nodded. 'Couldn't agree more. They're for ceremonial use only.'

Perak blushed, 'I see.'

'Look,' Taking both her hands in his, 'my people simply want you to love them. The trinkets are their way of saying welcome.'

'How do they know about me?'

Kaylak's eyes roamed her face with delight, 'Oh beloved, my people have yearned for me to bring them a princess. They are tired of my wanderings, and want me to settle down.'

'And what of *your* wishes, are you ready to give up your adventures?'

'I am, but I also want to show you some of the world beyond the Northland. I want to take you to places that will make your violet eyes sparkle like the jewels on your gown.' He held her hands to his lips never taking his eyes off her face. 'I want always to see them dazzle like they're doing now.'

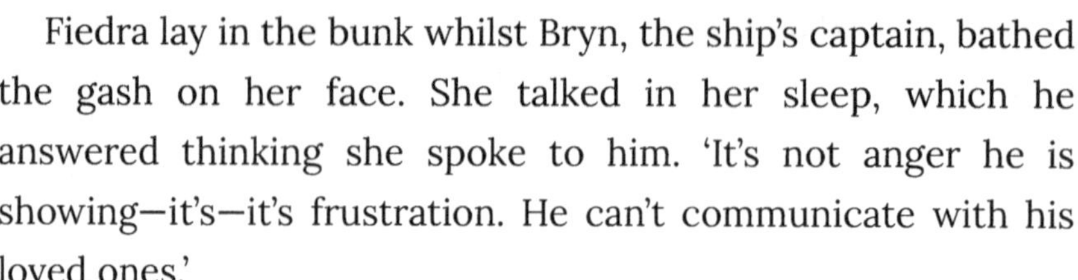

Fiedra lay in the bunk whilst Bryn, the ship's captain, bathed the gash on her face. She talked in her sleep, which he answered thinking she spoke to him. 'It's not anger he is showing—it's—it's frustration. He can't communicate with his loved ones.'

'Yeh well—yer see lass, that's the way with us men. Lack of communication—it's what we do best.' He teased away the fleecy swab stuck to the skin.

'His—fam-family,' she twisted against the pain.

'Sorry lass, nearly done.'

'His family - they need our help.'

'I know—and we'll give it to 'em, take my word, we'll give it to 'em. Now rest awhile lass, dunna fret about 'im any more.' He smeared a dollop of unction into the wound and pinched it closed between thumb and finger, holding it until the black ointment oozed through the cut. 'There's a brave lass. Not many sailors would've stood me doing that. Now rest easy.'

He washed the gungy mess off his hands and stroked her hair away from her forehead. When her breathing settled he moved to rise up and found Yorevyn had crept in and was stood leaning against the partition.

'The lake's gone flat—is she still talkin' crazy?'

'Yeah—some man not communicating with his family.' Bryn gathered up the soiled swabs and threw them into the bucket, 'hope it isn't her uncle.'

'It isn't,' Yorevyn smiled and took the pail from the captain's hands. 'We got a good deal. And he's negotiating to supply us with glue from his neighbours.'

'And the wee lass—did he ask how she is?'

'She's part of the deal—we're taking her with us.'

'By the gods, Yorevyn—what'cha doin' to me?'

Fiedra called to them in her sleep, 'I passed it on—your promise to help.'

'Yeh, yeh, lass—now rest easy.' Bryn looked to Yorevyn, 'Poor mite, she'll never be right y'know—not with an injury like that.'

'She'll pull through.'

Zak squelched his way back to the shadowy world of the Forgotten trying to retrace his steps. He was in no mood to save foolhardy fishermen, nor was he inclined to put up with kinsfolk bowing and scraping to old men. Besides, he had niggling thoughts about the kid he'd knocked over, how would he feel if some drunken brute did the same to his child? He wouldn't like it—and the kid meant no harm—he was sick. He would find him and make amends. Poor people forgive easily—they never hold grudges.

He found the intersection and the pool of vomit frozen on top of the layers of filth flattened into makeshift pathways—but no child lay whimpering. Grateful the injury wasn't serious, he breathed easier until his eyes focused on grooves made recently by a sled carrying a hefty load.

The ruts ran along the west gateway of the crossroad, close to where the boy had fallen. He followed the lines down the filthy back track until they led to an open piece of land.

There, crows circled in the murky sky and swooped down on a lone man heaving bundles of rags from the sled onto a frozen mound of debris. Zak inched close, but the stench halted him, rooting him to the spot.

Horrified yet fixated, he watched the figure pull hefty shapes and drag them to the top of the mound where they fell over the crest and out of sight. Those of lighter bundles, he cast towards the crows; as though to ward them off. When Zak saw the limp shape of a child being lifted from the pile he held his breath. Frozen to the spot, he watched the man drop it by one of the cart's runners before returning to empty more heavy items from his load. Zak stiffened—not wanting to know more. The bile, which he had managed to subdue, began to rise: hot and urgent in his stomach. The shadowy figure continued to disperse his grim cargo, slowly making his way around the heap and disappearing into a different direction from the one he arrived by. When he'd gone, and Zak had quelled the acid in his gut. He edged his way to where the child lay.

His life had been that of the warrior and huntsman. Never did he imagine he would strike a child, or if he did, not to kill. He bent down, kneeling in the filth to turn the child over and gasped at the whiteness of his face: even in the gloomy light, his skin glowed like candlewax. He turned away as the contents of Zak's stomach finally burst onto the ground beside him. Sweat poured over his skin and trickled through his scalp mingling with the tears of remorse running down his cheeks.

He didn't know how long he knelt there but when a crow came close to peck the child's flesh; Zak lost control and rose to his feet, lashing at the bird.

When Cadic returned to the Roundhouse, Zak's wife ran to greet him, asking if he'd seen his brother.

Cadic shook his head. 'We needed him, I can tell you. That freak storm churned the waters so fierce—it wrecked two fishing boats on the shoreline.'

Her eyes filled with tears, searching his face to tell her where his brother had gone. Urdeth came to her side. 'Come, my daughter, I will take you to be with your kinsfolk.'

'No,' she rebelled. 'This is Zak's family's problem to solve. Not a clan matter.'

Urdeth withdrew, though she watched Cadic take his sister-in-law's shoulders and speak in urgent tones to her. Skaldric came to her side, asking what was wrong.

'It's a worry for her. Apparently, he's been gone most of the day.'

'Zak's impetuous that's all. He has dreams and is impatient to see them come true. He will return to his wife's bosom when the cold out there begins to bite.'

'Oh how easy you make life sound, my husband.'

'Urdeth, life doesn't have to be as complicated as Zak makes it. Look at what he's got, a beautiful wife and handsome, sturdy son—what more could a young man wish for?'

'He must learn to temper his mood.' Said Cadic when he returned to Skaldic's side. 'I am sorry for my brother's inconsideration.'

'There is no need for apologies. Zak has good ideas.'

' Oh yeah? And he'll be out there, wandering around the lake, planning some hot-headed scheme he'll expect us all to listen to.'

Skaldric slapped Cadic's back. 'To be fair to your brother, not all of his ideas are bad—it's the timescale he seems to get wrong. Zak thinks he can change generations of tradition in just a few summer months.'

Chapter Twelve

Preparations in the Roundhouse were made ready for yet another evening of feasting. Logs were brought in and piled in the store; ice, cut into slabs and placed into vats to thaw for drinking and furs were shaken ready for sleepy heads to rest upon.

Perak sat in the anteroom watching Kira groom Urdeth's hair. Light, from the burning torches fixed to the walls, picked up golden strands as the comb slid through it. Perak's eyes began to moisten. Soon, she would leave her mama and dada to build a new life with Kaylak and his people; people who, though they had never met her, already loved her as their princess. She wondered whether she should ask Kaylak if Fiedra could be liked, if not loved, by them, and whether it would be possible to bring her along. Urdeth turned away from Kira's combing and looked into Perak's eyes, *don't even think about it*, the voice inside her head warned.

Kira dropped the comb onto the straw-covered floor. When she picked it up and wiped it down her tunic, ready to continue with Urdeth's grooming, her mistress said quietly, 'If you intend to stay on as Perak's handmaiden, then I suggest you learn not to put the dust back into her hair or mine. Do

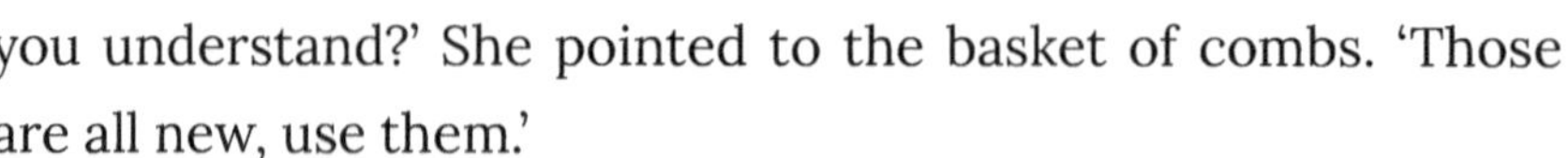

you understand?' She pointed to the basket of combs. 'Those are all new, use them.'

Inside Urdeth's head, a voice said, *Fiedra wouldn't need to be told something as fundamental as that.*

The gash to Fiedra's head grew red around the edges, and swollen across her cheek and forehead, distorting her right eye into a slit. The captain kept vigil, wiping her forehead with swabs soaked in ice-cold water. The ship gave a gentle roll; he stepped on deck to peer across the water. By the shoreline, layers of surf churned by the recent frothing of the waves, lay frozen and upended across the shingle. In the moonlight, they stood like child ghosts waiting to be laid to rest. Across the water, something sleek shimmered on the surface before sliding noiselessly into the depths. The captain frowned. 'Now - if you are what I think you are, what by the blessed gods are you doing here?'

'You should join your men,' Yorevyn said as he climbed aboard, 'you're starting to talk to yourself.'

Bryn turned round, his grin showing huge tombstone teeth, 'Yeh, and who'd look after wee lass then?'

'How is she?'

'The wound is burning her up. But she's a valiant little mite. I believe you're right in thinkin' she'll pull through.'

'Let's hope.'

'I see you've started to load the glue.'

'Yeah, and if our little girl's uncle proves true, we'll have double the amount by the moon's wane.'

They stood in the cold air watching the barrels of precious glue being fastened into place on the cargo ship. Before long the hull took on another shape with the oarsmen's seats catching glints of moonlight like they were lined up ready to be put to immediate use. 'She's lying low in the water,' Bryn said at last, 'can she take more?'

'That's what I came to ask of you.'

The captain grabbed Yorevyn's shoulders nearly lifting him off his feet. 'First you bring a lass on my ship, then you make me lie to my men by passing her off as a boy apprentice, and now you want me to ship your goods.'

'You're ch- choking me.'

'Good.'

The ship rolled as a wave washed against it. On the shore the mounds of frozen surf were gathered up by the wake and pulled into the water. Bryn let go of Yorevyn's tunic and turned to scan his eyes towards the lake's middle.

'What's the matter?'

'Not sure,' whispered the captain, 'but I think we've got a krill-eater trapped in the lake.'

Zak fought off the cloud of screeching black feathers and picked up the limp body of the child. He held it close to his chest, wrapped his fur-lined cloak around the bony, lifeless form, willing his own heat to penetrate and bring colour to the waxy cheeks. In the moonlight, he could see the child had traces of vomit around its mouth and nose. He looked around where he knelt, found a patch of unmarked snow and taking a handful, wiped the face clean. A tear fell from Zak's cheek to land on the forehead of the upturned face. Zak hugged the child to his chest, feeling his heart ready to break for what he had done. He let out a huge sob, looked up to the sky and prayed, 'Oh Mighty Lords of the Heavens, make me learn from this terrible deed. Take the fire from my veins and teach me wisdom.'

He could not, would not, leave the child on the stinking mound. Cradling him close, he rose to his feet and walked back along the track to the intersection. He would carry the boy to the stream of clean water. He would wash him with reverence and wrap him in Zak's own tunic, so he would look presentable when he reached the Gods. Numb except for these thoughts Zak walked between the hovels, hearing but not registering the coughs and retching going on within. Nor did he notice more recent pools of semi-frozen vomit strewn along the side alleyways. His mind was filled with giving the body held in his arms a decent burial. He would collect enough stones to build a cairn so high that no scavenger, whether crow, wolf, or boar, would be able to reach what lay beneath.

Elvad, brother to Kaylak and soon to be Perak's brother too, strolled to the water's edge with Meg, the faithful wolfhound. The water was calm now with small surges rippling onto the stony beach. Meg gave a mournful cry, causing Elvad to pat her mighty neck and ruffle her fur. 'I know my friend,' He assured, 'you miss your master and so do we—but we still have each other.' But Meg wasn't assured—nor was she crying for Methiu. Instead she pointed her huge nose inland and lifted her head to give another howl. In the far distance, where the plains stretched to the mountains, came the sound of another howl.

'Now see what you've done?' Elvad whispered into the dog's pointed ears, 'You've brought us to the attention of wolves.'

Chapter Thirteen

Zak laid the child's body onto the crisp, clean snow and began to strip off the filthy rags it was clothed in. He broke the ice and dipped the rags into the free running water of the stream and worked quickly to cleanse them ready to use as bathing cloths. Down by the lake, a dog howled. Its mournful cry seemed to be appropriate in Zak's mind, it felt fitting for the task that lay ahead.

The boy was pitifully thin, so unlike his own son. Again, a pang of guilt shook through him. Should someone, long ago, have done something to ease the lives of the Forgotten? Back in the purple mountains where Skaldric ruled, everyone ate good food, drank clean water and slept on furs, whether they were high born or not. Why? Zak lamented. How could it be that the Forgotten people were of no concern—pushed out of mind, to be truly forgotten?

He lay the boy down whilst he returned to rinse the cloths, and heard a wolf's howl—not near to, but too close for comfort. Zak squeezed the excess water from the rags and returned to attend to the boy. In the still light of the moon, the child looked to Zak like he wasn't dead at all, but sleeping. Numb to the icy air, Zak took off the tunic he wore under his cloak and began to dress the boy in it. Memories of his own childhood came to the fore, and of those with his young brother Cadic

and to days when he had helped the lad to dress ready for the hunt. 'There,' He whispered to the lifeless child after donning him in the tunic, 'the Gods will welcome you now.' He rose and began to search for stones heavy enough to build a strong cairn and far away, on the plains that stretched between the lake and the purple mountains, a lone wolf's howl sang a lament for the dead. And, lay by the stream, wrapped in Zak's warm tunic, the child opened his eyes for a moment before closing them once more.

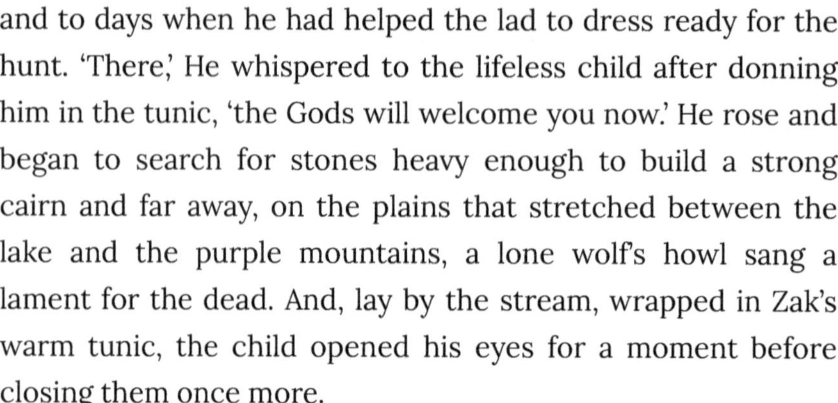

Elvad followed Meg as she circled in front of him, urging him to move faster but instead of boarding one of the ships moored by the wharf, she ran on towards the north end of the lake's shore. Normally, her movements would have suggested she wanted to play, but this time, Meg was sending Elvad signals of something more urgent. The distant wolves were too far away to be a threat, yet Elvad felt they were connected with Meg's behaviour. He stepped up his pace and broke into a jog, breathing in the cool air and purging his lungs from the smoke of the Roundhouse. Before long he came across a small river where the water flowed beneath its frozen surface and into the lake. With the heel of his boot, he broke off a portion of ice and stood back to allow Meg to drink. Somewhere upstream, the sound of rocks falling onto rocks could be heard.

Zak carried a large slab of stone and placed it by the circular wall he'd built. With each trip he glanced to where the boy lay, fearing the wolves would smell death and come to search for him before the grave was ready. Sweat ran through his hair and trickled down his back. It felt sticky without the woven fabric of his tunic to soak it up. He rubbed his cloak across his shoulders, hoping the fur lining would wipe the sweat away. When he looked up he saw a man with a hound walking towards him, the hound sniffed the body whilst the man continued up the hill.

Wiping the palms of his hands down his cloak, Zak walked to meet the man he'd taken an instant dislike to on the eve of the Midwinter feast.

Chapter Fourteen

Fiedra's burning was reaching the point where a fever either breaks or kills its host. Yorevyn watched as Bryn peeled the dressing off the wound on her face. He winced inwardly when the giant finally separated the two but stepped nearer to inspect the gash. 'Should I get Elvad to look at it?'

'Not yet,' whispered the captain, 'your cousin can't do any more than I'm doing. But if the fever doesn't break, then…'

'The air's chilling down fast. When, if, the fever breaks we may have to take her to the Roundhouse, get her to somewhere warm.'

The captain shook his head, 'She's better here where I can keep an eye on her. Besides, I've got stones warming under the braziers,' he gestured towards the wharf with his head, 'some I've packed around the cot, wrapped in fleeces to keep the bed heated.'

Yorevyn watched how Bryn gently examined the swollen areas around Fiedra's eye before applying the swab of sheep's wool soaked in water around the inflamed wound. 'See the centre where the unction has been smeared?'

'Yes—the red appears to be less angry.'

Bryn looked up at him, his face full of pride. 'That's the deepest part of the wound. With luck, by tomorrow, the rest will be less angry.'

'I owe you plenty.'

'How very true, my friend, how very true.'

'Get that hound away from him.'

'Meg—come here.' The dog gave the child another sniff before obeying Elvad and coming to heel.

'What do you want?' Zak examined the sides of the cairn's wall until satisfied it was strong enough to take the weight of the covering slab.

'I want nothing but Meg senses something is wrong.'

Zak glanced in the direction of the plains. 'Did you hear wolves?'

'Meg has been bred to fight wolves. She has no fear of them.'

'Then take her away from here, take her onto the plains, get rid of them before they get wind of us.'

'There isn't time to chase wolves. Our people may be sailing to the West lands soon. Yorevyn, our trading agent, has almost completed his task. All three ships will probably leave together.'

'Will Perak be taken from her family sooner than planned?'

'Probably.'

'Don't you know?'

'I'm not going with them.'

'Why?'

'My path is on a different course, I am travelling on a kind of pilgrimage, an exploration in the art of healing—I seek enlightenment.'

Zak stared at Elvad's open face and saw the truth in what he said. 'I er, I too have a thirst for wisdom. I, er, I caused the death of the child down there.' The words just blurted out. 'He came out of nowhere, vomited on my boots, I er, I'd lashed out without thinking. He, er, he's one of the Forgotten.'

'Forgotten?'

'Low born folk that live on the scraps even your hound would refuse to eat. They never leave their area. We call it the Shadows. A place respectable people know not to venture.'

'What were you doing there?'

'I, er, I wanted to, needed to think. Needed to be away from everyone. I strolled off the beaten track without thought.'

Meg inched away from the men, making her way back to the body, illuminated now by starlight. As she neared the boy's head, she sniffed the vaporised air leaking from his nose and gave a single, but excited bark.

Donated from the Roundhouse, extra food had been placed in wicker baskets and brought to the fishing village, where

volunteers were working to repair the damaged boats. A makeshift canopy lit by braziers had become their workshop and amidst it all, Bryn and Yorevyn's men had left the comfort of their lodging house to lend a hand. Soon, two musicians started to play their instruments giving the workforce tunes they all recognised and hummed to. The task of reconstruction became easier with talk of a monster the fishermen swear they saw being quelled by the longboat oarsmen. They, being more familiar with the ways of deep water, assured the simple folk that there was no creature and the whirlpool was nothing more than a freak of nature.

Along the labyrinth walkways of the Shadows, a sled is being pulled. A lone man stoops to pick up another bundle of rags and wedges it securely on top of his load. He bends to pick up his harness, but staggers to one side and vomits.

Zak cradled the child to him before placing him into the stone circle.

'I tell you, the dog knows something is wrong.' Elvad held onto Meg's ruff, preventing her from attacking Zak a second

time. 'She doesn't go for humans she's been bred to fight other dog-like creatures.'

Zak found it easy to ignore the outsider, but the hound was another matter. As soon as the burial of the child was completed, he would slit the dog's throat.

'I thought,' Elvad pleaded as he struggled with the dog, intent on being released, 'I thought you said you sought wisdom.'

'That was before your brute charged at me.'

'She knocked you over, that's all. She does it sometimes to prevent people either hurting someone or themselves.'

'Well I don't need a dog as a nursemaid.' Zak lifted one of the stone slabs and placed it across the top of the stones. The hound let out a howl. 'Take that mange-ridden mutt away—a noise like that will bring the wolves close.'

Elvad gripped the scruff of Meg's neck, bringing her to a firm heel. She whined—more at the frustration she felt rather than pain. He slipped the belt from his cloak and looped it across her throat, holding the two ends and locking them firmly around his wrist. He turned to head back to the shore but Meg resisted by placing her huge feet apart and bedding them into the ice. 'At the risk of repeating myself, Zak, son of Sarash and brother to Cadic, the hound knows something dreadful is about to happen. And it concerns either you or the burial of that child.'

'Well I don't want any help from your dog and the body in this cairn is beyond her help. Perhaps,' He curled a cruel lip, 'the wolf in her has developed a taste for man-flesh.' He lifted

the third and final slab and closed the top of the cairn with a satisfied release of air from his lungs.

Elvad tugged the corded belt and pulled the dog down the hill. As his stride got wider and faster Meg slid behind him, making every effort to hinder Elvad's step. Eventually, when they reached the stream's outlet to the lake, Meg gave up her fight, broke into a lolloping trot, and came to heel by Elvad's side.

Chapter Fifteen

The music from the boat mender's yard wafted along the shoreline, and to where Yorevyn and Bryn sat by the braziers drinking ale. 'So how did it get into the lake?'

Bryn scratched and tugged at his beard, 'Dunno, but if it wants to feed, it'll have to find its way back to the salt sea. Aren't no shrimps small enough in these waters.'

'Probably just as well—you know how territorial fishermen can be? They'd sooner let you have one of their wives than share any of their catch.'

Bryn shuddered, 'I've seen the wife of a fisherman. Not a good look.'

Yorevyn's laugh held deep bass tones. 'If my memory serves me well, your own wife's no pretty catch.'

'What 'd'ya mean? She's a wonderful woman. She's got special qualities.'

'Like what?'

'She likes me going to sea.'

'Aye,' Yorevyn reached for the flagon of ale. 'I'd forgot about *those* special qualities.' He poured a measure into his tankard before offering to refill the captain's. From the ship, Fiedra's

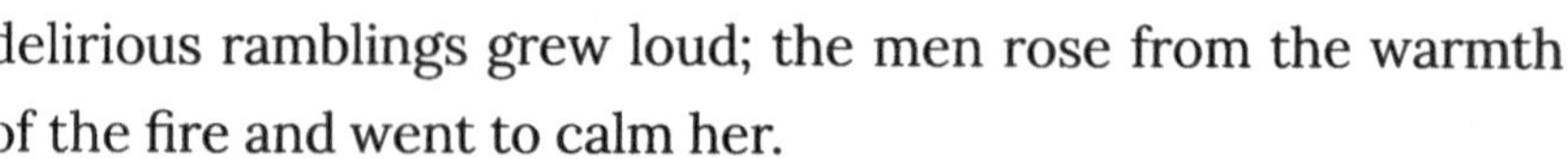

delirious ramblings grew loud; the men rose from the warmth of the fire and went to calm her.

Elvad reached the first of the line of torches lighting the shoreline, he slipped the makeshift leash from around Meg's neck but before releasing her fully, gave her the order to stay at heel. A few strides further, where the welcome braziers sparked and glowed, sat Bryn and Yorevyn. As he neared them, they leapt from their seated tubs to board Bryn's sleek boat. It was at that moment Meg turned around, circling once more for Elvad to follow her, he looked up and down the wharf and further to where music could be heard. But Meg wanted him to go back along the route they'd come from. She yelped for him to follow, circling tighter and tighter, coiling around and around, a knowing sign amongst his people that Meg had sensed a terrible wrong.

'I told his family you would help him.' Fiedra's head turned first this way and then that, her skin dry and hot. 'Yet he remains parted from them. He is bewildered, hungry and trapped.'

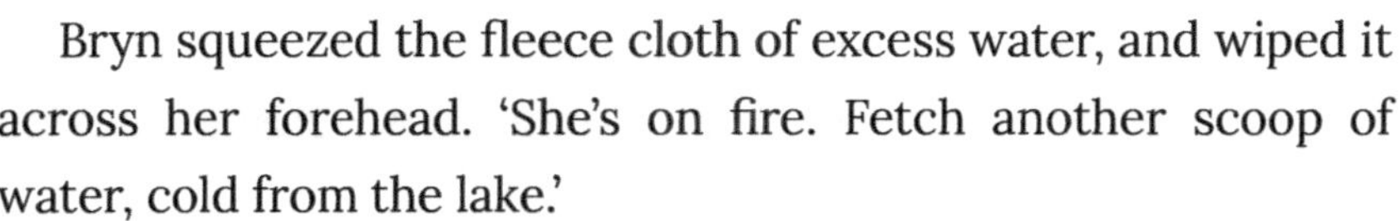

Bryn squeezed the fleece cloth of excess water, and wiped it across her forehead. 'She's on fire. Fetch another scoop of water, cold from the lake.'

Yorevyn ran to obey, grabbing one of the leather pails as he went. The ship gave a lurch. A wave rose up and broke across the wharf. Meg's yelping turned to a howl as she left Elvad to circle in front of his cousin.

'Don't have time for you now, my beauty,' Yorevyn gave a pat to the loyal hound's head, 'Bryn needs me.' He scooped the bucket into the lake and snatched it back before another surge rolled in. He ran onto the boat: Meg followed him. She stood trembling by the opening of the cabin, nose in the air, ears pinned back to her scalp.

'He needs your help soon.' Fiedra pleaded, her ranting filling the tiny space, 'Needs to be back with his kin. Will you keep your promise and help him?'

'Dear lass, if only we knew what's ailing you.' Bryn swapped over buckets, plunging the fleecy sponge into the fresh, icy water, then dabbed it—soothing and cooling Fiedra's skin with every move. Her head stopped rocking from side to side and her breathing relaxed, allowing the giant's hands to work their magic.

Suddenly, her voice rang clear in the confines of her bunk. 'Why have you brought that hound here?'

Bryn looked to Yorevyn and, crouched behind him saw Meg, jaw hanging, tongue dribbling and panting. '

'Why, lass,' said Bryn, 'Meg visits us often. She is part of our clan. Why shouldn't she be brought to us?'

Fiedra's eyes opened. They were heavy with fever but she turned them to where Meg sat on haunches behind Yorevyn. 'You meant me no harm. I know that now. You fret over a child. One you say must not to be forgotten.'

Elvad had boarded the ship. 'Did someone say Forgotten?' He asked.

Fiedra's eyes turned to the ceiling and her lids closed over them.

The lighted torch that Elvad carried gave off sparks, which circled in a stream behind him. Having no need for artificial light, Meg ran on ahead where she yelped around the cairn, leaping over Zak who was lying huddled by its side. Elvad wedged the stem of the torch into a crevice between two rocks and pulled aside one of the cairn's weighty stone lids. He picked up the flame and shone it into the grave. The light glinted on two eyes as they turned towards it. He jammed the flaming torch between the remaining slabs, reached arms into the opening and pulled the child out.

Using the furs taken from the ship, Elvad wrapped the boy up and held him close. He pushed the wad of wool Bryn had given him between the child's lips and squeezed the moisture it held so it would trickle down his throat. The boy coughed but began to suck on the wad again.

Meg gave a low growl when Zak came to and began to find his feet. 'By the gods,' he croaked, 'am I never to be rid of you?'

Elvad rummaged through the pouch, found more of the liquid he'd given to the child and offered Zak the flask. 'The boy wasn't dead,' Elvad blurted, offering the flask again. Zak shook his head, trying to focus on what was happening. 'Do you understand? You didn't kill him. The dog smelled the life in him, she forced me to come back.'

Zak wiped a hand across his face, rubbed his eyes and stared at the child wrapped in fleeces. 'Either you are mad or I am. I saw him being thrown on that stinking mound to rot. He was white and cold as the water I used to clean him. I know when someone is dead. What are you? Some sort of freak who, with a click of his fingers, thinks he can quicken a corpse?' His speech began to slur. He tried again to stand but fell back against the cairn wall.

'We need food, all of us. Come, Zak, brother to Cadic, my cousin Yorevyn has promised to cook us fish.' Elvad lifted the boy over one shoulder and held his free hand towards Zak. 'You have plenty to rejoice in.'

Bryn approached the brazier, retrieved his tankard from where he'd left it and took a long gulp of the cool ale. He wiped his mouth with the back of his hand and belched. Yorevyn scooped embers aside, making them flat enough for the purpose before pushing the fish onto them. They flared

momentarily before settling to a gentle sizzle. The aroma caused the juices in Bryn's stomach to roll. He belched again, grabbed his wooden platter from beside the beer flagon and wiped the frost off it. Yorevyn turned each fish over with the broad of his sword and stood back when they flared. 'What d'you make of our little girl then?'

Bryn's eyes never left the fish, 'Too soon to say. We must wait for Elvad to return. But if she saw what Meg tried to tell us, then she's something so special—it's scary. And, remember, she knew we had a cat. Maybe she's trying to tell us something about this man who has been separated from his kin and needs our help?'

'Could the man not be a man but the boy buried on the slopes?'

The huge head shook copper locks catching the colour of the brazier putting the fire's glow into shade. 'Nay blessed boy, that little mite's been ranting on about him ever since you brought her to me. No, he's someone else and she's holding me to my promise and not letting go.'

'What promise?'

'That we'd help him find his family.' Bryn curled his beard around his fingers, 'Are you going to feed me or not?'

The crows squabbled over the latest offering; causing a plume of angry feathers to conceal what they pecked at. Not having made it to the community dump, the sled lay on its

side, empty of it's gruesome cargo - its dead owner trapped beneath and still wearing the reins. Scurrying between the dump and the black-feathered cloud—rats twitched their pink noses, dragged their long pink tails across the filthy snow, and scratched with clawed pink feet at the fleas hidden in their black fur. They swarmed over the mound, snarling at the birds swooping upon them—showing their fangs of needle-like teeth. Life on the mound was thriving for those living off the dead of the Shadows.

Zak held the wooden platter in both hands, but made no attempt to eat the fish placed on it. He stared at the boy taking bite size junks of fish from Elvad's fingers. He was very much alive. Thin and still pale, even in the light of the brazier but nevertheless, the boy was very much alive. The boy's eyes darted from one man to the other before resting on the man that fed him, and his mouth opened like that of a pet dog to take the food without snapping; and when it closed to chew, every bone of his jaw showed through the gaunt, pallid skin. Zak's mind flashed back to images of his own boy—a baby not yet two winters old, but weighing more than the child in front of him. Were all the children of the Forgotten as thin as this one? He wondered. And if so, how by the gods above do they manage to reach puberty and adulthood?

Elvad took the offered cup of water and held it to the boy's lips, 'Sip,' He urged, 'sip.' The boy swallowed the chewed fish before freeing his arms from the fur wrap and taking the cup

with both hands. He gulped it down, draining the last drop into his gullet and burped.

The men around the fire burst into laughter, Yorevyn slapped Elvad's back. 'If you're going to teach him to quaff like that, take care when he develops a thirst for ale.'

The boy looked from Yorevyn to Bryn and watched as they picked up their own tankards and knocked them together in a way of camaraderie alien to him. He gave Zak a moment's stare before turning his eyes back to Elvad. Thrusting his cup against the brim of Elvad's, he yelled, 'Sip!'

Chapter Sixteen

The party of men repairing the broken fishing boats slept under the cover of their purpose-built workshop. Behind them, the waters of the lake rose and fell bringing a wave to roll up the shore before it was dragged back across the shingle then sending another, stronger surge of water to reach further up the beach. It gave a rhythmic sound, lulling those curled in the unfinished boats or on top of the heaps of fishing nets into a sense of security, sending them deeper into their slumber.

And inside the Roundhouse, folk slept on warm furs, their stomachs full and minds at ease having spent another evening in the company of kinfolk. Zak's wife tossed and turned under the woven blankets of her sisters and cousins, kinfolk ordered by Cadic to care for her. Her child slept with other members of her clan's children, the Shaman's gift still clenched in his podgy hand.

Only the elders and chiefs kept vigil by the fire. They talked at length about matters of state and the need to keep to the traditional way of life.

'It would appear,' said Skaldric the moment Mowdah, the elder had finished his turn, 'that change is upon us, whether we like it or not.'

'In what way?'

'I speak of recent times, like, for instance, my insistence that we pack up and return to our homeland before the thaw.'

Mowdah nodded gravely, 'I know I resisted that change to our ways but, you were right to overrule. It has kept us safe from the sickness.'

'Locals say the sickness didn't come last winter. Perhaps it has passed.'

'Nevertheless, Skaldric, the early trek back did little harm to our livestock, so, I think we should keep it and add it to our preferred way of life.'

'And what of other ideas—say for instance, Zak's plan to strengthen the settlement?'

'Foolhardy—Zak needs to gain more experience of life before spouting unrealistic ideals.'

'Yeah, there is merit in what you say, Mowdah, but we could at least give him a platform. Hear what he has to say—without the necessity of always talking him down.'

'Skaldric's got a point Mowdah,' One of the lesser Elders broke in. 'Remember what the Shaman said? We should give the young ones an ear.'

'Bah,' Mowdah sucked his teeth, 'my bones are too old to listen to more of this nonsense—time I went to my bed.'

Skaldric watched the old man shuffle away from the hearth to disappear into the shadows where his pile of furs lay. A shudder ran through his body, wondering how many more treks across the Great Plain the old man would make. His mind switched to Zak who still had not returned to his wife and

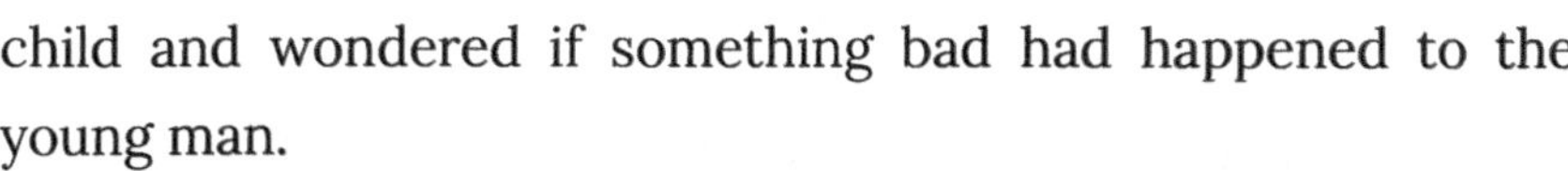

child and wondered if something bad had happened to the young man.

'Such contemplation should be wearing a gold crown.'

Skaldric looked up, his grin showing genuine fondness, 'Ah Kaylak, has my daughter run out of questions?'

'She's certainly inquisitive, that I'll grant you. Urdeth called her over a while back, I have been getting to know Cadic. He says your boys are interested in learning the skills of seafaring, is that so?

Skaldric filled Kaylak a measure of mead. 'Cadic is like his brother Zak, he says too much.' He handed the goblet to his future son-in-law and raised his own. 'My sons are like their sister, interested in everything under the sky. Your good health.'

'And yours.'

'Urdeth worries herself sick about them. They are strong and good huntsmen but she frets they will come to harm.'

'As do all mothers. But learning the ways of the sea is no more dangerous than hunting a boar. It's like all things—if we are taught by good masters, then the risks should be lessened, besides learning new skills should be a pleasure for everyone to enjoy.'

Skaldric nodded, 'Have your men teach my boys, I'll calm my wife's fears. Tell me, has Cadic had news of Zak?'

Kaylak shook his head. 'He didn't mention him. As you know, I have spent the evening being interrogated by your daughter, but if you like, I could do with a drop of fresh air, I'll walk down to the wharf, see if any of the men have seen him.'

As Kaylak walked along the shoreline, waves rolled, one after another, across the shingle. He paused to look across the water but the starlight was fading and the lake gave nothing away. Braziers burned ahead of his path; they arced tiny lights that outlined the curve of the bay. The village where the fishermen lived was dark. But near to the beach, torches flickered under the canopy of the repair hut and as he strode by, he caught the rhythm of synchronised snoring and smiled, wondering what manner of liquor the sleepers had drunk.

Ahead of him and against the dark backdrop, the flames of Bryn's brazier glistened. Movement leapt before it in a shape familiar to him as it headed his way. He braced himself for Meg's greeting as she ploughed into him, wrapping him inside her circling bulk, expressing her canine joy with nuzzles and groans. When she had settled down Kaylak allowed her to lead the way, filling his lungs with the cool air wafting from across the lake and toying with his thoughts of spending the future with a purple eyed princess.

Images of her heart-shaped face flickered across his mind—her spontaneity and untamed hair delighting him more than he could have wished for. And something else—something he couldn't fathom but felt was there, yet out of his reach. A trait he thought she had inherited from Urdeth, his beguiling mother-in-law to be.

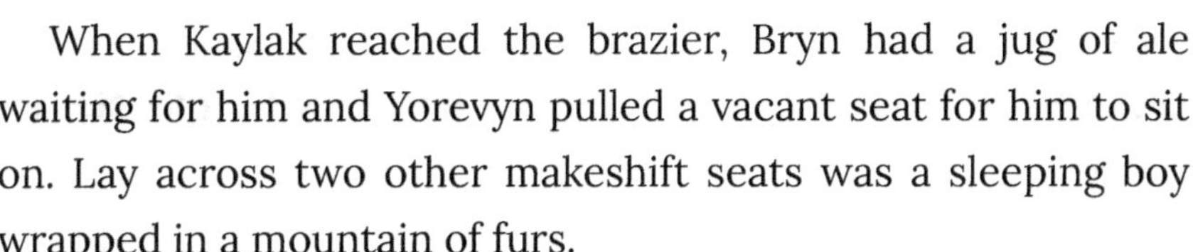

When Kaylak reached the brazier, Bryn had a jug of ale waiting for him and Yorevyn pulled a vacant seat for him to sit on. Lay across two other makeshift seats was a sleeping boy wrapped in a mountain of furs.

'This the new apprentice we're takin' on?' Nodding towards the child and taking hold of the jug.

'By the gods, is nothing secret here?'

'Cadic, brother to Zak has been making new friends with our men.'

Yorevyn glanced at the sleeping child, 'Yeh, that's him alright, though he's a puny mite, need to fatten 'im up before we take 'im on.'

Kaylak took a long drink of the ale, 'By the gods, but that tastes so good.'

'Sick of mead eh?'

'Too rich for my palate.'

'So—how's life in the Roundhouse, apart from the liberal flow of mead?'

Kaylak's eyes picked up the light of the torches, where it danced merrily for a moment. 'Good.' He took another draught and looked around the wharf. 'Have you seen or heard anything of Zak, brother to Cadic?'

'Yeh,' said Bryn. 'He's not feeling well—gone to cool off by the stream, Elvad's with him.'

'His wife is beside herself with worry. I said I'd go look for him.'

'When he returns, we'll send him to her. Though if its mead rotting his guts, then he's better staying with the stream water.'

Elvad watched the vomit gush from Zak's gullet and turned his face away from the stench. He'd smelled that stench before, seen the colour of bile before and remembered the fever that accompanied it. Many years ago, he and Kaylak had both nursed their father and later when they fell sick: their father took his turn to nurse them through it. The sickness had a name—yet to this day, superstition was so great that Elvad never heard anyone utter it.

He waited until Zak exhausted the contents of his stomach and crept towards him, urging the crouched man to his feet. 'Come my friend, the stream is near, the water will cool you, and cleanse your burning throat.' He wrapped his arms under Zak's belly and heaved him up, dragging him across the shingle and to where the rivulet met the lake. Once there, he broke off chunks of ice to cup the flowing water beneath and pour it through Zak's burning parched lips. Greedily, Zak took every drop Elvad could scoop until he succumbed to the fever and fell slumped on the spongy moss.

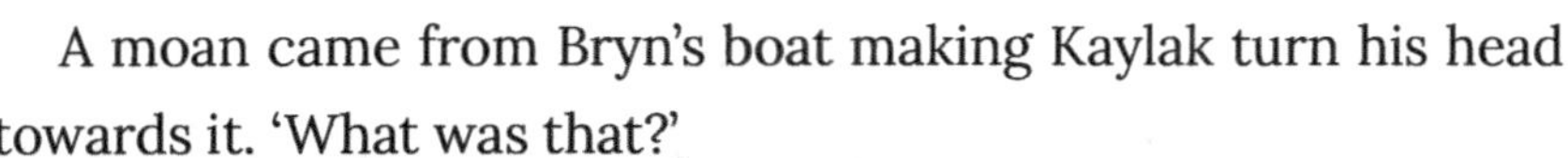

A moan came from Bryn's boat making Kaylak turn his head towards it. 'What was that?'

'The er, the….'

'The other apprentice,' Yorevyn interrupted, 'not much better than this, but Meg knocked him over and split his head.'

Kaylak looked to where Meg lay and noted her eyebrows twitch with guilt. 'What did the boy do?'

'Nothing,' Yorevyn reached for the flagon of ale, topped Kaylak's jug up and tried to change the subject. 'So how does your little princess like the gifts our people have sent her?'

'Never mind my princess,—why did Meg go for a child?'

'She didn't go for the child. She knocked him over when she greeted me, the child has a gammy leg.' Yorevyn stood up and walked towards the boat. 'I'll check on her, er, him.'

'Aye—and whilst yer do,' Bryn conferred, 'I'll catch up with my old friend Kaylak. Now tell me old friend, will your bride-to-be allow you to continue with your travels?'

Despite calling out moments earlier, Fiedra lay quietly in her bed, her breathing slower and deep. Yorevyn squeezed excess water from a handful of sheep's wool and dabbed it on her brow. She turned her head from it and grunted. He put the wad back in the pail and turned to leave. 'They thank you for coming to the aid of their kin.'

Yorevyn spun round, 'Who are *they*, Fiedra?'

'His family—they can't reach him—they don't understand how he got into the lake but he's going to die if he can't get back to the Salt sea. They are waiting for him.'

'He's the *krill eater*?'

'Yes.'

'Fiedra, how do you know this?'

'They speak to me.'

'Fiedra, did Meg speak to you?'

'About the boy?'

'Yes.'

'Yes the hound sensed life and knows living things mustn't be buried.'

Yorevyn knelt by the cot, 'Fiedra, does the wound still ail you?'

'No, tell the flame-haired giant his unction has worked.' She opened her eyes in time to see his twisted smile, 'Will you make haste to help the *krill eater*?' And this time her eyes did not roll to the top of her head, instead her lashes closed sleepily onto cheeks less puffy than of late.

When Yorevyn rejoined his companions by the brazier, Kaylak had taken Meg for a stroll along the shore.

'The fever's broken.'

Bryn's eyes reflected the joy they both felt. 'By the gods, but she's got more guts than you'd know by the look of her.'

'She's got more than guts Bryn my friend. She's blessed with insight.'

'Yeah, like I said, she knew we had a cat. Knew the crafty animal was playing with my unction.'

'She says to tell you it worked, the unction. And the help you promised is getting urgent. It's the *krill eater*, it's trapped and its ma and da want us to set it free and return it to the Salt sea before it dies.'

When Bryn's jaw dropped open, his beard lost its sparkle and drooped uncoiled on his chest. 'Oh is that all?' He said at length, 'that wee lass told you that—did she?'

'What wee lass?' Kaylak stood behind the brazier warming his hands. 'What's going on around here?'

Perak watched Kira pack the silk gown into the carved chest, 'Apart from Fiedra finding work with her uncle Kira, what other news have you of her?'

'None—you know more than any how she shuns society.'

'But she made it across the plain? You're sure of that?'

'Yes—I told you, she went to work for her uncle.'

'But who is he? Fiedra has never mentioned an uncle before —why would she suddenly leave us to work for him?'

'Except for the kindness you gave her, Fiedra never felt welcomed by the settlement. Perhaps she saw your betrothal as a signal to start a new life.'

Perak inhaled, began to unravel the ribbons from her hair, 'I don't want you to wear those clothes—it upsets me.'

When Kira's eyes glowed, their full orbs caught the light of the torches, 'But Fiedra gave me this dress.'

'I know and when I am made a princess, I will have you supplied with new ones. But for now, I can't stand the hurt of seeing you in my best friend's clothes.'

'What am I to do with them?'

Perak stood up from her stool and pulled the remaining ribbons from her hair, setting it free to spring in every direction. 'Take them away, anywhere, but don't let me see them again—now leave me. My mother is on her way. She will groom me tonight.'

Kaylak stood at Yorevyn's side, both hands gripping the cold bar of the ship. He stared at the entrance to the cabin where Bryn had gone to tend to his charge. 'So let me get this right: the lass in there isn't the boy apprentice the crew think she is. She is instead, the niece of the man supplying us with glue.'

'Yes.'

'And you bought her from her uncle.'

'Yes—well he actually paid me to take her off his hands. All part of the deal.'

Kaylak ran his hand through his hair, 'So why did we buy *this* little fella?'

Yorevyn stared at the child sleeping soundly by the brazier. 'You won't believe how we acquired him.'

'I won't?

Yorevyn shook his head, 'Trust me—the way this day is going—I'm not entirely sure *I* believe it. But all I can say is the little lady being nursed by our captain is so special—I think she may be a Spirit visitor.'

Kaylak's eyes widened, 'Can I see her?'

'Bryn doesn't want her taken to the Roundhouse.'

'But the women there, they can look after her needs.'

'Her needs have been looked after well enough. Besides, we may be putting to sea soon, and she insists we help in her "divine" works.'

'Divine? What on Earth are you talking about?'

'Sit down cousin, and when I finish explaining, don't say I don't believe it. Because, like I said earlier, this has been a day to remember.'

Chapter Seventeen

To the rear of the Roundhouse near the latrines, a pair of pink paws scratched the black fur of a fellow rat and twitched its whiskers. The scent of the creature revealed it to be a brother, yet no mourning for its death took place, it simply scampered over the body to follow the sweeter smell of cooked food.

At that moment, Meg came into view, and in one well aimed snap of her mighty jaws the rat lay dead and was tossed to lie in the ditch alongside its brother. She searched the area for more but found none. Job done, the hound returned to the wharf where Kaylak was in conversation with Yorevyn and Bryn.

Chapter Eighteen

Elvad woke to find Zak still asleep. He checked him over looking for the signs he had become familiar with—signs that told him what type of sickness Zak had. It was following a similar pattern to that of the fever he, his brother and his father had been struck down with several winters ago. A long time had passed, yet the memory of the bodies being carted out of the citadel to be set alight remained blazoned in his mind.

It occurred during their travels to the Southlands, a place of exquisite colour and warmth, yet had they been warned, they would not have anchored but turned back their ships instead. But the sickness had already spread among the residents in the poorer areas of the citadel and nothing had been done to prevent it reaching the palace, where Methiu and his family had been invited to stay. So rapid was the rising death toll that the army had to be brought in to take away the dead and burn them.

Afterwards, those who came down with but survived the sickness were held in contempt. Accused of being in league with a demon spirit—accused of being spared for some unforeseen purpose by the evil one. By comparison, those who had spent time amongst the sick, nursing them, mostly right to

the end, were considered blessed if they did not succumb to the illness.

Elvad came into the former category. Yet he had often wondered why the majority did die and in so short of time from acquiring the illness. He wondered whether there was some truth in what the Southland accusers had said. Not the demonic side of the accusation, but whether Kaylak, their father and he, had been spared so they could spend the rest of their lives doing good. Ever since, wherever they docked their ships, they had striven to find cures for fevers and searched for knowledge of remedies for all kinds of ailments.

He knelt down and removed a layer of ice from the stream, cupping the freezing water with both hands; he swilled it over his face. Droplets of ice clung to his hair and beard. He dried them off with the hem of his shirt and scooped more water to drink. He turned his gaze back to Zak, wondering whether to wake him and force him to drink or to leave him in peace. He decided on the former, a method used when Kaylak and Methiu fell ill.

He stood and wandered to the stream's outlet searching for a vessel in which to carry water and found a smoothed stone that had been hollowed out by the elements.

'Come, my friend,' he coaxed his patient, 'take the cool water into your system. It may cleanse whatever ails you.'

Zak obeyed and parted his cracked lips enough for Elvad to administer the liquid before returning to his deep slumber where he was left to rest.

Meg ran to greet Elvad as he approached the wharf, followed by the little waif holding the hem of the ankle-length undershirt he wore; and tried to keep up with the dog.

'Don't come near me,' He tried to ward off the boy. Too late —the child copied the antics of Meg and circled Elvad mimicking the hound's gleeful noises. Letting go of the shirt he leapt up until Elvad was forced to catch him. 'Bryn, Yorevyn— listen to me,' He called above the noisy greeting. 'I think Zak has the sickness. You know—the one Kaylak and Father and myself came down with.'

Bryn stopped in his approach.

Yorevyn finished putting fuel on the brazier and wiped his hands down his hide coat, horror streaked across both of their faces.

'I will stay with Zak,' Elvad yelled, 'but I need supplies, furs and things. Can you put them where I can collect them without coming close?'

They were all men who didn't ask questions when help was needed. They had practiced the drill so many times, 'Aye—we'll do that. But you should know, we intend to leave today.'

Elvad's shock caused the child in his arms to stop his play. Yorevyn's eagerness to return with the shipment of fish-glue was well known, but to leave so soon? 'Perhaps it is as well,' was all he could say without raising his voice, 'if there is sickness here.'

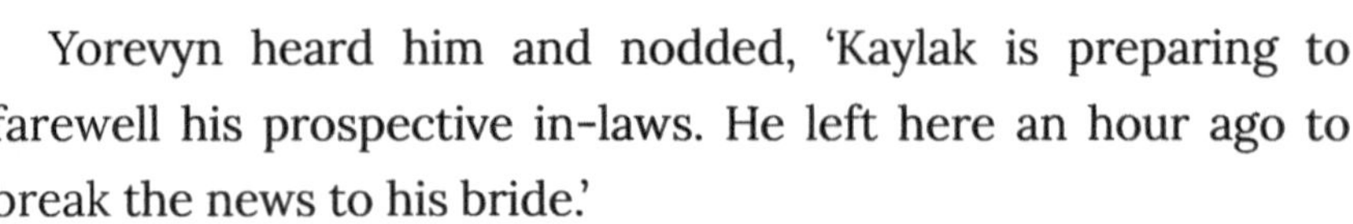

Yorevyn heard him and nodded, 'Kaylak is preparing to farewell his prospective in-laws. He left here an hour ago to break the news to his bride.'

'That is good—tell him I will keep Meg with me. Tell him my quest to find cures may have come sooner than expected. Tell him we will meet again perhaps for the Midsummer Feast.'

Yorevyn carried a bundle of furs and placed them on the ground, 'Take these for now. We will fill a sled and leave it for you. My men will not need the lodging houses any more, when you feel you need shelter, use them.'

Elvad watched them turn away, 'What am I to do with this little fella?'

'He belongs to Zak.' Bryn yelled.

'But what about the sickness?'

'He's like you—blessed by the demon spirit.' The giant turned to face them and grinned. 'I'll have warm clothes and preserved food and dry tinder left for you. Take care my friend, until we meet at the Summer solstice.'

Chapter Nineteen

Perak watched the youths of her own settlement carry her chests of clothes out of the Roundhouse and pile them onto the waiting sled. She pulled tight the fur-lined cloak around her middle and turned her eyes onto the lake.

This was the day she had dreaded, though in truth she thought it would come later. She had hoped to stay until the sun peeped above the mountains for a while longer before sinking once more to darken the skies. But that wasn't to be. She would leave all she had known to ride the salt seas to the land of the West where, according to Kaylak, it stayed green for ten whole moons of the solar cycle. Ten whole moons.

She looked towards the activity by the wharf, straining her eyes to catch sight of her brothers and found Kaylak supervising the loading of their ship. Apart from papa, he was the kindest man she had ever met. And amusing too, in the way he made her laugh, with his stories of far off places.

Her brothers crossed her vision, stopping to talk to Kaylak, he embracing them like they were his own kin - which of course, they would be soon; and Kaylak pointing to something aboard the largest of the ships and her brothers running off in that direction.

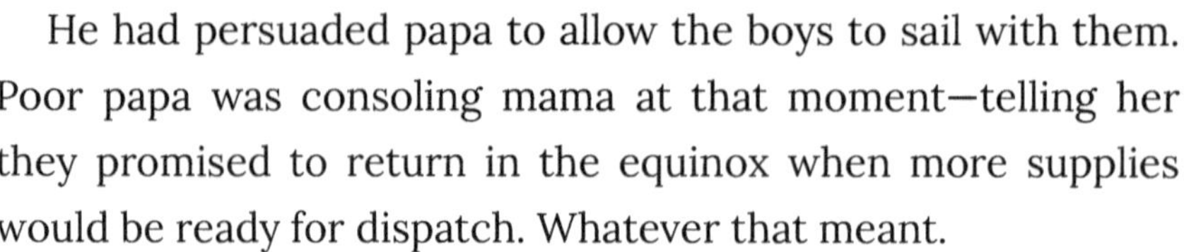

He had persuaded papa to allow the boys to sail with them. Poor papa was consoling mama at that moment—telling her they promised to return in the equinox when more supplies would be ready for dispatch. Whatever that meant.

Meanwhile Perak scanned the shores and the settlements around the lake searching for sight of Fiedra—whose disappearance from her life had left a hole so deep it threatened to drag her in. Once aboard the ship and away from mama's prying thoughts, Perak would ask Kaylak what his people's views were about lameness. And whether a person with such an affliction could befriend a princess. She knew her mama was distraught, otherwise a thought like that would be challenged. She turned and walked back to the Roundhouse— where with an aching heart, she would spend the last few moments with her beloved parents.

Chapter Twenty

The Shaman's reindeer trod through the deep snow with ease. Methiu held the reins loosely in his lap and dozed. He woke when the sleigh stopped and found the deer had reached their destination—a cave set deep under snow-covered rocks. He stretched his muscles and stepped down, feeling the crisp deep snow beneath his boots. The Shaman stirred.

'Come Wise One, take my hand, our journey is at an end.'

The Shaman reached out but instead of taking hold of Methiu's offered hand he fell forward and into the King of the Westland's arms. Being of little weight, Methiu easily carried him to the shelter of the cave where he placed the old man's frail body onto the dry ground. The air was warm and further back a yellow glow lit the rugged stone interior.

'Is there someone living here?' Methiu called, but no answer came.

He returned to the sleigh and unharnessed the deer. Without orders or the need to be led, they filed one after another through a gap between the cave opening and the steep side of the craggy mountain. Curious, Methiu followed and in the light of the rising moon saw the deer had found

mosses growing on the slopes of the rocks. He returned to unpack provisions from the sleigh and set to lighting a fire.

The smell of cured venison warming over the hot stones brought the Shaman out of his slumber. Methiu helped him to sit and placed fleeces to support his back. 'Has Mira arrived?' the old man whispered.

'Mira? Do you mean Urdeth's mother?'

The Shaman nodded as he took the offered skewer that was threaded with strips of tender meat. 'She promised she would be here for my return.'

'Perhaps the snow is too deep.'

'No—Mira will come. It is we who are early, my son. We travelled well.'

Methiu looked around the cave and to where the yellow glow had lit the back wall but his firelight now dominated and so he could not see it. 'Tell me, Wise One, does Urdeth favour her mother?'

The Shaman nodded; yellow flames caught the twinkle in his eye, 'Urdeth has her mother's beauty if that's what your question intended.'

Methiu smiled, 'Skaldric is a fortunate man. And now my son is to wed their daughter who also shares her mama's fine looks.' He twisted another length of cured meat onto a skewer and placed it onto another hot stone where it sizzled and sent swirls of blue smoke up to the dark heights of the cave. 'I also refer to something the Elders of the Roundhouse mentioned. That of Urdeth's other attributes, the gift of knowing things others don't.'

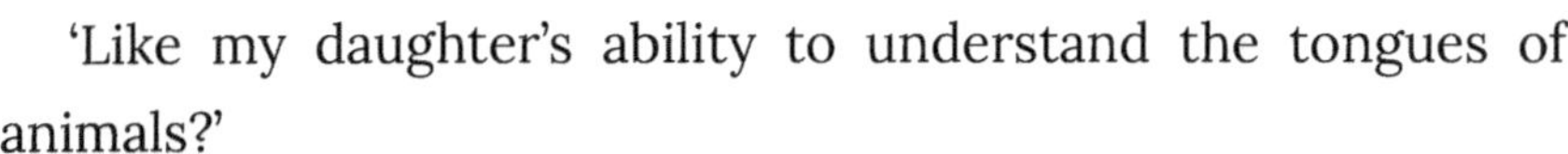

'Like my daughter's ability to understand the tongues of animals?'

Methiu spun to where the voice came from.

Stepping easily down the smooth slope and holding an oil lamp before her was Mira, the mother of Urdeth and grandmother of Perak. She was known in his homeland as the forest dweller, a queen amongst women and skilled in the art of medicine. He left the side of the fire and knelt before her. She laughed and held out her free hand. 'A king of the West does not bow to me.'

'This one does.' He took her offered hand and rose. 'Will you eat with us?'

Chapter Twenty-One

Bryn's ship was the first to leave the wharf. His course took them to the lake's centre where he knew the *krill eater* searched for food. Fiedra, wrapped in fleeces was lying, head propped by cushions, in the bunk. She slid in and out of consciousness, yet Bryn was sure her fever no longer raged. His crew had arrived at the lake via a network of deep rivers, a route he knew the creature would not have taken. The opposite side of the lake was new territory to his crew. But the only passage the krill-eater could have taken. Guiding a huge creature through the narrow cuts that linked one lake to another would be tough, but he trusted his men and their navigational skills. And, he reasoned, if the creature had found a way into the lake, then there must be a way out.

Yorevyn captained the cargo ship whilst Kaylak took command of his father's. Perak's tear-streaked eyes stared along the shoreline, sometimes resting on the building that dominated the hillside, other times searching amongst the crowd gathered to see them off. The view became smaller until the only sight that was left was that of the Roundhouse and the veils of smoke hanging thick in the murky air.

The last moments of farewell echoed inside her head, with mama being brave, striving to hold everything together, and dada, weeping uncontrollably, hugging her so she could not

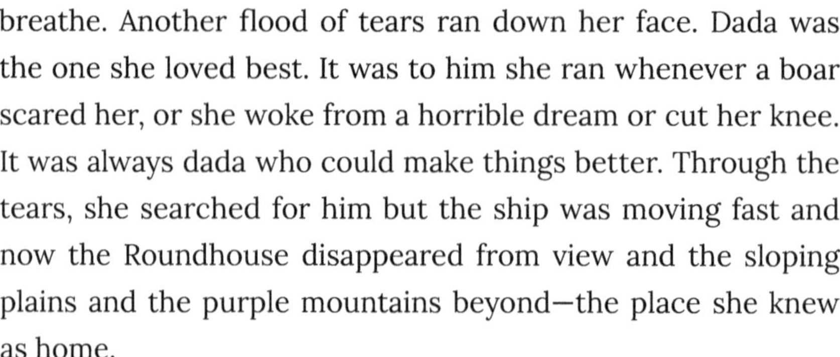

breathe. Another flood of tears ran down her face. Dada was the one she loved best. It was to him she ran whenever a boar scared her, or she woke from a horrible dream or cut her knee. It was always dada who could make things better. Through the tears, she searched for him but the ship was moving fast and now the Roundhouse disappeared from view and the sloping plains and the purple mountains beyond—the place she knew as home.

'Beloved, I wish I could heal your breaking heart.'

Perak felt Kaylak's gentle arms envelop her. She turned and buried her face in his chest, sobbed deep and hard, and drew lungs full of breath, inhaling his manly scent, his strength, and his love.

'I—I,' She sobbed, 'I am going to love you with all my heart,' She looked up to him. 'B—but I cannot love anyone as much as I love dada.'

'Nor should you Beloved,' he bent and kissed the tears that were already turning icy on her cheeks. 'Though I wager the day will come when you will love a child you gave birth to more than anything or anyone.' He laughed, 'Now that's made you think—dry your eyes and face, before the cold winds chafe your skin.'

The ship veered to the right as a swell of water hit the side, making Kaylak leave to attend to his duties. The crew held the course steady and Perak now turned her attention to the passage between the dark bluish purple hills where the carved head of a sea dragon pointed their way. She pulled the hood of her cloak around her face, pressed the fur to her cheeks and felt the surge of power as the oarsmen moved the ship on. She

had never ridden waves before. Though like all the settlement's children, she had played and swam in the shallow rivers that trickled through the forest. She watched her soon to be husband liaise with his men and noted the ease with which he moved around the ship. Kaylak had spent most of his life at sea. Would he—she wondered—really give it up to share a dull life with her?

Movement across the lake caused her to look towards the other ships that shared their journey. She spotted her brothers taking lessons from muscular men four times their size. In the background she caught sight of Cadic, brother to Zak and joy leapt into her heart sweeping away the ache threatening to pull her down. Cadic had made friends with Kaylak. Her brothers loved Cadic like he was a brother to them.

'Now those purple eyes are shining, I can relax.'

She turned to the voice. 'Thank you for bringing my brothers along,' She squeezed his arm, 'and for bringing Cadic too.'

'Cadic?' Kaylak shrunk his eyes into slits and peered towards Yorevyn's ship. 'I had nothing to do with Cadic joining us.'

'But you are pleased. I can see it in your face—I can tell in your eyes even though you've made them slitty.'

'Beloved, we are not even wed, yet already, you read me like a wife.'

'The further I move from mama's influence, the more I look forward to our wedding. Tell me again what it will be like?'

'It will be like a coronation. My people love an occasion. They love pomp and splendour and trumpets and feasts—especially feasts. You will be made my princess. We will wear

crowns and our people will adore you.' He rubbed his nose to hers, 'Now if you will forgive me—I am needed. We are about to enter the next lake.'

She watched him stride to the prow of the ship where he placed his arm on the carved shoulders of the sea dragon. To each side of the boat, steep jagged hills rose like trolls guarding the gap. At their foot, more jagged rocks jutted above the water's edge. The men slowed the boat, pulling just enough to keep it moving forward but slow enough for Kaylak's steersman to navigate a safe passage. Even for a girl knowing nothing of seamanship, Perak felt the increase of the current and knew the seriousness of keeping control and mastering the boat through the channel. She watched the men work, sensed how much in rhythm they were with the elements, how readily they obeyed the orders Kaylak called to them.

Once through the passage and heading to the middle of the second lake, she turned to watch Yorevyn's cargo boat follow and then the third ship, which was captained by a giant with flaming red hair. That ship, she saw, moved more than the others. It seemed to sway from side to side as though travelling on turbulent waters, though she knew that was impossible.

Chapter Twenty-Two

Elvad unloaded the first sled and took the provisions to the nearest of the vacant lodging houses. He returned to empty the second but paused to stare out to the lake. In the foreground Meg and the boy played throw and catch, but across the water, the outline of Bryn's ship could be made out before being engulfed in layers of mist.

Elvad mouthed a seafarer's prayer before he continued to sort essentials needed for immediate use, from those better stored for later. Amongst the vital items, he noticed Bryn had parted with a pouch of dried leaves he always sprinkled into his stews. Elvad pulled open the drawstring and took a long sniff of the mixture of aromas. At once his mind filled with the meadows of home, the woodlands and heaths where the plants grew.

Meg nudged his elbow, bringing him out of his reverie. He pulled the string closed making sure the aromatic smells were sealed tight. 'Do you miss home Meg?'

She snaked around him, rubbing both flanks in turn against his cloak. He reached inside one of the crates, pulled a strip of dried hog's skin from a sack, and placed it across the hound's open jaw. She bounded to the lake's beach and settled to chew

the tasty treat. The boy stared at Elvad. Elvad picked him up and was amazed at how warm the child's feet were. 'You don't feel the cold, do you?' he asked but the child didn't know Elvad's language nor did he understand any of the other tongues spoken by Elvad, Bryn or Yorevyn. Reaching into another crate Elvad found a strip of cured venison and gave it to the boy before sitting him on the furs stacked on the sled.

When they returned to the north side of the shore Elvad was puzzled to find Zak gone. Thinking perhaps a call of nature had awoken his patient, he set to stoking the fire, filling a pot with stream water and dropping in chunks of dried meat.

Pointing to where Zak had laid, Elvad asked Meg to find him. She put her nose to the ground and began to trace the whereabouts of what looked to Elvad to be that of an invisible person. Meg's nose discovered Zak had gone to relieve himself, then scuffed marks in the frosty earth revealed he must have staggered to the stream, then further on he had vomited. Elvad watched Meg zigzag along the stony paths of the sloping landscape. The boy jumped to the ground to follow but Elvad picked him up, took him back to the sled and set about clothing him in items gathered together by the thoughtful giant called Bryn.

The lakeside grew quiet since the departure of the three ships and the leaving of the crew. Fishermen continued to repair their boats and whilst they worked, talk of a monster in

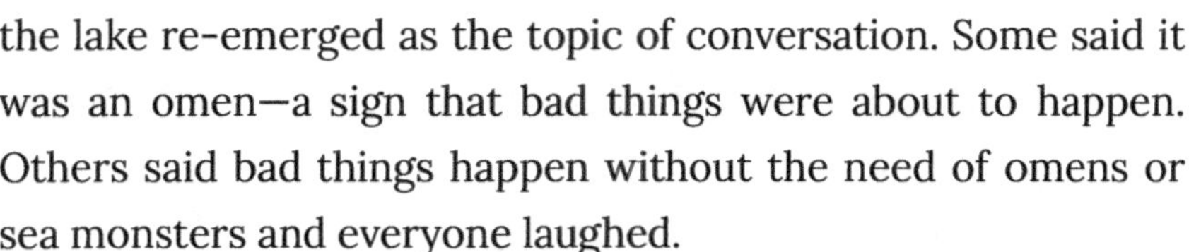

the lake re-emerged as the topic of conversation. Some said it was an omen—a sign that bad things were about to happen. Others said bad things happen without the need of omens or sea monsters and everyone laughed.

Inside the Roundhouse, the atmosphere was subdued. Families worked on their daily routines, yet a sense of foreboding hung over them, like the bad smell filling the air.

Urdeth wiped the mist off her polished metal mirror and stared at her reflection. Behind her, Kira came into view and began to prepare combs and ornaments to groom her new mistress. 'I regret my daughter's emotional outburst Kira, please find it in your heart to forgive her.'

Kira moved around the room picking up items she knew belonged to her. She stopped behind the mirror to face Urdeth in the flesh.

The once graceful lady had aged overnight. Her movements were slow and stiffened, and dark circles shadowed the socket lines of her lavender coloured eyes. 'There is nothing to forgive Urdeth, I have never been able to replace Fiedra nor striven to do so.'

'I too do not compare so favourably with Fiedra. She was Perak's closest friend, and in her eyes no one will come up to her standards.'

'I know that Urdeth. And I want you to know I am not sorry to be staying behind. I—er, I was going to ask to be relieved of my obligation to serve Perak. But her accusation I stole a bracelet has settled the matter. I will stay with my own kind.'

'And will you not settle to tend me?'

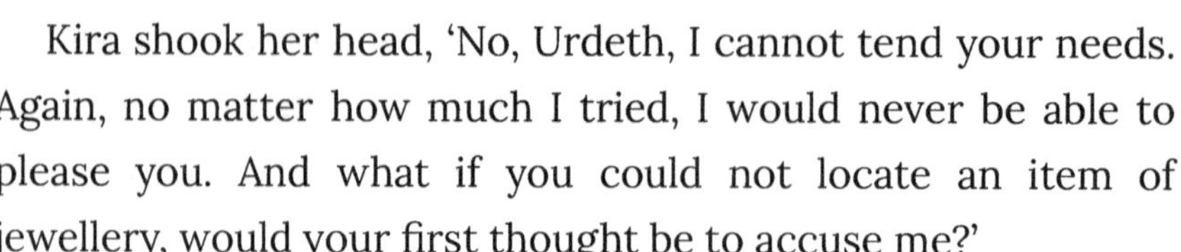

Kira shook her head, 'No, Urdeth, I cannot tend your needs. Again, no matter how much I tried, I would never be able to please you. And what if you could not locate an item of jewellery, would your first thought be to accuse me?'

'I am truly sorry, the bracelet was found, that should've been an end to it.'

'No, Urdeth, I should not have been accused, and that's that. Like I said, I will stay with my own kind.'

'And will you find satisfaction in the house of Zak?'

'Satisfaction has nothing to do with it. My new mistress needs me—as does her child.' Urdeth's sharp intake of breath told Kira she had touched a raw nerve. Emboldened by this she added. 'Urdeth, you may be Skaldric's wife but you don't have the monopoly on feeling hurt. You should know that others feel pain too and *they* didn't bring it upon themselves.'

'What did you say?'

Ignoring Urdeth's response, and fearing she had nearly disclosed she knew too much, Kira said instead, 'Zak's absence is affecting the whole clan and now we learn that Perak's new kin have persuaded his brother Cadic to forsake us.'

'But that's none of *my* doing.'

'Isn't it?'

'Certainly not—I would have you know I didn't want my sons to learn seafaring skills. It was Cadic who persuaded Kaylak to take them on.'

'Nevertheless, Urdeth, with Zak gone from us and Cadic taken by the lure of the Salt sea, our kinsfolk are now left without a leader.'

Chapter Twenty-Three

As Mira and Methiu prepared to settle by the fire for the night, the Shaman's breathing became more laboured. Mira reached out, taking the old man's hands in both of hers, encasing them in warmth. He smiled through gritted teeth showing the pain of his efforts.

'Be easy, O loved one,' She soothed, 'your path is set and the journey perfumed with sweet memories of your blessed life.'

His eyes rested on her and glowed though no words of reply could be formed. She kissed his fingers one by one until the rasping of his breath ceased, his gaze softened—and then dulled.

Methiu placed his hands over hers forming a seal around their threesome.

'When my time comes,' he whispered, 'I could wish for no better send-off.'

Mira lifted her tearful eyes to him and smiled, 'It is only as it should be for everyone.'

'It is.'

'I have prepared his place of rest. It is in accordance to his wishes.'

Methiu smiled, 'Of that, oh gracious lady, I have no doubt.'

Fiedra's mind was deep below the waters of the lake where the young creature circled. Feeding her thoughts were the instructions of his kin—his mother, who waited in the far off Salty Sea for him. To Fiedra, these thoughts sounded like stretched into strange, mystical tunes. She felt their slow rhythm run through her body, passing into the young krill-eater, still blind to where he was and confused about how he had come to be there. She could feel his huge backbone sway to the song being sent from his mother - first to her before being relayed to him. He surfaced and let off a stream of water. Bryn and his men had seen many a whale spout, but never had they seen one on a freshwater lake. The creature's size was magnified many times, almost dwarfing the dark hills in the background.

When the whale dipped below the surface his nose headed towards the narrow gap—the only way towards the Salt Seas.

The men gave a cheer. 'Nay lads,' warned Bryn, 'we're not ready for cheering just yet.' He stepped into the cabin and cast a glance across to his patient. Fiedra was humming a strange tune. He smiled and returned to manning his ship.

Through the gap and heading onwards to where the second lake emptied into a third, Yorevyn looked back and scrunched his neck into his shoulders and told his crewmen he had no idea either why Bryn's men had erupted so joyfully. But that wasn't the truth, he figured the krill-eater and little Fiedra had something to do with making Bryn's iron-hearted men raise a cheer.

He studied the boat abreast of them were Kaylak and his men also turned their heads towards the captain's boat. Whilst under the shelter of the awning, stood Perak, his cousin's bride to be who was not taking part in the shared seafaring moment. It moved him to watch her. She looked so young, and her eyes full of tears made him wonder if she would ever smile again. He turned away when the ship gathered speed, to concentrate instead on the fast moving waters that were taking them towards the next gap.

Meg caught up to Zak where he rested against a rock, but she did not approach. Instead she gave one bark to alert Elvad where she was. Zak slowly turned his head towards her and groaned a curse before straightening and moving on.

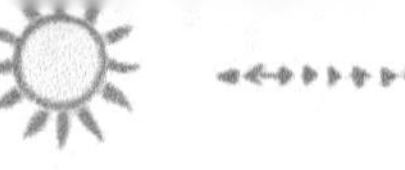
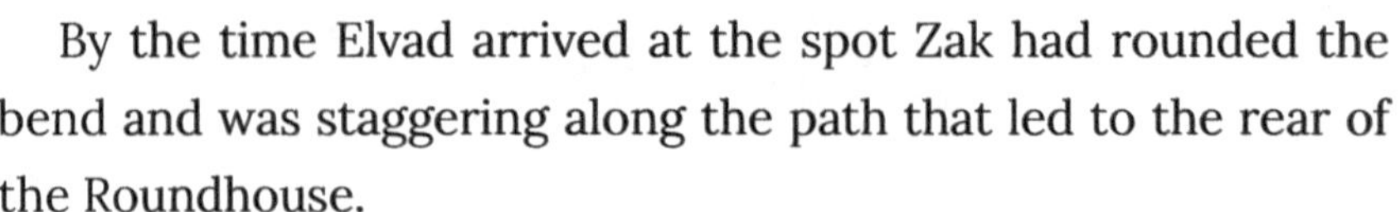

By the time Elvad arrived at the spot Zak had rounded the bend and was staggering along the path that led to the rear of the Roundhouse.

'Wait,' Elvad called, 'Zak, listen to me—you can't go down.'

Zak turned and pointed a shaking finger at Meg. 'Keep that mutt from me. And him—' his trembling finger moved to the child clutching Elvad's hand—'that spawn of evil, raised from the dead. Don't let him anywhere near me.' He swayed on the spot, struggling to stay focused, then turned back to his path and dragged one foot after the other.

'You have a terrible sickness, Zak. It will leap from your body to take up residence in someone else.'

Zak's footsteps faltered. He turned to face Elvad, a sneer cutting his fevered cheek, 'So why then, haven't you succumbed to this sickness?'

'I have—many years ago. For some reason unbeknownst to me, I seem to be shielded from it now.'

'So,' Zak coughed, 'can't be too terrible, can it?' He turned back and staggered along his track, choking and coughing as he did.

Elvad lifted the boy into his arms, thankful he could not understand the bitter words Zak had uttered. He turned to Meg and said, 'Seize him, Meg, and bring him down to ground with a thud.'

Chapter Twenty-Four

Fiedra's song carried deep below the ship as Bryn's men kept pace with the water's flow and they entered the third lake. They felt the music's timbre vibrate through their oars, giving a rhythm not unlike that of their own coxswain but giving a rhythm much like that of their own coxswain, only smoother and faster. The oarsmen of the two other ships also felt the change in tempo as they too gathered speed to head for the sheer-sided cut between the mountains. As they neared the gap, the sight beyond it brought a cheer so loud that gulls took flight. Sparkling in the weak glow of the setting sun, the Salt Sea winked and glinted a hearty welcome.

Elvad looked down at Zak's prone body and shook his head. 'I know I said bring him down with a thud, but you didn't have to take it literally.'

Meg twitched her ears. The boy tried to move Elvad's, emulating the hound's every move.

Elvad shook his head. He was in no mood to be frivolous. He sighed, knowing he would now need the sled to transfer Zak back to their campsite. Should he leave Zak alone, or leave Meg and the child with him? He was growing weary of Zak's outbursts, already regretting the care he'd lavished on the ungrateful wretch. He took in a lungful of clean, cold air and jerked his head in the manner that told Meg to follow.

When they reached their camp, the aroma of meat stew made the juices in the child's stomach churn. Elvad felt the gurgle. 'That Zak,' He cursed, 'I will despair of him. He makes me forget the simple duties of life.' He sat the boy onto the stack of furs and placed logs in the brazier. 'Come little one, first we eat.'

He watched the boy's hunger gather momentum as the child blew and sipped the hot broth from the bronze goblets provided by Bryn. 'What shall we call you?'

The child looked up from his cupped hands and grinned, 'Sip.'

Elvad gestured towards himself. 'Elvad, my name is El-Vad.'

The boy continued to grin, and nodded, 'Vad.'

Pleased with the gentle progress Elvad nodded and returned the grin before pointing to the child, and hunching his shoulders and opening empty hands, he urged, 'You, what is *your* name?'

The boy punched a closed fist to his own chest. 'Di-on.' Thrusting the half- empty goblet towards Elvad he grinned, 'Sip. Vad.'

'Sip—Dion.' Their cups met with a metallic ring that brought a touch of warmth to the bleak midwinter afternoon.

The folk staying in the Roundhouse were too busy preparing their furs and blankets for the evening to notice the comings and goings of others who were not from their clan. Mothers settled their children, taking them to and from the latrines, whilst the men gathered as always, to talk of cured meats, hunting techniques and the new sharp tools brought for trading by the three ships.

Kira knelt on a pile of furs behind Zak's wife. She pulled the comb through the long blue-black hair of her cousin and new mistress. She stopped mid-groom and gripped her cousin's shoulders. 'Sheena. Look over there,' She hugged. 'Didn't I say he would return?' They both looked across the crowded, smoky hall and saw Zak's sweat-smeared face etched in the glow of the huge fire. His movements were slow, like he was loath to be amongst them. 'I will take the baby and leave you two together.' Kira whispered as she wrapped the sleepy child in his fleece and silently slid to join her other cousins and their babies.

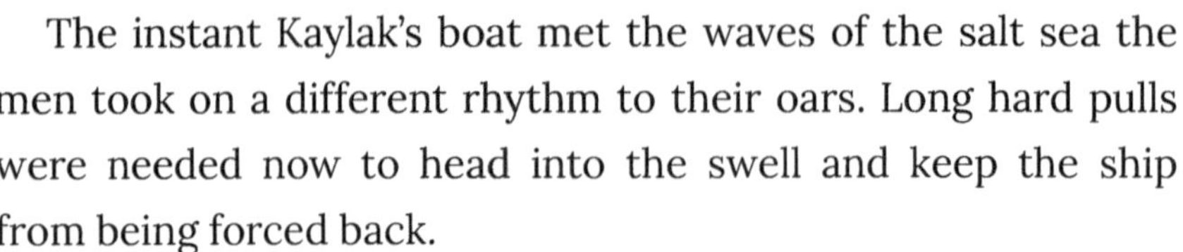

The instant Kaylak's boat met the waves of the salt sea the men took on a different rhythm to their oars. Long hard pulls were needed now to head into the swell and keep the ship from being forced back.

Yorevyn's ship took on the same tempo and followed Kaylak's across the shimmering surface, now turned creamy-yellow as the sun's last rays were dowsed and swallowed by the ocean which lay towards the lands of the West, their home.

Bryn's men took a different course. Guided by his instructions, he ordered them to keep straight where flakes of snow hit the faces of the rowers and threatened to needle into the backs of their muscular hands. From below, the song Fiedra hummed could still be felt as it travelled beneath the waves and up, through the handles of the oars. As though in some kind of trance, the men pulled Bryn's boat with ease, taking it further north and into the pitch-black waters of unknown territory.

Surfacing and diving to the beat of the evening, a dark sleek creature headed past them, gaining strength with every move. Refreshed by its return to the salty waters, the young whale smacked his mighty tail with glee—a sign to the crew that he could at last hear the cries of his kin, far to the north, urging him on.

'Where have you been?'

'Is there accusation in your words?' Zak slurred, waving away the offered goblet of mead.

'You look dishevelled—where have you been sleeping?'

'I—er, I've been unwell. I suspect it was too much of that filthy stuff Skaldric swills around this place.'

She pushed back her glistening strands to study him more closely. 'You're sweating, yet it must be bitterly cold outside, I ask you again where have you been sleeping?'

Zak grabbed her arm, 'I will not have you talk to me like that.'

When she wrenched her arm free, Zak's cloak opened to expose his bare chest. 'Where's your undershirt?'

When he looked down, images flooded his mind with memories of a boy he buried. 'I used it to shroud a child for burial.'

Eyes full of disbelief stared back at him. 'You've been wenching down by the wharf, haven't you?' Anger flashed as she got to her feet and kicked him hard in his stomach. 'Keep to your own clan, Zak, son of Sarash. I will no longer be your wife.'

Others within earshot tried not to stare or listen to their kinsfolk's domestic quarrel. They too suspected Zak of taking the pleasures of those women who frequented the lodging houses beyond the fishing village. They considered it was none of their business, after all, they reasoned, Zak's blood line was that of high birth, so a lesser chieftain's daughter must put up with her lot.

Zak clutched his stomach as his vision wavered. Rage burned within him. A man deserved more respect from his wife. How dare she insult him in front of his kinfolk? How dare she accuse him of—of visiting the wenching houses? He straightened, trying to focus his eyes on her as she stepped between members of her family who moved aside to allow her to pass. His eyes fell on Kira and the child she held in her arms —his son. He made to move towards him, meant to take him in his arms and hold him close. Someone's foot tangled with his, bringing him down so that he collapsed unconscious onto the furs his wife had just vacated.

Chapter Twenty-Five

Elvad's rage and dismay at Zak's disappearance stabbed pain through his chest. He shouldn't have left him alone. He should have ordered Meg to watch over him. But Meg was tending little Dion—she couldn't be expected to do everything. He flashed the lighted torch back along the track, desperate to find a prone body but all he discovered was another pool of vomit.

Reality hit him harder. Despite the warning given earlier, Zak must've headed towards the Roundhouse and taken the sickness straight to his loved ones.

Resigned to the fact he could do no more, and with a weary heart, Elvad pulled the empty sled along the high ground and to where he had made camp. There, settled by the glowing brazier lay Meg, and curled within the hollow of her tucked-in legs was Dion—fed, watered and fast asleep. Elvad's mind flashed with the image of Zak's baby son. Before he knew it, he was kneeling and pleading with the gods to bless those in the Roundhouse. He asked the gods to arm them with the same shield that had been given to Kaylak, their father Methiu and to Dion. But in his heart, he knew what really lay ahead. He knew they would vomit and cough until they died of exhaustion like his mother and sister had done.

The Shaman was wrapped in his red-deer cloak and placed in a crevice at the back of the cave. Methiu stood back to allow Mira to scatter possessions of shell and antler carvings beside the body.

'These were given to the Wise Man during his lifetime,' she said, before nodding to Methiū to cover the hole with the boulders gathered for the purpose. 'Like all men of wisdom, his was a life of simplicity.' She swallowed as Methiu wedged the final rock that sealed the crevice tight. 'Tell me Methiu, King of the West Land, what plans have you now?'

'None, I told my sons to reign without me. My youngest has a thirst for knowledge—he seeks wisdom in healing. He could do with meeting you, perhaps?'

'Perhaps he will.'

'And you, what plans have you now the Shaman is at rest?'

Mira lifted the lamp to guide their way, 'Oh I don't have a planned life as such. I live within the boundaries of the seasons. Unlike my feathered friends, I cannot flee the winter months, nor can I curl up and sleep like my furred companions.' She knelt by the fire, warming her hands and spreading the heat over her tear streaked face. 'We must look forward,' She smiled, 'It helps to live in hope of spring, when the sun's rays will warm my face as my hands do now.'

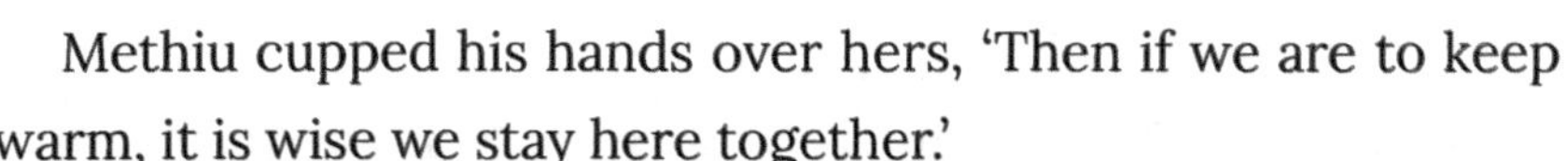

Methiu cupped his hands over hers, 'Then if we are to keep warm, it is wise we stay here together.'

'He said you would say that.'

'Who did?'

'The Wise One, he doesn't get his name by being wrong.'

'What else did the Shaman tell you?'

'That his successor will be a spirit visitor.'

Methiu sat back on his heels. 'You? Will you be the next Shaman?'

When she shook her head, silver lights picked up hues from the fire and turned her hair to the colour of fox fur, she looked at him slyly, 'Not me, but I think at some time in the near future, the new Shaman will need my assistance—possibly yours too.'

'Why? Do I know who it is?'

'Not yet—but I think the child who will become Shaman is travelling with your kin. One is crossing the North Salt Sea, one is heading eventually to settle in the West, and one is raising a waif destined for greatness.'

'By the gods, where on Earth did you learn that?'

Mira looked up to the cave's entrance where a straggly branch of a tree had vined its way across the top. She whistled. A raven flew down and landed on their still entwined hands. 'This is Dandijack,' She cooed, 'at the moment, he carries the spirit of Idra, my other daughter. She was the rebel of our family, the one who fell for a great swordsman of the Silver Falls..'

'The Silver Falls—but surely, to love one such as they, isn't an act of rebellion? I thought they were one of the most noble families in the north.'

'They were—and through the swordsman's mother's line, there is real greatness. My youngest daughter gained her bad reputation by deserting him to join the wild women of the plains.' Mira looked up to Methiu, her eyes no longer amethyst but dark, almost purple. 'Dandijack keeps a close eye on Fiedra, my granddaughter; who was put in danger by her paternal grandmother for bringing shame to their family. I cannot be sure, but I think Fiedra will be Shaman one day.'

'To be considered for such an honourable role is wonderful, you must be so proud.'

'Pride has dangerous edges. I fear if she is to become Shaman, it will put Fiedra into focus, bringing her under the scrutiny of her other grandmother, Dahron, the Guardian of the Silver Falls.'

'Dahron is Fiedra's paternal grandmother? Oh but surely, she can be no match for you.'

'I'm hoping you are right.' Mira leaned close and placed her head on his shoulder, 'Do you know something? The way the future is unravelling, my dear friend Methiu, *we* may become kinsmen too.'

'How do you know that?'

'Oh a little bird told me.'

Chapter Twenty-Six

Perak held onto the framework of her covered shelter and tried to roll with the waves as Kaylak had told her. But it was impossible. As the boat dipped and rose so did her stomach. She glanced to one side trying to take her mind off the constant motion and studied the men at work. Over the passing days, Kaylak had taken the place of an oarsman so another might rest. *Slept?* How could anyone sleep whilst being tossed and thrown from side to side? She scanned them again—but they were not being tossed or thrown, they were either manning the oars in regimented fashion or snoring in the bunks below.

A bird flew aboard and landed on the shoulder of the carved sea dragon. It's blue-black feathers ruffled in the strong breeze and its yellow eyes darted this way and that before settling to stare at Perak.

Breathe easy, said the voice in her head.

Perak's intake of air came not from instruction but from shock. *Mama?*

That's right—nice and deep—feeling better?

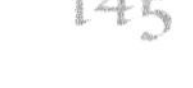

Perak shook her head, causing a cascade of white curls to swirl in the wind like a frenzied halo. *You're not mama—you are the other voice. Mama said you didn't exist. Who are you?*

How's the stomach?

Perak took another deep breath and scanned the deck once more. Kaylak sat in the middle of his men; they rowed as one entity cutting through the water like a many-legged serpent. She could hear the sleeping men below; their snores rhythmic and steady. She no longer felt at odds with the motion of the waves, her breathing fell into pace with ebb and flow, rock and roll of the boat. Perak turned towards the ship's prow and focused on the neck of the sea dragon. The raven's eye flashed, and before she could formulate a thought, it spread its wings and flew away until it became a black dot in a grey sky.

When Fiedra opened her eyes, it was Bryn's fiery coloured beard that filled her vision, along with his huge tombstone teeth spread in an enormous grin. 'Yer did it wee lass, yer guided yon krill-eater back to his mammy.'

She nodded and reached to remove the fleece wad from below her eye. His frown knotted the red eyebrows that grew furiously across his forehead. 'Leave it be,' he whispered. 'You're not quite healed yet.'

She moved her hand away and ran it through her scalp. 'Is there somewhere I can freshen up?'

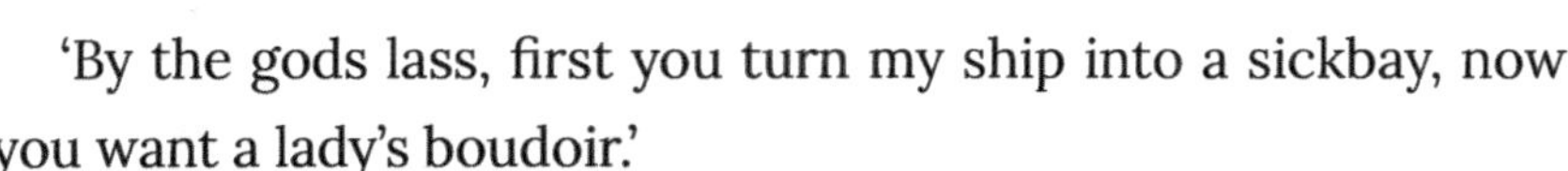

'By the gods lass, first you turn my ship into a sickbay, now you want a lady's boudoir.'

'A what?'

'Never mind.' He twirled his beard, curling the locks around his fingers in deep thought.

With stiffness, Fiedra sat up. 'A bowl of water and a cloth is all I need.'

'Aye, I know—I'm not used to girls aboard my ship you see. Not used to being asked for *bathing* facilities. A bowl of water and a cloth, you say? I think I can do better than that.' He shot up from the chair beside the bunk, 'Give me a heartbeat or two and I'll be back.'

Chapter Twenty-Seven

Zak slept undisturbed all the following day.

Kira glanced back at him several times, checking that he still breathed, and was relieved to see he did. She shared her cousin's anger, knowing now that he had spent the missing days and nights with wenching girls. She too felt like kicking him though, she mused her foot would have found a lower place than his stomach.

The baby toddled towards her, holding up his arms to be picked up and cuddled. He was the image of his father, strong in build and rebellious in nature. Even at his tender age, he often clashed with the other children of the clan. She stooped to pick him up and turned her attention to watch over Sheena.

Her cousin lay on top of Kira's firs and stared up at the thatched ceiling with unseeing eyes. Dark circles shaded her eye sockets. Aware of Kira standing over her, she blinked and smiled at the baby in Kira's arms.

'He needs to be fed,' she whispered, her voice hoarse.

'I gave him barley broth,' Kira said, shifting the child to her other arm, 'he loved it.'

'That's good—with all the worry over Zak, my milk has gone.'

'He was ready to sample tastier stuff anyway. You look exhausted Sheena. Why don't you curl under the furs, I'll look after this little man.'

Zak's wife managed a weak smile as she rolled over, pulled the skins up to her shoulders, and closed her eyes.

Around the huge hall, people went about their duties. Logs were stacked and ice brought in to melt, furs were shaken clean, and food was made ready. Older children took younger ones out to play down by the lake, whilst those in their teens wandered to where the fishermen worked repairing their boats. The fishermen found labour for the young hands, and soon they were mending nets, daubing grease onto raw timbers and learning stories their parents might not want them to know. Fishermen spoke in a crude manner, their wives even cruder.

Beyond the activity by the lake and the Roundhouse were the hovels of the poor. They were crowded together and set back, away from everything else. Nobody ever spoke of the Shadows; no one questioned why no smoke had risen from the pathetic reed-covered roofs for days. No one knew anything about the Forgotten, nor did they care.

Urdeth rinsed water over her face and scooped some to run over the back of her neck. As with every female, she had

knowledge of women breaking out in sweats but she thought she hadn't quite reached that age. Besides, she reasoned, this was midwinter, hardly the time of year to be plagued with too much heat. But sweating she was, and uncomfortably so. She made her way back to her sleeping place and lay on top of the furs. She reached across to where she could hear Skaldric's steady breathing. He was cool. She let out a deep faltering breath, wondering whether perhaps her body was old after all —much older than she had previously thought.

Skaldric stirred, rolled towards her, and whilst still in slumber, patted her arm as though to console her, soothe her back to sleep.

Above the place where they lay, a sparrow slept between the overlap of the roof's thatches and close by him, a blue-black raven looked down onto the sleeping horde as though to keep vigil until dawn. Midwinter was passing and the space between the rise of dawn to the setting of dusk was lengthening, but only by a short margin in time.

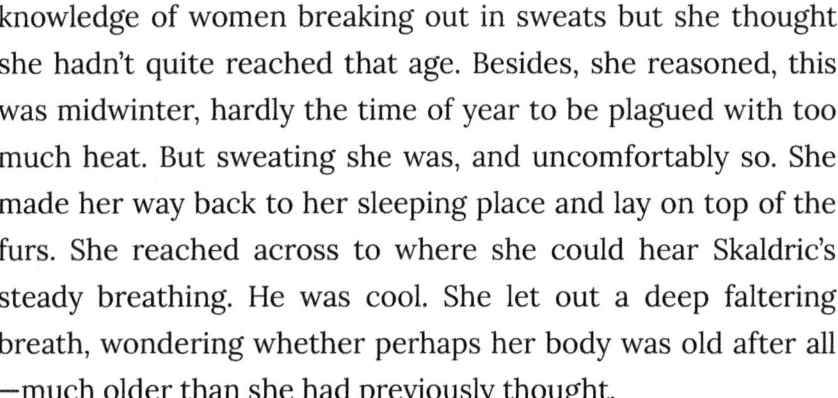

Chapter Twenty-Eight

Elvad scooped out the remaining chunks of meat left at the bottom of the cauldron and dropped them into the waiting goblet. Dion blew a stream of cold vapour to cool them, then reaching in finger and thumb to fish one out. He looked up and asked with pleading eyes if he could share it with Meg. Elvad shook his head. 'No. Meg must never eat cooked food.'

Dion gave Meg a look of sorrow before taking a bite of the chewy meat. Meg twitched her eyes back at him, sharing his mournful look. Elvad let out an irritated sigh, picked up his sword and brought it down on the side of the dried goat that lay across the sled. He hacked a fore-shoulder loose and whistled for Meg. She carried it in her gentle jaws to her favourite mossy spot, held it between her massive front paws, and began to lick the surface. Elvad rewrapped the carcase and pushed it back into one of the barrels. He turned to Dion, who watched his every move. 'Later Dion, I will show you how to catch fish. Then tomorrow, we will venture towards the woods over there, and we will see what fresh meat can be hunted.' The boy sensed the gist of the topic and grinned.

'You learn fast, my little friend. And since it seems we may be destined to be alone in this part of the world, I'll teach you to become a great hunter. Would you like that?'

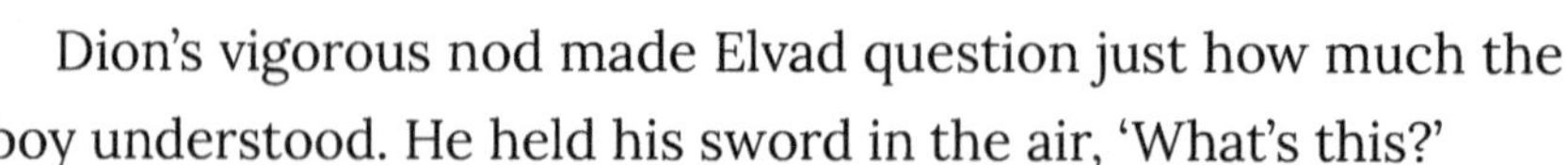

Dion's vigorous nod made Elvad question just how much the boy understood. He held his sword in the air, 'What's this?'

'Kri-kri.'

Elvad shook his head. Taking his knife from his belt, he asked, 'What's this?'

'Kri.'

'Kri is knife, but kri-kri is sword?'

Dion nodded. Pointing his finger to the knife he said, 'Kri,' then pointing to the sword, he added, 'kri-kri.'

Elvad paused, 'Ahh—so in your tongue a knife is called kri, and the bigger it is, the more it doubles its name.'

Dion grinned and pointed towards the hound gnawing at her hunk of meat, 'Meg-meg.'

'Yeh, you are not wrong there my little friend, she's a big 'un alright.'

Mowdah the Elder staggered to the latrines. His visit was urgent but his limbs were old. He leant against the timber support and coughed, sweat rolling through his sparse hair and trickling into his eyes, blinding and stinging. The cough hurt his old lungs yet he struggled to regain his composure, steadying his gait he trudged on. Blinded and gasping for breath, the oldest member of Skaldric's clan veered off the well-used track and fell face down onto the scree behind the Roundhouse.

Chapter Twenty-Nine

Fiedra sat up drinking the cup of hot water infused with a sprinkle of Bryn's precious dried fruits. She watched him come and go with pails of steaming water, which he poured into a half-barrel, filling the air with fragrant fog.

Piled onto the furs of her bed were woven squares of cloths and clothes crafted from similar material.

She didn't ask where he was finding this stuff. During her phases of consciousness, she had learnt many things about the ship and its cargo and especially, its resourceful captain.

'There,' he said at last, 'a boudoir fit for a princess.'

'How will I ever be able to repay you?'

'Oh, dear wee lass, you owe me nothing. But that rogue of a man Yorevyn—well, his eyes will water when the account is settled.' Her laugh caused the wadding on her upper cheek to pull against the skin and she gave an involuntary wince. 'Ah, see what I said about leaving the wadding to do its work? It is still early days. Promise me now, that you won't touch it, or let it become soggy?'

'I promise.'

'Good, then I will leave you be. These are washing cloths, newly bartered for, so good and clean, and these are clothes

bought for my youngest wee lass. They should fit a scrawny little waif such as you.'

She drained her cup, passed it over to him and watched him pull the heavy screen to. Unfolding the stack of clothes, she stood up and held them to her. Woven from strands of fine wool and crafted into layers, pleats and folds to give warmth without weight. She marvelled that such garments could exist.

Soon she was sitting in the barrel with the dried petals of some sweet-perfumed flowers floating around her. She breathed in the scents, allowing them to fill her lungs before setting out to rid her body of the lingering stench of fish-glue.

'Wad of wool or not,' she whispered, 'my hair will be perfumed and stay scented from now on.'

Tilt your head back. I will wash your hair, just like your grandmother used to do, remember?

Fiedra looked around the cabin, 'Mother?'

Shush—better if we can't be heard.

And what poor creature's body are you haunting this time?

Not haunting my daughter, borrowing—for the use of.

Fiedra twisted round and laughed, bringing fresh pain to her gash. *You're borrowing Grandmother's raven? And she let you?*

Why shouldn't she?

Fiedra knew very well how distrusting her grandmother was of her wayward daughter.

Does she know where I am?

Yes, I report back to her.

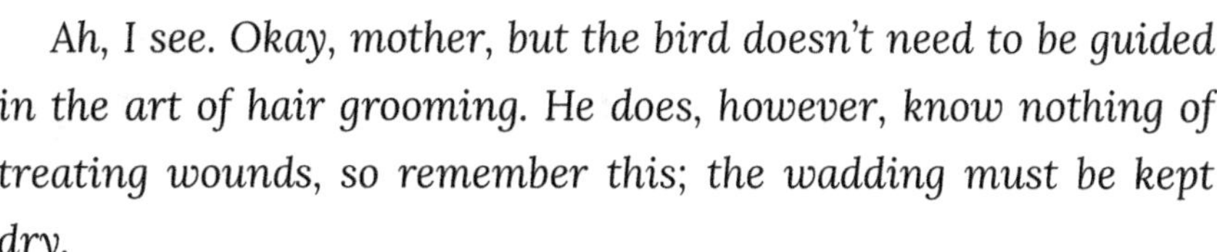

Ah, I see. Okay, mother, but the bird doesn't need to be guided in the art of hair grooming. He does, however, know nothing of treating wounds, so remember this; the wadding must be kept dry.

It will be.

'So where has your spy flown to now?'

'Dandijack isn't a spy.'

Methiu stacked the firewood by the cave's entrance and took the cup Mira held towards him. He sipped the hot fusion. 'You haven't answered my question.'

'He's gone to check on Fiedra again.'

'I see—and that's not spying?'

'No,' Mira snatched the goblet back, 'it's simply keeping an eye on one's kin.'

'He caught the poor girl bathing last time.'

'Look, he's not *he* when he's, er...'

'Spying?'

'Visiting. Look, he carries the spirit of my youngest daughter—Fiedra is alone on board a boat with a giant and forty oarsmen. Surely you understand a grandmother like me must use whatever powers she can to reach out to her? Give her some motherly comfort?'

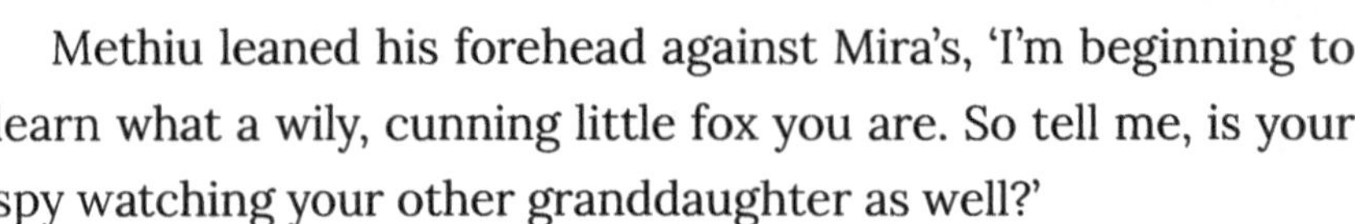

Methiu leaned his forehead against Mira's, 'I'm beginning to learn what a wily, cunning little fox you are. So tell me, is your spy watching your other granddaughter as well?'

She nodded, 'Of course he is, and my two grandsons, who are learning seafaring skills on board the other vessel. What's he called, Yorevyn - his cargo ship?'

His eyes glowed with amazement. 'If only Yorevyn knew what powers you possess. He'd make you empress of the world. The man has spent his life smelting ore and refining metals for peaceful use. Now he must fashion metal into arms, for he fears we will need for warfare. And all he had to do was train a couple of birds to find out what the invaders are doing, and report back to tell him before they reached his shores.'

'Perhaps it isn't too late to help him. After all, he has Fiedra now.'

'What can a little girl like Fiedra do?'

'Oh, you have much to learn. But remember this, it isn't power we possess, it's being able to see what others cannot. That, my dear Methiu, King of the West Lands, is all there is to it.'

'If you say so, my cunning little fox, my Lady of the Forest, wise witch of the woodlands and all the creatures who dwell within them, if you say so.' He took back the cup and raised it to his lips. 'You do know I am falling under your spell, don't you?'

Bryn tapped the cabin's screen and waited.

'Bryn, you don't have to knock.'

'Aye, I do—now that you are up and about, and no longer in my care.'

'I'm hardly likely to be doing something secret, now am I?'

'I've been brought up to respect a lady's privacy and it's too late to change me now.'

She wrung the water from the cloth and gave the table another wipe. 'Well, I wish that horrible uncle of mine had had the same upbringing. I don't understand why Yorevyn wanted to trade with him. He's nowt but an oaf.'

'If Yorevyn hadn't needed the glue, he wouldn't have found you and Meg wouldn't have knocked you over and...'

'...And I wouldn't be here wearing your daughter's lovely new dress.'

'Nay, you wouldn't. I came to tell you we will be arriving tomorrow.'

'At your island?'

'Yes, my kinfolk will look after you, whilst we prepare the ship for our next journey.'

'Will we see Yorevyn?'

'Why?'

'You are teasing me, I can read it in your eyes.'

'Yorevyn has to take his cargo to his people. They fear the invaders will resume their march before the Equinox.'

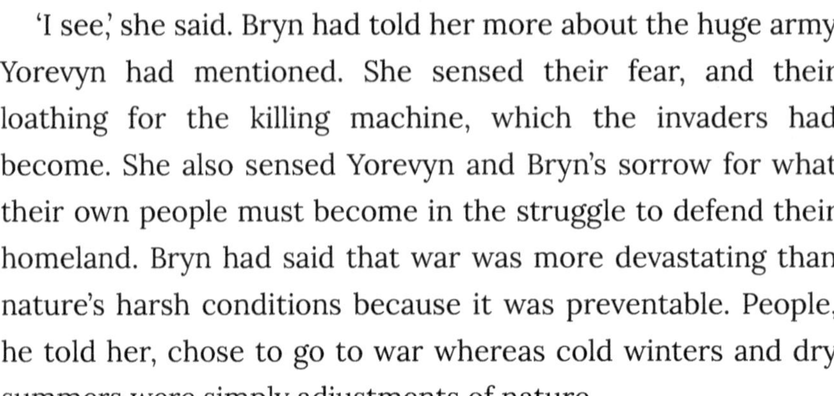

'I see,' she said. Bryn had told her more about the huge army Yorevyn had mentioned. She sensed their fear, and their loathing for the killing machine, which the invaders had become. She also sensed Yorevyn and Bryn's sorrow for what their own people must become in the struggle to defend their homeland. Bryn had said that war was more devastating than nature's harsh conditions because it was preventable. People, he told her, chose to go to war whereas cold winters and dry summers were simply adjustments of nature.

He returned to his crew whilst she continued cleaning the cabin, washing the polished timbers, shaking the furs and filling the lanterns with the aromatic oils Bryn had given her. Through the sides of the screen she noticed the days were lengthening, she had asked if it would be winter on his Island.

'It will get warmer the father south we travel,' He told her, 'not that my island is in the real South, you understand, just a little more southerly than your homeland.'

She wondered where Yorevyn's homeland was and what kind of people smelted ore into metals. She had learned that such people were considered to be magicians; *alchemists*, Skaldric had called them, people who had the knowledge to turn rock into bright, shiny metal that could be tempered strong enough to slice a man in two with one hefty blow. Could a man, who had shown such kindness to a glue-maker's niece, be capable of slicing another man in two? Could a man with a twisted smile lead other men to do such things?

Fiedra held the neckerchief she had found under the fleeces in her bed to her good cheek, and breathed in the scent of Yorevyn. Was she doing what she had vowed she would never do? Was she falling in love with a magician?

Chapter Thirty

The sled glided easily across the iced surface of the shoreline, which lay to the north of the bay. Here, the air was clean and the waters ran pure under its covering of ice.

In the dimming afternoon light, Meg ran ahead, her huge nose picking up scents left by the creatures of the woodlands that came down to the lake's edge.

Dion took long strides, trying to keep in step with Elvad. He was learning to be a man. That morning, he had caught two good-sized fish, which dangled behind him from the makeshift rod resting on his shoulder.

Elvad gave him a side-glance. 'See yonder, Dion, where Meg is?'

The boy's gaze followed Elvad's. He nodded.

'Good, then that's where we will make camp tonight.'

Dion grinned, and lifting the rod from his shoulder, he laid it carefully on top of the moving sled before running ahead to join the hound.

Elvad shook free his thoughts. He couldn't fathom why the boy spoke few words, yet seemed to understand everything

said to him. He watched Meg curl around the child as though she was shielding him with her body and he marvelled again at the determination she had shown when seeking help to prevent him from being buried alive. Elvad's mind flashed back to Bryn's cabin, to the bunk, and to the strange person with the wound on her face. She had read Meg's frantic fears and passed them on. What kind of power, Elvad's awe-struck mind shouted: what kind of power would a person need to have to be able to read the minds of animals? And what kind of person would they have to be to handle such power?

When Zak finally woke, it was the acrid stench of vomit that filled his nostrils. Immediately his mind flashed to the day when his boots were covered, and to the little child who ran into his path. His mind filled with the image of the intersection and the piled high sled carrying its gruesome cargo. He shook the image away, leant on one elbow and propped himself to stare around the huge Roundhouse.

Someone close-by him was coughing, he turned to find one of his kinfolk struggling to his feet, retching at the effort. His mind reeled, where was his wife and their child? He sat up just as the coughing man fell forward and onto the stack of furs Zak had been sleeping on. In the murky, smoke-laden light, Zak could see the man's sweat-coated face, heard the painful, coarse cough as he laboured to breathe. He got to his knees and leaned forward to assist him, but shot back when a stream

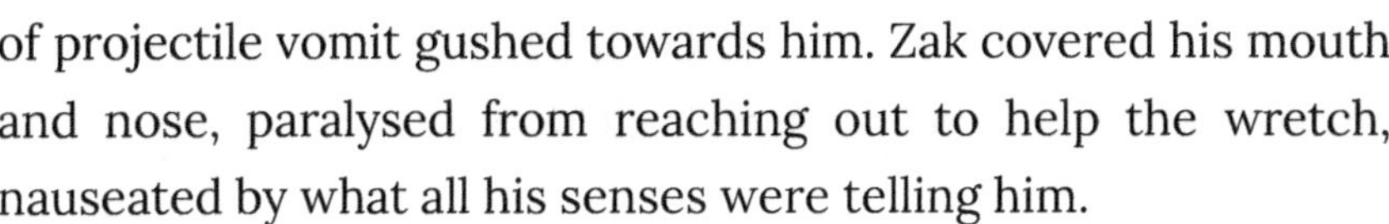

of projectile vomit gushed towards him. Zak covered his mouth and nose, paralysed from reaching out to help the wretch, nauseated by what all his senses were telling him.

He got to his feet, staggered towards the side door and headed for the latrines.

Kira rinsed the cloth and wrung out the excess water. With the back of her hand she pushed her hair from her forehead before slipping her arm under Sheena's head. She wiped her cousin's face clean from sweat and vomit before tilting the goblet of ice-cold water to the cracked lips. 'Drink, Sheena, drink.' Sheena turned her head aside, 'You must drink.' Kira cried, tipping the goblet, watching the water trickle between the parted lips. "That's it—come on—a little more.' When Sheena swallowed, Kira saw her pain. 'I know it hurts, but you're burning up, it's all I can think of to do for you. Another... drink another mouthful, that's it—now you can sleep.' She turned her cousin over, pulled furs around her and went to check on the baby. He slept in a niche, away from those coughing and retching up their guts, she placed a hand on his chubby cheek, and was relieved to find it warm but not raging like that of his mother's.

Kira took the pail of washing water through to the back of the anteroom and tipped it into the frozen gulley. On her return, she glanced across to where Zak had slept, and in the dim light, mistook the man sleeping on Sheena's original furs

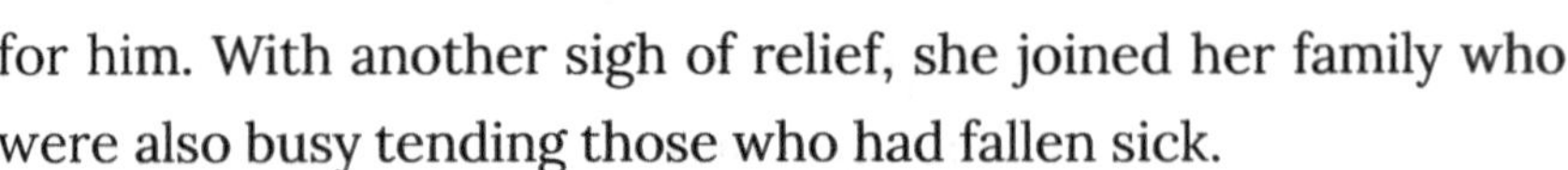

for him. With another sigh of relief, she joined her family who were also busy tending those who had fallen sick.

Smoke lay between veils of grey around the rafters of the Roundhouse. Below it, families—some of high birth, others not —huddled in frightened groups. Teenagers had been given the task of keeping the little children away from their sick parents, told to tend to their needs outside until their mothers regained their strength.

Along the walls torches left unattended, spluttered and flared. The sudden flare of one such torch reflected in the blue-black feathers of a raven as it ruffled its plumage. It swooped onto the two people who slept fitfully below its roost and began to nudge the hair of one with its beak.

Urdeth, the raven's host spirit, urged, sending a message deep into her senses, *Urdeth you must wake up.* The raven ran its yellow beak through Urdeth's hair, stroking her scalp as a mother would sooth a child, *Urdeth—wake up, there is great danger. You must wake up. Skaldric needs you.*

Urdeth moved her head; the bird swapped sides and continued to part strands of hair on the other side. *Urdeth, you must wake up— Skaldric is dying.*

Between cracked lips, Urdeth whispered, 'Skaldric, my darling, forgive me. I caused the curse on our brave boys. I—I did what I thought was best. I know it was for the best. You love her as much as if she were our own. I—I could not have done otherwise—please forgive me.'

Above where the two lay, a spluttering torch sent a spark into the air where it was sucked upwards to wedge between the timber rafters and the woven thatch. Upward draughts blew life into it and the spark became an ember and an ember became a glow.

The raven nipped the lobe of Urdeth's ear. She moved her head away, irritated by the sharp pain. *Urdeth, what did you do?*

Someone held open the door bringing cool air into the Roundhouse, and the raven nipped another pinch of Urdeth's ear. She raised an arm, sending the bird up to the spluttering torch, catching its feet in a flame. It squawked, swerved and headed for the gap left by the open door. With another fluttering of wings, the injured raven was followed by the sparrow.

Chapter Thirty-One

As Zak walked across the shores of the lake, his muscles gained strength with each stride. He scanned the craggy hillside, looking for inlets of clean water to wash away the stench of sickness from his nostrils. As he inhaled, his lungs burned with cold, crisp air, giving him flashes of the care he had received from the foreigner Elvad. Why had the man nursed him? Why had he bathed vomit from his face and made him drink icy water? Why—when, as Zak recalled, he had made it clear foreigners were not welcome in his land?

He broke the ice and knelt by a rivulet trickling over the rocky scree and cupping his hands, drank his fill. With his numbed fingers he rubbed the tingling water into his beard, rejoicing as his blood started to circulate beneath his skin. He was alive. He had come through the sickness just like the boy had done. Did that mean he too was an aberration—a creature that had come back from the dead? An involuntary shiver ran through him. Using the hem of his fleece-coat, Zak rubbed his face and neck dry. He stood tall, eyes searching the flat, smooth surface of the lake. It was freezing over. How long had he been sick? He had no answer. Slowly, he turned and walked back along the shoreline, towards the Roundhouse.

A group of youths filling a sledge with cut logs came into view. Zak knew them—had taught some to hunt. Other boys

were breaking ice and piling the slabs onto another sled. As Zak moved to help them—they shied away.

'What's the matter?'

'They say you carry the sickness,' one boy said.

'They are saying you brought it to the Roundhouse,' said another.

'Who is saying?'

'Everyone,' said the first boy. Keeping his distance, yet showing no fear, he pointed an accusing finger at Zak. 'Our people are dying. Three Elders are dead, including Mowdah. Our brothers and sisters have taken it upon themselves to keep the littl'uns out of the Roundhouse whilst vomit fills the air. Skaldric and Urdeth burn with fever, as does Sheena, your wife.'

'No,' Zak cried, 'it can't be.' He held up his hands palms facing the boy, 'See—I am whole and clean. Not sick, not sick.'

Unconvinced, the young men continued to back away from him, using the sledge as some kind of shield between *them* and the approaching Zak. They watched him gain on them, and suddenly horror filled their eyes. One youth held his fingers to his face and made the sign of warding off the evil eye. 'If you are not sick, Zak, son of Sarash,' he cried, 'then you must be damned.'

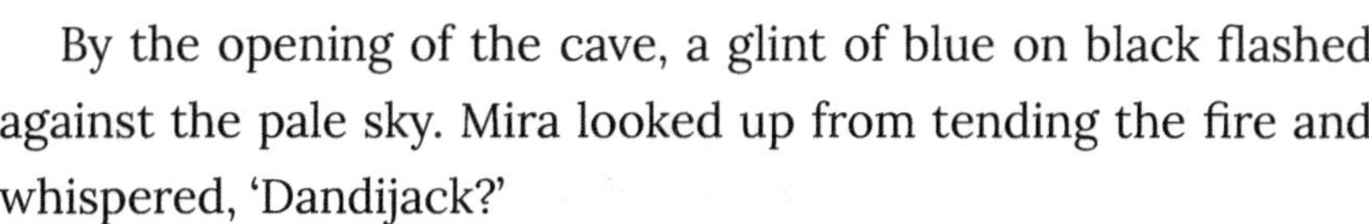

By the opening of the cave, a glint of blue on black flashed against the pale sky. Mira looked up from tending the fire and whispered, 'Dandijack?'

The bird continued to circle outside the cave's mouth, telling Mira something was wrong. She rose to her feet, picked up her fur cloak and went to greet it. 'Dandijack—*what ails you?*' The raven fell from the sky into her open hands—its scaly feet blistered.

'What is it?' Methiu asked.

'His feet—his feet are burnt. My daughter's spirit has fled. What could've happened?'

'I have salve—it soothes human skin. It might work on Dandijack.'

Mira shook her head. 'It would be the cruellest of things to do.' She was massaging the bird's neck—Dandijack's eyes struggling to keep open. 'A bird can manage without one foot, but with none....' She started to hum as her fingers smoothed the feathers and slowly, Dandijack rested his head and fell limp into the palm of her hand.

'You've killed him.'

'I have done no such thing!'

'But, he's gone limp.'

'I've numbed his pain. He will sleep—his sleep will grow deeper—he will not feel any more pain.'

'You're about to kill him then.'

'No—I am not. He merely sleeps.'

'But he won't wake up?'

Cradling the bird in both hands, she gave a deep sigh and returned to the cave, stopping in its entrance. 'If you want to help,' she whispered over her shoulder, 'then bring me a handful of clean snow, we've got work to do.'

The sickness was no stranger to the folk of the fishing village. Experience told them it took highborn folk with the same ease as those like themselves, poor and lowly. Yet their hearts filled with pity for the children gathering in increasing numbers on the lake's shore. The fisherwomen took food to them and bid their own children to show them where to find fresh water to drink. And when snow began to fall in huge flakes, the fishermen's children brought them in, to shelter with their families in the warmth of their humble homes.

On the northern shores of the lake, Elvad taught Dion to track without being spotted. Then to kill an animal swiftly and cleanly. They had made camp between the lake and the edge of the forest, choosing a sheltered cove where sparkling fresh water ran under sheets of crystal clear ice. The tall trees protected them from the cold winds and from the heavy snow that whirled in swathes across the frozen surface of the lake.

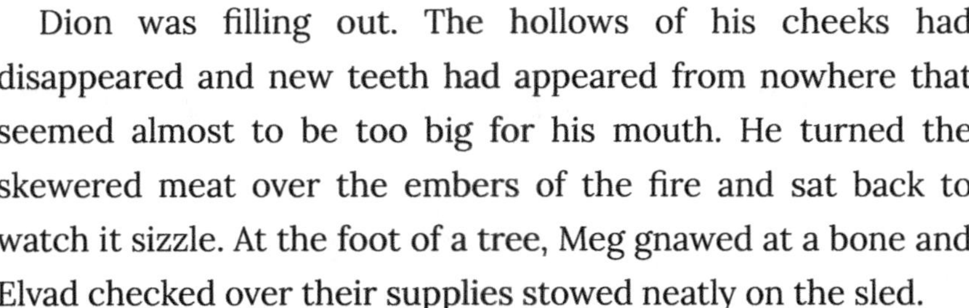

Dion was filling out. The hollows of his cheeks had disappeared and new teeth had appeared from nowhere that seemed almost to be too big for his mouth. He turned the skewered meat over the embers of the fire and sat back to watch it sizzle. At the foot of a tree, Meg gnawed at a bone and Elvad checked over their supplies stowed neatly on the sled.

Meg gave a low growl, alerting Elvad to danger. He drew the knife from his belt and put a finger to his lip warning Dion to keep quiet.

In the midst of the swirling snow, dark shapes hovered in and out of view, making it difficult to see what they were and how many. Meg stood ready to leap and Dion took his place by her side. As the shape neared the light of the fire, it became clear that it was a small group of people. Some carried children wrapped in bundles of snow-covered furs, one carried a new born close to her breast, all clutching hold of each other, propping one another up. They trudged towards the sled, and fell exhausted at Elvad's feet.

Chapter Thirty-Two

Fiedra held onto the cabin's partition wall and watched as Bryn's men negotiated the swell of the tide. Beyond the heaving sea, the craggy outline of the island's shore dipped in and out of sight. As the ship's prow neared the coast, rows of russet red buildings stood alongside white ones, lining the walkway at the water's edge. Fiedra could make out their shuttered windows and sloping, snow-covered roofs against the brown and grey backdrop of the rocky landscape.

This was Bryn's homeland. This was where his wife and wee girls, as he called them, lived together with other members of his clan. Fiedra had learned they stemmed from a nation of giants and although they were not exactly Titans, they stood head and shoulders above ordinarily tall folk.

She stared at the quayside as the ship edged towards it and marvelled at the charm of the single dwellings, each painted in a different, bright colour. The only single houses known to Fiedra were hovels similar to those of her uncle, and the homes of the fishermen and their families, which to Fiedra's eyes were dull and miserable.

She scanned the air above the ship, looking for a glimpse of the raven in the pale grey sky. A sense of unease had entered her soul, and she wondered if it had come to harm. Winter was a dangerous time of year for all creatures, yet she felt somehow, that a raven filled with her mother's spirit, would easily be able to weather a storm or outwit any predator.

The coxswain shouting his orders brought her out of her reverie. The ship was entering the harbour, a sheltered area where the waters were calmed, allowing the men to steer safely to their mooring. On the quayside, men and boys pulled wheeled carts stacked with cargo. Their voices shouting orders as more goods were brought from other vessels tied along the wharf.

Bryn waved at a group of women. 'See yon lasses,' he grinned, 'they be mine.'

Fiedra saw the twinkle of a tear in the giant's eyes and loved him more than ever. The 'yon lasses' had hair redder than a setting midsummer sun. Even in the pale light, Fiedra caught the glints of copper from their curls as they bobbed up and down on the excited girls' shoulders. Soon, squeals of delight reached the ship as other children and women joined the welcome party, and before long the quayside was ablaze with the many coloured clothes they wore. Colours Fiedra had never seen except on the heads of flowers in the summertime. She stood aside. 'Go greet your family first,' she urged Bryn, 'then you can explain about me to them.'

And she watched from the ship as he swept his wee girls into his arms, giving each one a special hug. And their faces lit with joy to see their father home safe after months on the Salt Seas. And Bryn's wife, waiting patiently for her turn with eyes flecked green like shards of emeralds set in amber.

Movement above Fiedra's head caused her to look up, a sparrow circled before landing on the ship's prow. She watched it for a while, trying to puzzle why she sensed it was no ordinary sparrow and why she felt it was somehow connected with Dandijack.

Perak stretched under the smooth sheets of her bed and listened to the strange language spoken by the members of her new family, as they chattered between themselves in the room next to hers. Sunlight poured through layers of thin-woven cloth that had been draped across the slatted windows, casting delicate shadows that danced in shimmering spasms across the smooth ceiling. The days were lengthening.

She swung her legs free and reaching for her robe, wrapped it round her shoulders to join the other ladies.

'Good morning,' greeted Abelia, one of Kaylak's many cousins, 'I trust you slept well?'

'I have never slept so well or for so long,' Perak took the offered cake, served hot from a griddle that was fixed to the chamber's crackling fire. As was the custom of her new home, she trickled it with honey before nibbling the edges. 'Mmm,' Her eyes rolled, delighting those in the room, 'can a girl ever tire of such cakes?'

'Well if you do, we have many more delicacies waiting for you,' trilled Abelia, as she gestured with one hand towards the

side table where confection of many kinds were stacked in layers.

'Please,' Perak held up a hand, 'I must decline—lest greed should enter into me. My dada brought us up to resist gluttony.'

'As does our King Methiu,' Abelia chided, 'he also frowns upon overindulgence.' The back of her hand failed to hide the smirk, as she turned her attention from the side table and began to arrange clothing made especially for Perak, spreading gowns and petticoats over chairs, ready for the new girl to make her choice.

'You jest with me, Abelia.'

'You learn fast Perak.'

'You didn't mean it when you said the King frowns on overindulgence?'

'Sorry, it is our way,' She teased, 'to imply what is clearly not true.'

'I see.' Perak didn't quite see but was beginning to learn that Abelia spoke in riddles. 'So when you said that I must always wear fine clothes, such as these—you didn't mean it?'

Abelia lost her appetite for jesting. 'You are to become a princess. Our people expect you to look splendid.'

'At all times?'

'At all times.'

Perak paced the floor. 'But surely, whilst I am learning the ways of the West, and spending so much time here, away from court, I see no reason why I couldn't wear something, er, more casual?'

'Like what?'

'Oh, I don't know,' Perak licked the honey from her sticky fingers, 'perhaps you could fashion a simple shift for me and have it studded with gems, and rucked with ribbons to show the multi layers of coloured silks that have been trimmed with rare furs—don't you think?'

'I think—you jest with me.'

'You too learn fast.'

The other females in the room clapped their hands and shouted encouragement to Perak. 'So,' Abelia said at length, 'when my dear cousins have control over their mirth, what would you like to wear?'

'I will wear the clothes you have chosen for me today, but instead of the music lessons, I would like my new cousins to help me to design clothes better suited for freedom of movement.'

'Are you jesting again Perak?'

'No, Abelia, I am deadly serious.'

Omi, one of the other ladies appointed to attend Perak intervened, 'Come, Perak, if you have eaten your fill, I will help you bathe.'

Perak nodded and followed Omi to the marble stand where a basin of warm, scented water was placed. She allowed the kindly woman to strip her of the sleeping clothes and wash her skin. All the while, she kept her eyes on Abelia as she ordered unknown females to take away the platters of cake and others to enter Perak's bed chamber where the silky sheets were replaced with freshly laundered bedding.

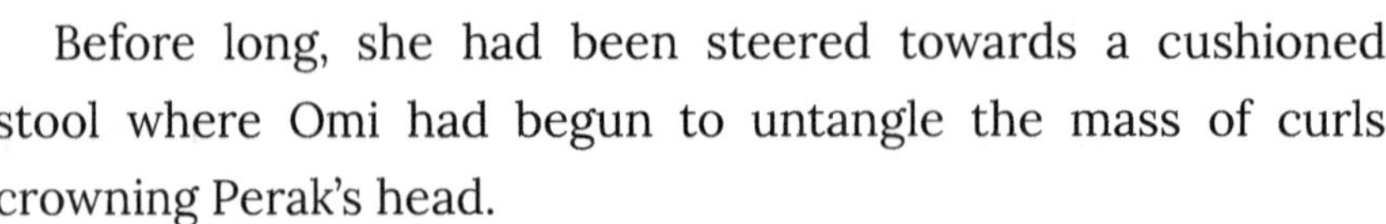

Before long, she had been steered towards a cushioned stool where Omi had begun to untangle the mass of curls crowning Perak's head.

'Are you not happy with us?'

Perak's intake of breath was ragged. 'I thought,' she confided to Omi's ears only, 'that Kaylak would have visited me, but since we arrived, I have seen nothing of him.'

'Did he not explain our ways?'

'You mean about the rules of our betrothal? Yes, my mother explained all that. It is similar to our custom. When a daughter from another clan is betrothed to one of our young men, they can be together in public, to talk and get to know one another, but must not get intimate until after the wedding.'

'Prince Kaylak has important work to do, and cannot afford to spend time chatting with you. Besides, he wants you to learn our ways, so that when you and he are wed, he can ask your advice about affairs of state.'

'I am not qualified to advise on affairs of state!'

'By the time you finish your training with us, Perak, my cousin, you will be.'

'I have much to learn.'

'And, may I say, you have passed your first test. Abelia has found her match, which is good, but I warn you, she doesn't take kindly to being bettered.'

'Now I know her true colours, I will take care.'

'Good. So, when you are ready, shall we begin by finding out what kind of casual clothing can be designed that will meet the

high standards of our court, and those of yourself? How does that make you feel?'

Perak's eyes lit up, 'Omi, I feel I am spoilt.'

'Good—because you are.'

Chapter Thirty-Three

Methiu held the raven in his warm hands and felt the snow melt and trickle through his fingers as Mira sprinkled flakes onto the blistered claws. 'It would have worked better if we could've got to the burns sooner,' he heard her say.

'So you think snow is better than salve?'

'You felt how hot his feet were. I'm simply cooling the burn down, hopefully preventing it from spreading. Your salve can come later.'

'What will happen to your daughter's spirit?'

'I wish it to be taken by the ancestors to find peace at last.'

'Why can't it?'

'My youngest daughter has caused many eyebrows to be raised. Her spirit is restless because of the selfish life she lived.'

'So, whilst the heavens debate your daughter's fate, you have no spy?'

Mira shrugged her shoulders, his mirth not sinking in. 'My daughter's spirit is resourceful, it will have found another host.' She lifted a claw, examined it closely, 'Dandijack is a dear little friend—spy or not, I don't want to lose him. See how closed his foot is, he thinks he is roosting, gripping onto a branch.'

Methiu shuffled on his knees, taking the weight from one to another. 'Will he waken by himself, or must you bring him round?'

'Bring him round? That's a strange expression.'

'They say it in a land far away to the east. The people have a sport where they throw each other onto mats of woven grass, sometimes a competitor is knocked unconscious—they throw water into his face to bring him round. It has become an expression that my people now use.'

When Mira was satisfied the bird's feet had cooled, she lifted him from Methiu's open hand and placed him in a hollow of rolled up furs. 'What strange people you encounter, don't they realise life is hard enough without knocking each into a daze?'

'They do it for sport. There is much aggression in their young men, it is a way of releasing it.'

Her tongue and teeth formed an audible tut, which echoed around the cave. She wandered into the darkness and returned with a large flagon and two goblets. She handed the flagon to Methiu, 'I was saving this for the Shaman's return, but his end came sooner than I expected.'

He poured the liquid into the goblets, replaced the flagon's stopper and propping it by his seat of furs, he asked, 'What are we celebrating?'

'Nothing, but I feel I must find out what happened to my daughter's spirit.'

'You think it has come to harm?'

'I worry what mischief she is making.'

His laugh echoed around their cavernous abode, Mira leaned close to him,

'Would you accompany me on a journey to meet up with my granddaughter?'

'Which one?'

'The one who may one day, become a Shaman.'

'Try leaving me behind.'

Elvad built up the fire and gave the broth another stir before cutting more strips of meat to sizzle on the hot stones. Anyone could tell the little group of people were starving. The leader, a man about ten winters older than Elvad, was explaining why they had no provisions with them. They had to flea their home, a settlement in a valley north of the lake, in a hurry because of an unexpected freak of nature.

'We should've joined the rest of our clan before the Midwinter feast, but our chief's wife was heavy with child. We belong to her family, so voted to send the majority on as scheduled, whilst we stayed with her until after the birth.'

'Are you saying the others joined those in the Roundhouse down there?' Elvad pointed back to the shore and in the direction of the wharf.

'Yes, they're safe, thank goodness, safe from the terrible thing that happened to us.' The man's haunted eyes looked to

his people, who stood, huddled in silence, listening to his every word. 'Without warning, a great wall of snow came rolling down from the mountains. Its roar deafened us. It was tumbling towards our settlement with such speed; we knew we could never out-run it. The ground trembled as it reached our community house then silence. It was engulfed by it, buried beneath its weight.' He started to tremble. A woman broke away from the gathering, wrapped her arms around his neck pulling his head down, striving to calm his shaking body, smothering him in the process.

He broke free, took a deep breath and warned her, 'If I don't tell them now how we got out, I never will.'

'Come, my friend,' Elvad interrupted, 'the broth is hot. Eat first, your story can wait. Give thanks you all got out.' He offered skewers of sizzled meat to be shared amongst the ravenous company, all the time, his mind fearful for them, dreading how they could take news of what was to come. He scooped broth into the only two cups he had, bid them share it between them, embrace its warmth, taste the goodness of the freshly hunted meat. He talked non-stop about how Bryn's tasty herbs had flavoured it. He chatted to them whilst they ate. Fearful of the moment when they learnt what fate their kinsmen had succumbed to. Dreading the moment they found a Roundhouse piled with the corpses of their clan. Compared to the sorrow that lay ahead, the avalanche experience could be a mere nothing, a minor mishap eclipsed by a mightier tragedy.

He looked at the little gathering as they shared their meal in silence, five children, a baby, three women and one male leader: all that might be left of their whole clan. Then his eyes

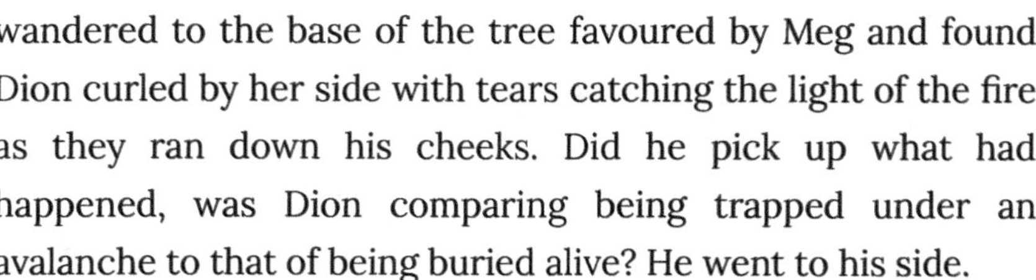

wandered to the base of the tree favoured by Meg and found Dion curled by her side with tears catching the light of the fire as they ran down his cheeks. Did he pick up what had happened, was Dion comparing being trapped under an avalanche to that of being buried alive? He went to his side.

'Sad story, hey, my little brother?'

The boy nodded.

'Have you met these people before?'

Dion hunched his shoulders, telling Elvad nothing—*could have* or *don't know.*

'They will have to put their sorrows behind them, like we have. They will become our brothers and sisters from now on, you do understand what I'm saying, don't you?'

Elvad hunkered down by Dion's side. He sensed Dion knew more than he could say. The boy turned to face him and nodded.

'Come on,' Elvad said at length, placing a brotherly arm across the boy's shoulders. 'Help me make them welcome. Help me unpack the sled—we have spare furs, they have nothing.'

Chapter Thirty-Four

Zak watched the boys flee towards the Roundhouse, heard their cries of superstition, warning those inside that, '*Zak, Son of Sarash was possessed with demon spirits*'.

Whether they liked it or not, he would help his people. He took the sled's rope and began to pull it toward the abandoned pails of broken ice. Despite the logs' weight, the sled glided easily across the frozen shoreline. As he picked up the first pail he noticed the colour of the ice. It was streaked with brown. Surely they didn't intend to use unclean water for drinking purposes? He examined it again. He would be loath to wash in water as foul as this looked—loath even to sluice the latrine channel with it.

Suddenly a terrifying thought caught hold of him. He looked up and to where the Roundhouse stood, his gaze following the track meandering downwards him. Ice collected from below the building could be, *would be* sullied by the latrines. Disgusted, he flung the ice slabs across the frozen scree. Why had no one supervised the quality of the ice?

The youths accused *him*, the son of a great chieftain, of taking the illness into the Roundhouse, yet all the time, they had been drinking foul water. He could not be held responsible

—would not be held to account. They were leaderless now that Skaldric had come down with the sickness, and Mowdah the Elder was dead, and other minor heads of clans. He looked back to where he had found clean water and followed the iced-over path upstream. From now on, he would take charge: he would command they use only pure ice from *that* rivulet.

When he returned his gaze back to the Roundhouse, Kira, his wife's cousin was walking towards him. In her arms, she carried his son.

Fiedra sprinkled crumbs onto the smooth surface of the tree stump and waited for the sparrow to appear. She turned her face to the sun, feeling its gentle warmth healing the scar on her cheek. The tiny courtyard where she stood had become her favourite part of the gardens. A sheltered spot tucked away from the formal grounds that surrounded Bryn's magnificent house, and one where she was left alone to gather her thoughts, and to converse in private with the spirit that dwelt within the tiny, feathered creature.

Before long, the flutter of wings caught her attention. Fiedra watched the delicate beak peck at the tit-bits and the little feet dance nimbly around the sawn edge of the stump.

She knew now what had happened to her grandmother's raven, Dandijack. Knew too that he had made his way safely to the cave, knew grandmother would care for him, like she cared

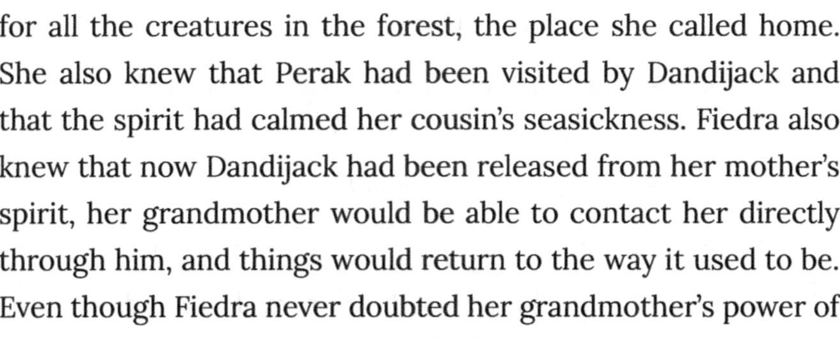

for all the creatures in the forest, the place she called home. She also knew that Perak had been visited by Dandijack and that the spirit had calmed her cousin's seasickness. Fiedra also knew that now Dandijack had been released from her mother's spirit, her grandmother would be able to contact her directly through him, and things would return to the way it used to be. Even though Fiedra never doubted her grandmother's power of healing, she sent a silent prayer for his recovery.

When the bird had finished eating, and had flown to a nearby tree branch to clean its beak and preen its feathers, the voice of Fiedra's dead mother came into her head. *My visit is short. I cannot return for a while.*

Why not?

Your grandmother needs me.

Really? Why?

She has left the cave—I must keep an eye on her.

Grandmother has never needed to have an eye kept on her. What other reason are you hiding?

Urdeth's husband, Skaldric—he also needs me.

You surprise me mother, what possible comforts can you give to poor Skaldric? From what I know, there has never been any love between you and Urdeth's husband.

Perhaps time has come for forgiveness?

Forgiveness? Oh, mother, have you forgotten? You had the old witch curse his male children.

Skaldric had no part in it. He was punished for Urdeth's wrongdoing.

And what was Urdeth's wrongdoing?

She refused to love you as her own.

To curse her like you did was an evil thing to do and you know it. Besides, I didn't need Urdeth's love.

No, you took her daughter's instead.

And she got mine.

Anyway, now Urdeth is dying, the curse will be lifted.

Urdeth dying? What makes you so sure? What's happened to make her die so young?

She's pining away—her daughter has fled the nest—together with her only surviving sons.

But what of Skaldric—what of the love she has for him? Urdeth wouldn't pine away—she's far too strong.

Well—she's dying of something. I feel it. And now the curse is lifted from the surviving boys.

Why do I get the feeling you are hiding something?

I'm hiding nothing. I haunt a bird, Fiedra—there is only so much information a bird can hold in its head. I have to work with what I can.

Maybe so, but my heart goes out to that poor bird—I wouldn't like your spirit haunting me.

You grow more like your grandmother every day.

That's the nicest compliment you have ever given me. So before you fly off, allow me to ingest what you're implying. You are certain Skaldric's boys are safe from the old witch's curse—is that true?

Oh yes, the boys will live to see Urdeth in her grave.

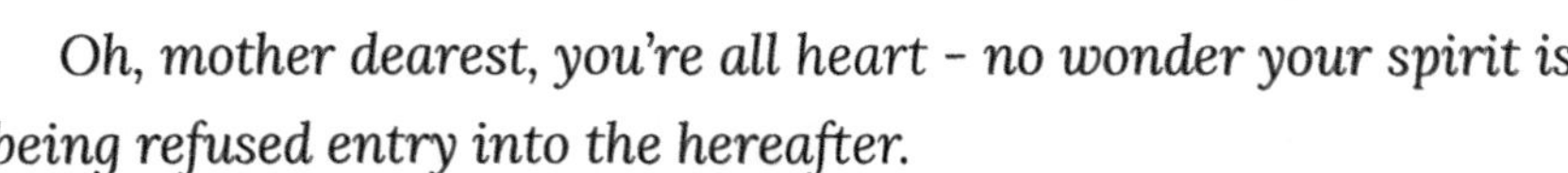

Oh, mother dearest, you're all heart - no wonder your spirit is being refused entry into the hereafter.

Ugh—and do I feel blessed - do you think I care to bide for an eternity with those judgemental souls?

He was looking for signs of the sickness on the baby's face, and found none. Nor did Kira have the sheen of sweat, or the stench of vomit as she neared.

'They are saying you carry the evil-eye,' Her voice frantic and breathless as she took long strides, carrying the sleeping child across the slippery, icy shoreline, 'I don't believe them, yet had to see for myself.'

Zak wiped his hands down the nap of his fleece cloak. Aware the foul ice had wet them. He bent to scoop fresh snow. 'There is no evil-eye, Kira. And I will show them.' Rubbing his hands clean, he ran to her, using his sharpened senses, to examine them closely, searching for any sign they were sick. 'He grows well,' he whispered, wanting to, but not daring to touch the sleeping child's face.

Her eyes were searching too. Looking for the signs she had become too familiar with of late - cracked lips, feverish sweating and uncontrollable shakes, coughing, retching and vomit. She found nothing save weight loss around his cheekbones, gaunt jawline and the wild eyes she had worshipped from childhood. 'I have fed him broth made from barley. He likes it.'

He didn't want to ask if his wife was ill, instead he asked, 'Does Sheena no longer feed him?'

Tears that filled her eyes overflowed in fat droplets down her cheeks. Unable to answer, she looked to the baby in her arms and shook her head.

'So the boys spoke truly—they said my wife had the sickness. Is that so?'

Suddenly angry Kira flung back her head, driving the tears from whence they came. She turned towards the Roundhouse and snarled, 'It's hell in there, like a vomit-ridden charnel house. Folk, some dying and some dead, are left in heaps. There is no one with the strength to separate them, to drag the dead bodies out—let alone to give them a decent burial!' Her sob was amplified bouncing back at them from the hardness of the scree, and the stillness of the frozen lake behind them. He moved to comfort her, but she turned her back on him.

'I'm sorry, Kira. Believe me, I have been sick—truly sick—but it has gone. Perhaps the boys are right in thinking I'm dammed —spawn of some demon now meant to roam the Earth in torment. But I didn't take the sickness to Sheena, or to anyone.' He grabbed hold of her shoulders, and when she didn't resist, he pulled her into his embrace, his child nestled between them, and never had Zak felt so much in need of her comforting and understanding as he did then.

Chapter Thirty-Five

'We thank you for your kindness, but we must press on. We have to find better shelter before the snow thickens.' The leader of the group said, as Elvad unpacked the ties holding the rolls of fleeces onto the sled.

'You need to rest,' Elvad urged, 'these furs and fleeces will protect you from the cold. And our camp is sheltered from the gales. The boy and I have survived, I am sure you will.'

'He is right, Volta, Lourah needs to rest, we all do, but *she* needs to keep her milk flowing. The baby needs her to rest.' The woman patted Volta's arm, took a bundle of furs from Elvad and returned to distribute them to the little gathering.

Dion helped two of the children make a temporary bivouac between the stumps of trees close to where his bivvy stood. It afforded shelter combined with warmth from the fire.

Exhausted but well fed, before long all four children were snuggled down and fast asleep, leaving the women and the baby wrapped in fleeces in their section and the two men around the fire. Meg was curled by the side of Dion, ever watchful, ever caring.

'Your manner of speech tells me you are from the West, yeah?'

'Yes.'

'Did you come for the Midwinter Feast?'

'Yes, en route from a trading expedition.'

'Ah, the ships moored in wharf. We saw them, three—were there not?'

'Yes. They are gone now.'

Volta nodded, 'They left without taking you with them?'

'Yes.'

'Just as well my friend - there was a monster—we could see it from up in our valley. There is a saying amongst folk around here: the monster brings bad omens.' Suddenly, Volta began to tremble. 'I am sorry, I realise what my foolish words must sound in your ears. The monster followed the ships. Oh dear, I really am sorry.'

'There is no need, my countrymen had no fear of the so-called monster, they simply left early to guide to its own waters. I stayed back because, I wish to study and seek enlightenment.'

Volta fell silent and looked across to the women; nestled together, eyes heavy and ready to slip into deep slumber. 'You are a learned man, you speak our language well and you have travelled to many places, am I right?'

'I am fortunate in being able to learn.'

'And the boy, he isn't of your kin?'

'He has become my adopted brother. Our paths follow the same route.'

'I am glad that route led you to us.'

'So am I.'

As Fiedra watched the bird fly off, she wondered if her mother's spirit would ever settle to normality—and knew the answer would be probably not. She turned to follow the sunlit path that led to the main garden and as she neared, she could hear Bryn's children at play. Above her head, chirpy birds sung in the trees, and away from the house, gulls were calling, excited, she thought, perhaps at the prospect of scraps thrown by the fishing boats that frequented the island's harbour. She rounded the corner and two of the girls were hitting a ball to each other using a paddle-shaped bat in each hand. The ground under their soft-shoed feet was raked with tiny shale, flattened to give them a smooth surface for during their game. She skirted around their court, and found a seating area where the last rays of the sun dallied and lingered above a tree. Sitting in the shade and enjoying the match was Tura, Bryn's kindly giant of a wife.

'Fascinated with my daughters' game are you Fiedra?'

'I am, though ignorant of the rules.' She put a hand to shade her eyes. A bird flew to the top branch of the tree and spread its wings, casting a shadow across Fiedra's face, shielding it from the sun.

Tura watched how Fiedra took it for granted the way creatures responded to her discomfort. 'Bryn has told me how you helped the whale calf reunite with his mother. Where did you get your gift?'

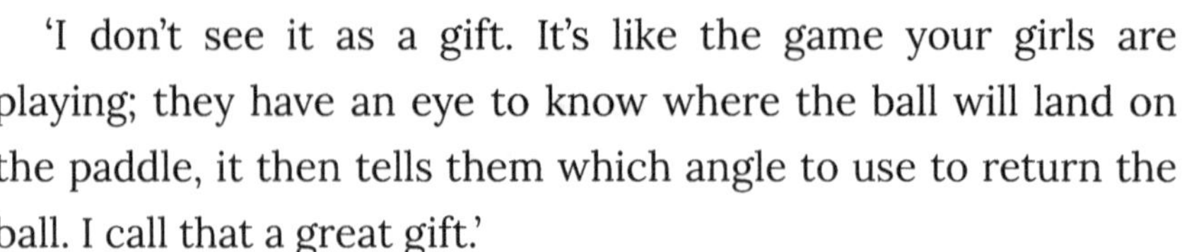

'I don't see it as a gift. It's like the game your girls are playing; they have an eye to know where the ball will land on the paddle, it then tells them which angle to use to return the ball. I call that a great gift.'

'Tomorrow, if you like, I will teach you to play.'

'Oh,' Fiedra blushed and gave an involuntary glance at her deformed foot, 'I have never been able to participate in....'

Suddenly, and from out of nowhere, an animal bounded across the levelled shale, making deep ruts in it with its huge paws. It leapt and with its mouth, caught the ball mid-air. Holding it between its mighty jaws, it turned and ran towards the seated women.

Fiedra froze, sending a silent command to the hound. It skidded to a stop and obediently dropped the ball at her feet.

Tura took in a deep breath, 'By the gods, what happened?'

'I er, I am sorry,' Fiedra reached out a hand, patting the beast on the head. 'I am truly sorry,' she tried to assure the trembling creature. 'I didn't mean to frighten you.' She let out a sob, and turned to Tura, 'I think I've scared him badly, it was instinct, I thought he would knock us over.'

Tura had turned pale, her emerald-flecked eyes questioning Fiedra's face, 'But you halted him without a word,' She whispered.

Before Fiedra could reply she was aware of men approaching from the far side of the court. A familiar voice caught Fiedra's ears, her name being called, its rhythmic accent like poetry set to music, sending her skin to tingle. She took her eyes off Tura and stood to glance towards it. Joy filling her heart, she picked up the layers of her new dress and

ran across the tiny pebbles, her lopsided run making uneven footmarks in her eagerness to greet him.

He crouched ready to embrace her, catching her and folding his arms around her, lifting and spinning, making her cling onto his neck and draw her face close to his, breathing in his scents, the flinty essences unique only to him, his lips hard and full of longing, pressing onto hers.

'By the gods, I reckon the wee lass has missed you too, Yorevyn, my friend.' Bryn observed as he strode past them to greet his own loved ones.

Chapter Thirty-Six

Skaldric woke from his slumber, his throat dry, head thumping, and sending pulsing throbs to boom in both ears. He needed the latrine, needed to quaff water, buckets of it. He crept around the sleeping families, using the dimmed torchlight to help him make his way out of the smoky Roundhouse. Once outside he gulped in lungs full of chilled air —breathing it in as he had never breathed before. Something in his brain was shaking his wits—making him wake up—telling him, warning him to listen. He tried to shake the thoughts aside but they came back almost screaming at him from the inside of his skull: insisting that he understood something was very, very wrong. He took another deep breath and noticed that within the iciness of the air, there was a rank and nauseous stench catching hold of his senses, forcing him to bypass the latrine and to stagger further up the hill. Above Skaldric's head, a tiny sparrow dipped then rose; its little wings fluttering wildly to keep its body aloft—striving to keep it airborne.

Zak looked over Kira's head to see Skaldric stumble against the store shed and shuddered when he caught sight of the bird, his mind flashing to the time when crows swarmed over bodies on the Shadow's filthy mound. He watched to see if Skaldric recovered and for some reason, noted that the bird

was zigzagging as though it too teetered on the brink of consciousness.

'Kira?' He asked, his eyes not moving from the scene on the hill above them, 'does Skaldric have the sickness?'

She nodded, 'I think so, hasn't moved for days—same as everyone.'

'Kira, have you had it?'

She shook her head, 'Keep thinkin' I'll come down with it. Bathing my kinfolk day in day out, but somehow, it...'

'Kira, are others tending the sick?'

'Yes, we, er, what's left of us are so few, and so very tired Zak, we shuffle around like dead men.'

'Have you tended Skaldric?'

'No, he hasn't woken yet. Some just sleep—like you did—I watched over you, but you slept on. I checked when I could—but couldn't get to everyone —there's so many to tend.' He felt her shoulders shake and tremble, he held her close, mindful of the child in her arms.

'Kira?' She stopped trembling, 'Kira—are you listening to me?' she nodded letting him know she was, 'I don't want you to go back to the Roundhouse. I will get fleeces, and bring them to you.'

'B-but my kinfolk.'

'Those tending the sick I will send out with provisions, furs to keep us warm. We will need Skaldric's barrels of food; I will move them from the Roundhouse stores. Don't drink water from the pails, go up to that inlet,' He pointed to where he had

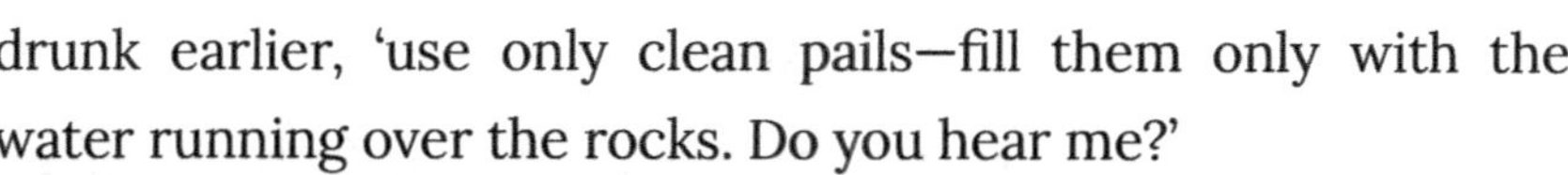

drunk earlier, 'use only clean pails—fill them only with the water running over the rocks. Do you hear me?'

She nodded.

'Good, now listen Kira, we're going to be alright—we'll get through this, believe me.'

'I do.'

'Good, now wait here, I'll fetch furs.'

'B-but—what if the sickness gets you?'

'It won't, I've had it and according to Elvad, that gives me a shield.'

'What has Elvad to do with the Roundhouse?'

'He doesn't have anything to do with the Roundhouse, but he tended my sickness, and for that, I think I owe him my life.'

'I've come to take you to my land.'

'What? Now?'

'Now. My ship is waiting in the harbour.'

'Ah—the joyful cry of the seagulls,' She reflected, 'I should've picked it up, but wait—I need to arrange things—I don't have any clothes—these belong to Bryony—she is the only child my size.'

'You shall have all the garments you want. You can wear four a day if you wish—so come, my ship is waiting.'

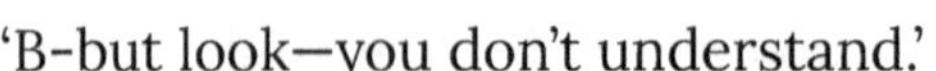

'B-but look—you don't understand.'

Yorevyn took his arms from around her, held them open, feigned sorrow, 'Are you trying to tell me you don't want to meet my people?'

'Not in a child's dress—and my scar—what will they make of me?'

'My people see only the person within, they are too worldly to judge by the cut of their clothing.'

'But you are wrong, People have always judged me as someone to be ashamed to be with, because of my foot and how I spent the first years of life.'

'My people will love you for what you are, as I do.'

'And what am I?' She stood back and smoothed the skirts of her childish dress, 'I am a waif brought up by the charity of Kira's family. I am not even a glue-maker's niece—he was paid to care for me by my mother before she died. Even then he sent me back to the Marsh Wives, complaining I was nowt but a burden.'

'You are nothing of the sort. You heard the cry of the *krill eater*'s mother. You have the power to hear, and see, and speak to those we cannot. Nature sparks in you like nobody else. Bryn has told me about the bird who combs your hair like he is preening his own feathers, taking delight in what he does. So don't tell me you are a nothing. You are so special. So very special, my people will want to make you their...' Interrupted by something brushing by his leg, he turned and looked down, 'what's this? What's happened to my hound?' Creeping and hunched, the huge animal came to heel at their feet, and slow and deliberate, he laid the ball onto the ground and nudged it

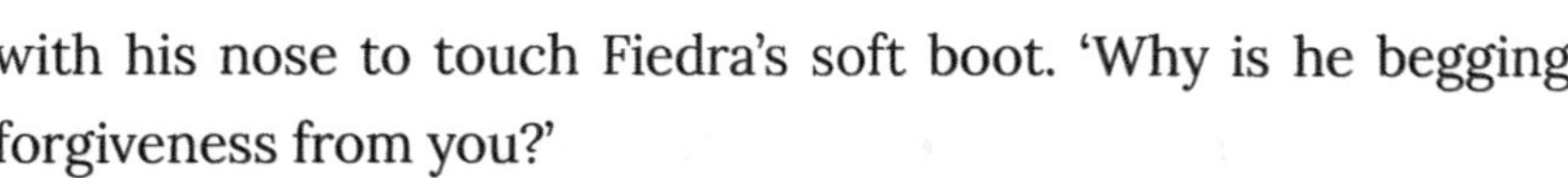

with his nose to touch Fiedra's soft boot. 'Why is he begging forgiveness from you?'

She patted the dog's scruff. 'It happened moments before you arrived. He hurtled towards Tura and me. I made him stop mid charge. I sent the command straight into his brain. I had to think quickly. I didn't mean to frighten him, honest.'

'Frighten him? He's fearless—he's Meg's son—one of eight she gave birth to a couple of winters back. Glue-maker's niece or not, it would take a mighty strong will to scare a hound such as him.' He looked into her eyes, seeing her anxiety. He held her close, calming the worry he saw, searching for some way to reassure her. 'You haven't hurt him. Look—he's reacting like all hounds do when they've been disciplined. And he's not used to seeing me hold a person for as long as I have held you. He's picked up that you are special to me and he's creeping around you because he senses my love for you—he's getting on your side.'

She smiled at his twisted smile. 'I'm glad to hear that. So, if he's yours and one of eight, then I must learn to relax around hounds of this size then?'

He took her face in his hands, bent and kissed her nose. 'You've seen nothing yet—I have his pa back home. Mark my words, you'll not scare *him* so easily.' With finger and thumb, he tweaked the end of her nose before taking her back into his arms. 'I can't wait for my people to see you. They've been going through a bad time. They also need someone to love.' He kissed her forehead.

'Bryn told me about the invaders who are heading for your island.'

'Yeh—I'm having to teach my people to become warriors instead of craftsmen—killers instead of artists, and it leaves me feeling I've failed them somehow. I wish I could stop these invaders mid charge. I wish I could stop them as easily as you halted Uka here.' He stretched a hand towards the dog, giving its flank a hearty slap. 'Imagine that, eh boy? Imagine having the power to stop an army on the march—imagine being able to give 'em the shits—and send 'em home, tail between their legs; and all without a drop of blood being spilled—imagine.' He gave the dog another slap, and laughed when the hound responding to his master's attention, lashing his tail wildly to beat against Yorevyn's thigh.

Fiedra chewed over the words Yorevyn spoke to the animal. She knew he meant them to be in jest, yet it sent a vision into her head, one that somehow she felt was shared with the creatures around her, especially the birds. 'Yorevyn—what you just said. I think it can happen,' Fiedra stood tall, her lavender eyes turning deep purple as she spoke, 'but I need to see your island, know its coastline, its forests and all the creatures that dwell on it, everything. So you are right in saying we need to board your ship as soon as possible, in fact, we need to leave immediately.'

Chapter Thirty-Seven

Zak carried the bundles of furs to where he had left Kira and the baby. He dropped the bundle by her side, shook one fleece loose, and wrapped it around her shoulders. The baby slept in her arms, he bent to kiss his cheek, felt her closeness and kissed her full and urgent on her lips. He heard her breath ragged before she pulled away, 'No,' She whispered, 'this is obscene. Your wife lies dying amongst my kinfolk. She could even be dead already for all I know.'

'She is,' His eyes were hard, dark as a starless night. 'I meant only to kiss our child, but lost my head. Forgive me Kira. Believe me when I say I'm sorry—I try to do what I think is honourable, yet,...' Now those eyes filled with a sea of tears, '... something out of my control takes over and I can't seem to do what's right.'

Kira reached with her free hand, brushed his cheeks with her soft fingers, wiping away the torrents of grief she knew Zak felt, whether they were for his dead wife, or for his motherless child, or for himself, she couldn't be sure, but her heart, as always, was full of love for him, and never more so than on that blustery, snow driven, icy shore of a lake frozen in mid winter.

Members of her clan came into view, some carrying bundles of fur, some baskets of food, others boxes of vitals ordered by Zak. Kira's aunt brought baskets of clothes, trinkets left in the ladies anteroom, combs, oils, and grease used to protect lips from the bitter winds.

Kira nudged Zak out of his misery, 'Come, this is no time for tears, these people need a strong leader.'

Yorevyn stopped his play with the hound—his manner serious once more.

'I have much to learn about these invaders,' Fiedra was saying, 'have any of your scouts sighted them?'

'Yes their ships make slow progress. But nevertheless, they are heading toward us from a land we trade with - or should I say, traded with. My sources tell me they have left that land sacked. They have scorched it, leaving its fine cities in ruins— its talented people desolate, and without hope.'

'Why do they do this—war thing?'

'Power and greed—they have ships larger than any of mine and some are filled to capacity with the treasures they have looted from all the countries they have invaded.'

'What do they want from your people?'

'More treasure - my island is rich in metal ore. We've learnt to blend some of these metals—made them stronger—thus

more valuable. Our biggest fear is they will kidnap some of my people to use as slaves.'

'Why would they do that?'

'Because of the skills they possess—craftsmanship handed down over many generations. My people can forge metal into wonderful materials—material that can and is being crafted into many uses.' Fiedra's concern faded momentarily, she smiled, prompting Yorevyn to ask, 'Did I say something amusing?'

'No, I was reminded of a wonderful work of metal Bryn showed me. Sorry, I didn't mean to distract you.'

'It is I who should say sorry; in my quest to save my people I get carried away. I need someone to distract me now and then. So what did Bryn show you?'

'A piece of your people's handiwork.' Although aware his people were still on his mind, she rolled up her sleeve to reveal a delicate bracelet, 'This was supposed to be a present for one of his daughters. He said they have too many trinkets, and gave it to me. I have never worn such a lovely gift. Nor have I ever been so well treated as I have with Bryn. I have grown to love him so much.'

'We all love Bryn,' He bristled, 'but beware, when you get to really know him, you'll find he's a canny old so-and-so.'

'No he isn't—he's resourceful and I love him for it.'

'I'll say he's resourceful all right. He's given me a bill for your keep and for your medical treatment and for storing some of my cargo on his ship. I know what you are doing - you're just trying to make me jealous. Well it worked and I am because he

doesn't deserve any of your love—I am the one you should be loving—not him.'

The sparkle in his eyes had returned, she continued to tease him—taking, she hoped, his mind from impending war. 'You cannot stop me from loving him—after all, I've spent more time with him than with you.' Suddenly feeling she had made him squirm enough, she added, '*Jesting apart, Yorevyn*, my love for him is different and can never match my love for you.'

'Why does that sound like birdsong in my ears? I've been told I'm rough as an uncut diamond, but I've seen what can be done to rough edges, once the right person has knocked them into shape. Could you knock a *ruffian* like me into shape, Fiedra?'

'Could you put up with a fickle wench like me Yorevyn?'

He took hold of her hands. 'Let us wed—right now on my ship.'

'But—but who will conduct the ceremony?'

'The harbour master—he owes me a favour.'

'Owes you a favour? But marriage is supposed to be a serious matter!'

'Well Bryn can perform it—they say it's lucky to have a ship's captain wed you.' Her laugh filled him with courage; suddenly he tightened the grip on her hands. '*Frivolous matters aside;* you have brought me to life. Ever since we met on that icy cold shore, I've been drawn to your laugh and the way your eyes peeped at me from under your hood. I knew from that moment on that I would always love you—knew that you would be the one for me. I want you to be my right hand, to help me guide my people: I want you by my side forever—and when we are

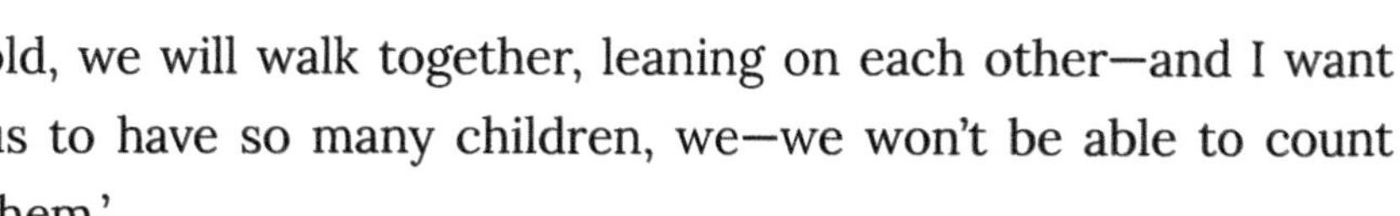

old, we will walk together, leaning on each other—and I want us to have so many children, we—we won't be able to count them.'

Fiedra's eyes danced from Yorevyn's to take in the final rays of the sun that haloed around his head, she stood on tiptoe and reached to kiss his lips, 'I will be *honoured* to share those things with you.'

Pulling her to join him, 'Come then,' he urged, turning back along the path he arrived from, 'Bryn has arranged a farewell supper down by the harbour, we can turn it into a wedding feast but first, we must ask him to marry us.'

Chapter Thirty-Eight

Skaldric found his strength failing with every step, but the urge to flee the stench and the strange voice *inside his head* pushed him on and upwards. At the top, he found a frozen-over rivulet and kicked at the ice with the heel of his boot.

Below him Zak gave orders to those gathering around the lake's shore, telling them to stack the supplies onto the empty sleds. Reiterating his words to Kira for them not to use any of the water supplied previously to the Roundhouse. He turned from them to walk up the hill to where he had seen Skaldric earlier.

The snow was coming fast and blowing in squalls and gusts around him, making it difficult to see beyond an arm's reach. Zak tumbled on something half buried in the snow—the body of a woman. Stiff with death and freezing temperatures. He skirted round the body, his brain telling him there was something he'd missed about the little child he had buried. He wasn't dead. If he had been dead, he reasoned, *surely he would have been stiff?* But the child he bathed and wrapped in his undershirt was limp. Pale and cold, but limp.

As he stumbled on, he stepped into a hollow where snow covered his legs to above his knees. Beneath his boots, the ground felt uneven. He kicked his way out, scrambling up the bank to stand back and peer through the swirling snowstorm down into the drift—slowly, his focus came clear enough to reveal the sight of more corpses lining the ditch's bottom.

'What are you looking at?' asked a croaky dry voice.

Kira found her aunt and took her aside, out of earshot of others, 'Zak says Sheena is dead—is it true?'

Her aunt nodded, 'There's no one left alive—or if they are, they're only just.' She looked at the sleeping baby in Kira's arms. 'Miracle he's not caught it. His mother coming down so bad.'

'None of us can breathe easy, Aunt Bel.'

'Aye, yer right there Kira, no saying which of us'll get it next. I keep drinkin' plenty of water, but now Zak says that's what caused it. Says we must climb the soddin' 'ill to fetch it.'

'We must do as he says, Aunt Bel, he is all we have to lead us.'

'Then may the gods have pity on us—that's all I can say.'

'By the gods—you gave me such a fright.'

'So did you jumping out of a ditch like that.'

Zak stared through the swirling snow into the face of his clan's leader. Skaldric was gaunt—even in the dim light, a shadow of his former self. 'Do you have the sickness?'

'What sickness?'

'*The* sickness—you know, the one we've tried to avoid for all these years.'

'Is that the stench filling the air down there?'

'Could be—but come the thaw—the stench will come from here.' He raised his voice above the roar of the wind and pointed into the snowdrift.

'Ugh—how long have they been dead?'

'I don't know, Kira tells me you and I have slept for days—meanwhile it's been running rife.'

Skaldric wiped icicles from his beard, saw the hollowed cheeks of the young man in front of him, 'But you've survived, and Kira, perhaps if we move fast, we can....'

'A handful, Skaldric—only a handful have survived. Sorry to tell you like this, but Urdeth...'

'No!' Skaldric moved to run down the hill, Zak reached out, held him back.

'She's gone, Skaldric—as is my Sheena.'

Skaldric stopped his urgency, placed his hands on Zak's shoulders, 'And the baby Zak, don't tell me....'

'He's well—for the moment that is. Kira took him into her care. She and her kin have been tending the sick. I fear before long, it may yet reach its ugly talons to pull them down.'

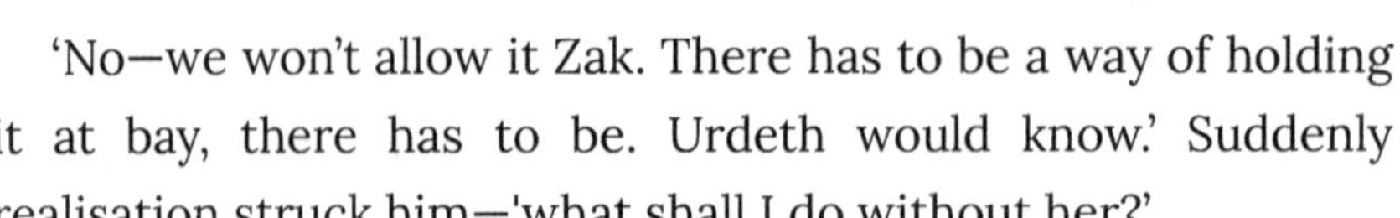

'No—we won't allow it Zak. There has to be a way of holding it at bay, there has to be. Urdeth would know.' Suddenly realisation struck him—'what shall I do without her?'

The great man's eyes began to fill. 'Skaldric, this is *no time for tears.* You and I must show our strength. Those survivors down on the shore, they're spent. They have nothing left. They don't walk; they shuffle, like they are dead on their feet. We have to find them shelter—somewhere away from the Roundhouse. Then when they have rested, we can come back—and bury our loved ones—and then we can cry over their graves—but now—we must attend to the living.'

Kira placed the sleeping child amongst the furs stacked on one of sleds and turned to walk up to the inlet where Zak said must be used for drinking water. She carried a pail previously held for storing the barley grain she fed to his child. Following his instructions, she rinsed the pail out before filling it from the water flowing over the rocks. The swirling snow was easing off, leaving in its stead, bitter winds blowing from across the lake. Despite the cold, she loosened her clothing and began to wash her face and neck; rubbing the cleansing waters into her flesh—scouring away the smell of sickness that clung to it. Blood surged below the surface of cheeks—tingling them with a mixture of iciness and burning. She rubbed her face dry. Picked up the pail and returned to the shores of the lake.

Someone had lit a brazier, and as she moved closer, she saw Zak working close to Skaldric. Skaldric was alive. The two men were lifting barrels between them, placing them onto the carts, which until now had lain under a blanket of snow. Someone else, a youth was leading an ox towards it—making it ready to be hitched up—like life had returned to normality. She saw aunt Bel—her toothy grin caught in the light of the flames. Kira's heart was given uplift at the sight of her kinfolk—what was left of them—moving with purpose—and amongst the little group were more teenagers—those who had been taken in by the fishing village and survived. The water inside the pail felt lighter as she carried it along the frozen scree and towards the welcoming flames.

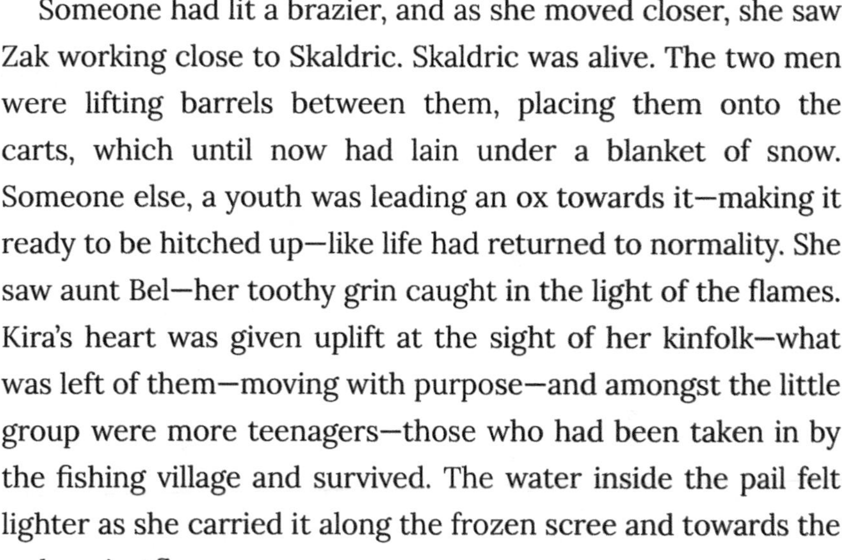

Chapter Thirty-Nine

'So when I begged you to guide the whale calf to the sea, you left your cousin to look after a sick man?'

'Yes—his name is Zak.'

'I know Zak—is he a kinsman?'

'No. But his wife's kinsmen are part of the clan who raised me.' Fiedra took a sip from Yorevyn's goblet. 'I could get used to this—what is it?'

'It's made from a fruit that grows on an island where the sun shines so warm—its people have skin that glows with its radiance.'

'Will you take me there?'

He took the goblet back, put it on the shelf built into the cabin's wall and kissed her for the hundredth time that night. 'Have I not told you,' he said as he leaned down to kiss her neck, 'that now we are as one,' his lips moved to her shoulder, 'wherever I go, you go too.'

'As one?'

'As one.'

Perak stood in front of the polished metal mirror and studied her reflection. Behind her Abelia was shaking her head, Omi on her knees was adjusting the hem of their latest creation.

'You really are the limit. I thought your previous outfit was bad enough Perak, but this time you have gone too far.'

'Don't you like them?'

'It is an outrage. Women are meant to be women. Not to scamper around the place mimicking youths. You look like a knave.'

'She doesn't look like a knave. As usual Abelia, you are prone to exaggeration.' Omi fastened the hem with a temporary stitch before nudging Perak to turn so she could measure the second leg to the outrageous outfit. She now had a full wardrobe of clothes that she and Omi had designed. All of which were comfortable and easy to slip into and made from material woven from silk that felt both cool and warm to Perak's skin. She wore her new clothes for all her lessons, telling her tutors they were the reason why she was able to concentrate of what they taught, rather than being stuffed with layers of tight clothes. They agreed among themselves that perhaps there was some merit in casual clothing, causing some to consider similar attire for students elsewhere.

Abelia fussed around the sewing room, picking up samples of lacework done by Perak during one of her lessons. 'You have a talent with lace—why don't you create a respectable piece of clothing made entirely of lace?'

'What a splendid idea,' Perak's reflection enthused. 'Perhaps I could use lace for my wedding dress.'

'Outrageous—who would make such a dress from something as flimsy as lace—you go too far with your jesting Perak. Too far by half.' She turned with a swish of hidden petticoats and made for the sewing room's door. Coming in the opposite direction was Kaylak and the two collided into each other. 'At last,' Abelia cried, 'someone has arrived who can talk some sense into the girl.'

He spun as she flew past him and watched her knock over stands of unfinished needlework in her wake. 'Have I called at a bad moment?'

Skaldric hitched the ox to the loaded cart and pulled the harness to ease the first movement of the wheels over the icy shale. Once they had turned, the ox took the load and slowly carried the cargo towards the vacated lodging houses by the wharf. The other people had gone on ahead, taken kindle wood and logs to heat the rooms and prepare warm food for their evening meal. They no longer had thoughts of celebratory feasts: no melodies played in their heads or songs of past heroes. Only the wind made a noise as it howled against the shuttered windows, moaning a mournful tune—a dirge lamenting the dead.

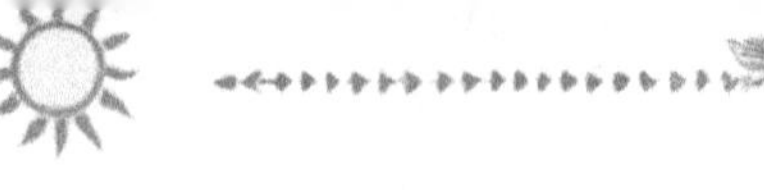

By the time Skaldric joined them and took his place beside Zak, the sound of logs crackling in the grate had brought a semblance of order to the clan. He ate heartily and listened whilst his people brought him up to date, telling him how the sickness came upon them too quickly to prevent it spreading. None mentioned they blamed Zak, instead they hinted the swiftness left them no time to make proper arrangements—like the plans they had discussed over many years. He nodded agreement with them, assured them they did well to do what they did do and not to reproach themselves for anything. As the night closed in, the firelight flickering across the stone of the lodging house's interior began to give off cheery comfort— its crackle, easing their ragged souls. Sizzling venison aromas filled the air, and Zak's baby brought gentle laughter when he blew a rude noise and clapped his plump little hands together delighting in the attention.

Slowly, human nature eased the torn spirits of the clan. Free from tending the dying, they settled down in their new abode to sleep the sleep of the exhausted.

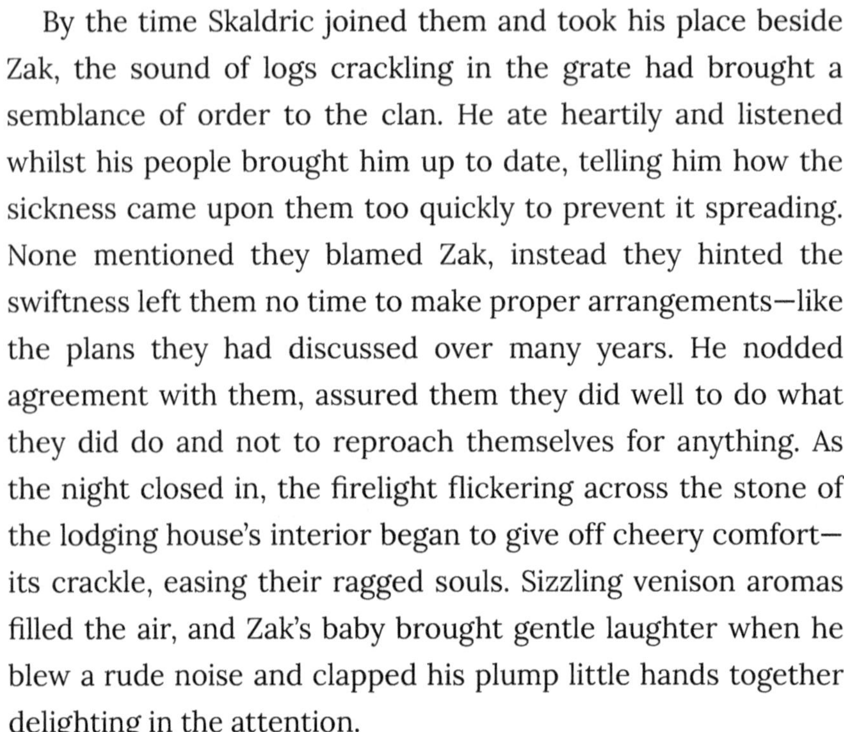

The spark that grew into an ember, then a glow, found nourishment when the Roundhouse doors were wedged open during the transfer of essentials. Fuelled by this sudden movement of air, the glow spread upwards to feed upon the rafters and upward still, to singe the edges of the tightly woven thatch. Once there, it nibbled and smoked and smouldered to

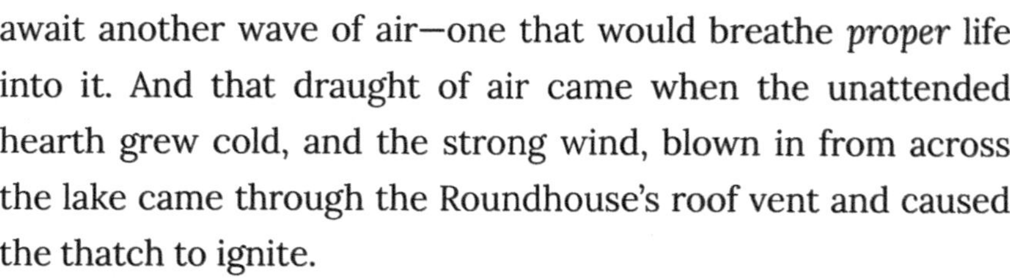

await another wave of air—one that would breathe *proper* life into it. And that draught of air came when the unattended hearth grew cold, and the strong wind, blown in from across the lake came through the Roundhouse's roof vent and caused the thatch to ignite.

Smoke began to stream from the rear of the roof. Carried in it was an occasional spark, rendered harmless when it landed on snow, but as the smoke wafted towards the hovels of the Shadows, some of those embers found more fertile landing places. Places rich in rotting timbers and thatches stuffed with ancient crows' nests. Here, amongst the withered reeds of the poorest dwellings, embryo sparks flourished. They sprung into life by feeding upon the crumbling dry ruins. In no time all, they had grown into gorging monsters of fire: aided by the strengthening winds, they set the Shadows alight, moving at speed from one hovel to the next, each providing fuel for the other moving onwards and turning, swirling like fieldfares, the fire monster trapping everything within its circle, and consuming it, rats and all.

Chapter Forty

Still wrapped in each other, Fiedra woke up to the sound of waves lapping the side of the ship. She opened her eyes but everywhere was in darkness. Yorevyn breathed easily by her side, she found his face in the dark and stroked it, tracing her fingertips over its contours, finding the lean line of his nose. He twitched, making her laugh.

'I will always love that laugh, it is so—*earthy*,' He whispered before taking hold of her hand, kissing the fingers, one by one. 'Good morning—my darling little imp.'

'It isn't—morning, I mean—it's still dark. But I think we're moored up somewhere.'

He rubbed his chin, sat up and leaned to pull the grill covering the shutter aside—an orange glow trickled across the ceiling. 'Yeh—we must've arrived early.'

'It's so quiet—where have the crew gone?'

'The tavern—*knowing them*.'

She uncurled herself from him and scrambled over the layers of woven blankets to reach for the jug of water and poured some into a goblet. 'Do all ships have cabins like this?'

'The ones I build do. We go to sea for a long time. A *good sleep* makes for a strong crew.'

'Bryn has a vast yard set aside for nothing but the building of his ships. Tura says the sea is his life.'

'We are island people. The sea surrounds us; when we breathe, we taste the salt in the air. Eat the fish it provides us with, and until recent times, we thought it also protected us—but...'

She passed the goblet to him and began to dress. 'On those charts you showed me yesterday, you have the invaders coming to your island from the south, will they make their way here, in your harbour?'

'Aw, if only they did, that would be wonderful, we could trap them, kill everyone before they neared our wharf. But their ships can't navigate the waters around the southeast of our island.' He drank from the cup, handed it back to her and reached for his clothes. 'Unfortunately, I fear they will anchor their ships off the west coast of our island, bring their war machines across by raft and come ashore using small boats that can be pulled onto the sand. From there, they'll march and try to surprise us—on our undefended side.'

'And that's where their expertise in battle lies—waging war on land?'

'Yes—they're strategists—their men are disciplined to format into certain groups—groups that work as one man—groups that deceive and trap opposing armies.' He pulled her close. 'My people have had to learn to fight like them. I fear they too will become human fighting machines. I have had to drive them to be like that—put a friend to pretend to be the enemy—another to pretend to kill him.' He stroked a lock of hair from Fiedra's brow and gently teased it back, tucking it

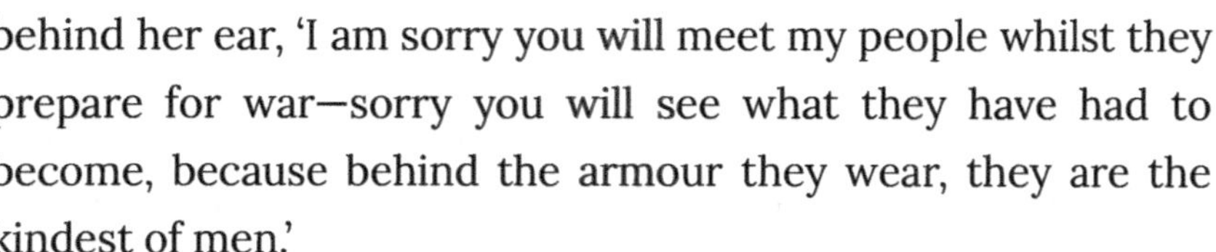

behind her ear, 'I am sorry you will meet my people whilst they prepare for war—sorry you will see what they have had to become, because behind the armour they wear, they are the kindest of men.'

'I too can be worldly in my assessment of strangers—I will not allow their attire—albeit glorious armour, to cloud my judgement. I will love them for what they are.'

'And they will love you—they already love you, after all, they sent me to fetch you.'

'They did - why?'

'Because I talked endlessly of you, so much so, they yelled "by the gods, go, bring her here, let us see her." So I have.'

She pulled on her boots. 'Right then, let's go meet them. But Yorevyn—I don't want any fuss, we've work to do. You have to show me where you expect the battle to take place. Like I said back at Bryn's house, I need to see everything and if the invaders are on their way, we don't have much time to lose.'

Like a pair of stowaways they sneaked off the ship, Yorevyn taking hold of Fiedra's hand and leading the way. The quayside was cobbled, made shiny by a cool mist that hung in the air. The braziers lighting their way were fashioned as globes of fire and the coals they burned gave off little smoke.

'What fuel do your people use?'

'The cinders left over from our smelting furnaces. They have *life still left in them*. My people—*our* people, are extremely inventive, they find a use for everything.'

She squeezed his hand, 'I look forward to learning about your people's talents.'

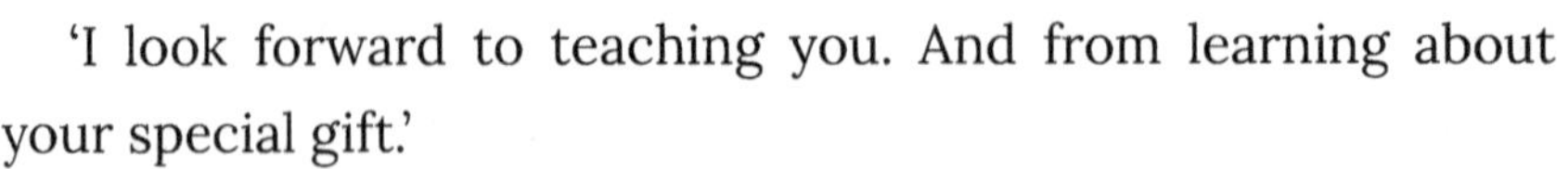

'I look forward to teaching you. And from learning about your special gift.'

Leaving the harbour behind them, they walked up a rise that opened onto a wide flat area. Again the ground was cobbled and lit by braziers, but these were sculpted to resemble ornamental trees, and set in symmetry across the square so that their lighted coals could reflect in pools of water surrounding the smooth stones beneath them.

The gates to Yorevyn's home were open - pinned back by planters that held sticks of lit torches. He grabbed one and proceeded to escort Fiedra upwards, along a path that turned this way and that through a garden of low clipped shrubs—the branches still without their leaves, whilst their roots slept the mild winter away.

'You leave your gates open, do you not fear wolves?'

'Wolves have never colonised this island. But there are bears in the forests to the north. And boars that keep the bears from leaving the forest.'

'I wonder your hounds haven't run to greet us.'

'Do you fear they might?'

'A little—yes.'

'Then rest easy—I had the crew send word to keep them kennelled up.'

'Did Meg give birth to other litters?'

'Of course—she is the best of all mothers.'

'I still have a sense of her, even though she is far away. She *mothers* the boy you saved from the grave.'

He stopped and stared in awe. 'You can see what she's doing?'

'It's not like that—it's her protective nature I feel. Like she's sleeping with one eye open, watching over him.'

'And Elvad—is she looking after Elvad?'

'Oh yes—it's like the three are welded in *bondship*.'

'*Bondship?*'

'Strange word I know, but that's what it feels like.'

'I like it—and I hope *we* are welded in *bondship*.'

'We are—or to be more precise, we will be when we have countless children.'

'Then oh wife of mine, allow me to show you to my quarters. It's this way, and to put your mind at ease, it's very private.'

Perak thumped at Kaylak's chest. 'Why didn't you send word you were arriving?'

'I wanted to surprise you.'

'But look at me—these clothes are for fun. Meant for no one but the ladies here to see. Wait here—give me a moment to change.'

'No—I don't have time to spare.'

Her eyes lost their sparkle: 'You're not staying?'

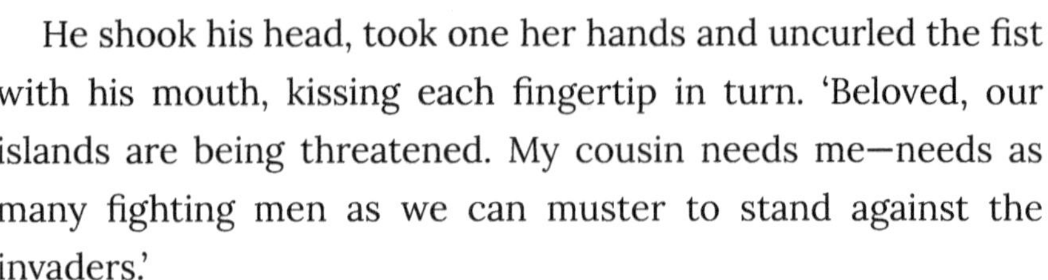

He shook his head, took one her hands and uncurled the fist with his mouth, kissing each fingertip in turn. 'Beloved, our islands are being threatened. My cousin needs me—needs as many fighting men as we can muster to stand against the invaders.'

'Is this cousin the one who has my brothers? And Cadic—are all of them in danger from these invaders?'

'We are all in danger from them. That is—if we don't stop them by joining forces with Yorevyn.'

'So when will you return?' Her heart-shaped face *looked so childlike and appealing.*

'As soon as I can, I promise.'

Her bottom lip protruded, 'I have only Omi for company. There was something I wanted to ask you—but you were always busy with other matters.'

'What was it my sweet? Whatever you want—I will give.'

'I had a friend at the settlement. She is lame but the most wonderful companion and she can tame the curls of my hair better than anyone. Can you send for her? Say when your men return for the cargo you ordered?'

'Is that all? Of course you may have your companion.'

'Oh thank you Kaylak. Mama said it would bring shame on our family to invite her—but you don't mind if she's lame?'

He picked her up and kissed her cheeks. 'Why no, Beloved. In fact, when we've dealt with these marauders—we will hold a celebration and your companion can meet with Yorevyn's new lady. She too is blessed,' He caught the confusion in Perak's eyes, 'it's what we call people born with a blemish, anything, a

birthmark, extra fingers, something out of the ordinary—we call these people blessed because we believe they are closer to the gods than us. Like they've been singled out to do good work for us—divine work. So don't worry about shaming any family with your friend—she will be exalted by us all, even amongst the mightiest of hair tamers.'

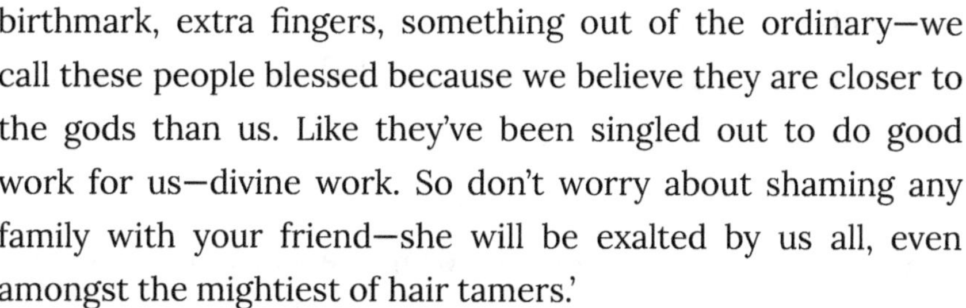

Outside the windows of Yorevyn's palatial quarters the birds were making a racket. He pulled a blanket around him, held back one of the shutters and looked down onto their garden where he saw Fiedra, who was also wrapped in a blanket, and surrounded by flocks of birds. Some were little garden birds, others large birds of prey. She waved an arm to one side and they took flight as though she had scared them off. But from his vantage, he saw them fly in formation across the bay. When she moved her arm to the right, they banked and, as one, turned to follow.

When she relaxed her arm, they broke their pattern and returned to settle in the bushes, or on the roofs, or on the stretch of water that glistened in the morning light at the bottom of the courtyard.

'I am learning not to ask what you are doing,' He said as he approached her, 'but watching the air display, I have to say, it is very impressive.' He stooped to kiss her. 'Good morning, my little imp.'

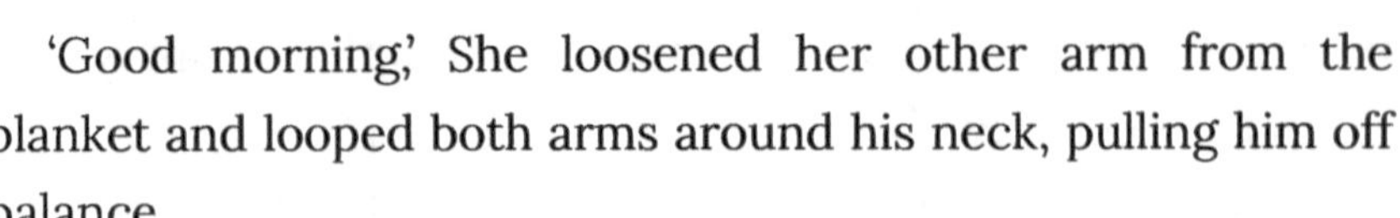

'Good morning,' She loosened her other arm from the blanket and looped both arms around his neck, pulling him off balance.

'Whoa!'

They fell together, rolling down the bank and into the ornamental lake. The water's iciness took their breath, causing them to gasp. Swans reared from the water, flapping their wings and geese honked their displeasure at the naked couple's laughter. On the sloping bank, their discarded blankets offered warmth and modest coverage. 'Oh my, did anyone see us?' Fiedra shivered.

Yorevyn held is head back and roared with laughter, 'Only every waterfowl in the land, and every sparrow, eagle, hawk, crow. You name it—you invited all your feathered friends to our honeymoon.'

'I didn't invite them, they found me.' She wrapped the blanket tight around her body. 'They are going to help you win your war.'

'How?'

'They are going to put the fear of the evil eye into that superstitious army. Like you said, we will send them away, scared shitless, tail between their legs.'

'This—I must see.'

'Now that—could be tricky.'

The invading armada had been making good progress until a gleaming opening gap in the dark grey sky caused panic and sent them blind to head for the rocks. It started like an *accusing finger from the heavens*, a beam of intense sunlight that seared from above and struck the guano-coated, limestone cliffs before them. Dazzling white light flashed across the waters in an instant and took those aboard the ships by complete surprise.

The helmsmen who steered the massive vessels were the most affected by the glare. Dazzled—they clung to the tillers—muscles bulging against the sudden surge of water. It threatened to hurl the ships forward onto the jagged rocks that lay unseen just below its surface.

On deck, lookouts, perched nearest to the prow, blinked away the flashes blinding their eyes, and once their sight was restored, screamed for the helmsmen to beware of the rocks. Masters and generals picked up the chaos and ordered those manning the tillers to steer the ships towards the west. Some screeched at those below who were strapped to the rowing seats to slow down the speed of their heavy-laden vessels; others yelled to everyone to avoid the jagged-edged rocks that had now become startlingly visible beneath the waves.

The leading craft, the one carrying the generals' chariots and most of the officers' tents, hit the submerged rocks and came to a scraping full stop when it ran aground on a platform of massive boulders.

The oarsmen were ordered to reverse—their masters whipping them, urging them to use every tissue of muscle to lift the enormous craft from off the shelf.

Augers—residing below the decks of the ships filled with loot, were sent for, and ordered to interpret the meaning of the sudden dazzling light. They ran amok consulting their runes—examining the entrails of the last sacrifices—looking for something missing, something they neglected to spot when they had offered the victims' souls up to the gods. But nothing could be read than a promise of safe passage—nothing in the runes or innards predicted they would be hurled into a blinding white wall hiding treacherous rocks.

As the men aboard the stricken ship were struggling to lift her free, a strange mist came rolling across the water—blocking out the sunbeam and returning the scene to its original cold, dank murk. From their nests perched precariously on tiny ledges dotted across the white face of the cliffs, gulls swooped down and darted towards the creaking vessel trapped below them.

The order to man the small boats was given, setting the exhausted oarsmen free to unleash themselves from their seats and to untie the rowing boats stacked above them. Again, the generals demanded answers from the augers, screaming at them to appease the gods so they could continue with their quest.

The small boats brought the saved men alongside the larger ships, disembarking them before returning to save more. Even in the misty light, it was evident the hull-wrecked ship was listing—its heavy cargo shifting and creaking audibly above the

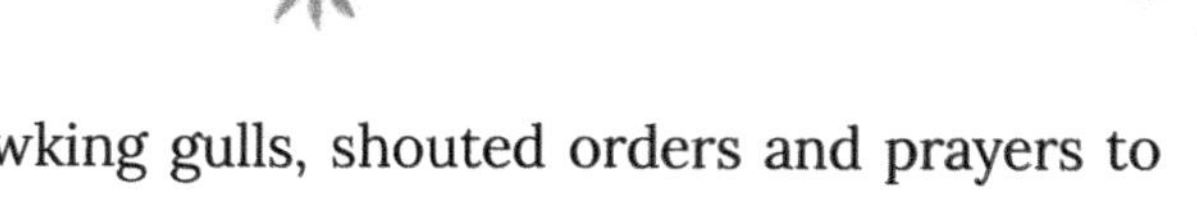

cacophony of squawking gulls, shouted orders and prayers to *deaf gods*.

'It has begun.' Fiedra said as she emerged from beneath the thermal-fed waters of the spring in Yorevyn's underground chamber.

He swam close, 'I'm learning not to interrupt you when you lose yourself in another world, you drift, dreamlike and go somewhere far, far away. So tell me, what exactly has begun?'

'The invaders are starting to doubt the wisdom of their priests.'

He laughed, 'You can see them?'

She threw water at him with the back of her hand. 'Of course I can't see them—I sense the chaos that surrounds them. That's all.'

'They have chaos surrounding them?'

'Yes,' She reached to grab hold of the pool's edge and pulled her body towards it. Pushing her hair away from her face she turned to him—her eyes catching the sparkle of the waters. 'One of their ships is stuck on the rocks below where the gulls nest. It contains chariots and living equipment for their high ranking military men.' She shook water from her hair. 'The ship will free itself in two days, when the full moon rises the sea levels. They plan to unload their warriors onto the west coast, just as you said, to prepare for battle, but the ships' masters

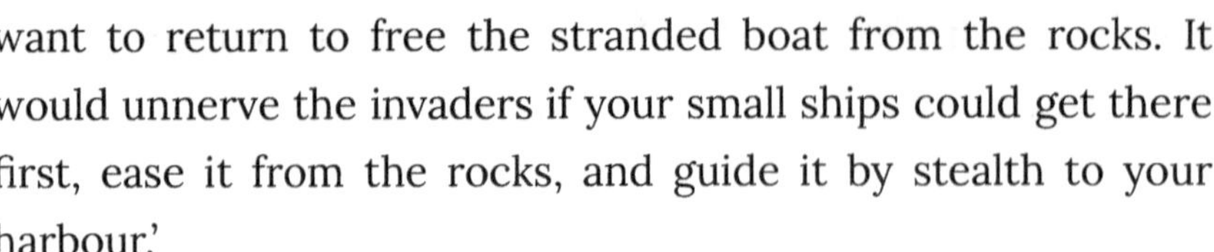

want to return to free the stranded boat from the rocks. It would unnerve the invaders if your small ships could get there first, ease it from the rocks, and guide it by stealth to your harbour.'

'I'd say unnerve was too weak a word—do you mean give 'em the shits?'

'Nah—that will happen on the morning of the battle.'

'Why morning?'

'Because that's when it must take place.'

'You make it sound so ordinary. Like when my mother could smell rain was on its way.'

She reached across the pool and pulled him close, her eyes turning deep purple—boring into his. 'Oh, my handsome husband, there is nothing ordinary about being able to smell the onset of rain. The invaders must attack after dawn, when the sun has risen above the hilltops on your charts. The ones that lie between the place where they will camp and here.'

On one of the ships, where the temples to the gods had been stored, acolytes re-examined the putrid intestines they had spread across the sacrificial altar. With an air of authority, they held the innards to their noses and shook their heads, confirming the truth in what the priests, their masters, had originally said. The gods—the novices reaffirmed—had given no warning with regard to a blinding white light. Therefore it

must've been a freak of nature—something that happens to all ships sailing on uncharted waters.

Not satisfied—the masters staked their claim to salvage what could be saved from stricken ship and turn back—go home with the treasures they had. The generals would hear none of it—they wanted one final battle—one that would yield the greatest rewards - one that would please their emperor—give him a gift he'd never been given before—the gift of alchemy.

Whilst the military personnel shouted it out, the priests set to making preparations to foretell omens for the new path ahead. They searched the waters around them, spied a couple of seals diving among the treacherous rocks beneath the cliffs and ordered their acolytes to prepare the altar for a new offering—one they were certain would please the gods mightily.

'My men are ready to bring the invader's ship to my yard. From there, they will do as you advise and strip her bare of the goods she carries. After that, they will sail it north and place it by the rest of the anchored ships under the cloak of darkness. Stealth at sea is what my men do best, apart from alchemy of course.'

Fiedra nodded as they walked along a track that led along the edge of woodlands. She could hear the birds twittering in the trees, felt the sun warming her face, gentle as late winter

sun can be. Inside her head, the twittering was passing images relayed from happenings on board the auger's boat. She turned her mind towards it, trying to tune in, to interpret what was going on.

'Where are your thoughts taking you now?'

Fiedra blinked, focussing her mind on the scenery around her. 'I was bewildered by the sight of sacrificial altars.'

'You mean you know nothing of making sacrifices to the gods?'

She blinked, stopped in her tracks and turned to him. 'Where is the logic in killing animals—creatures that have no other laws than the ones of nature?' She studied his frown. 'Don't tell me your people practise the dark art of ritualistic slaughter?'

'They used to—many generations back—when their metal making was linked to magic. My ancestors believed the magic was given by their close affinity to the gods.'

'But that was in the past—surely they don't do it now?'

'No—well not often anyway.'

'What sort of family am I married into?'

Yorevyn tried his twisted smile, but the look of horror on Fiedra's face told him it hadn't worked. 'You are married into a family whose people have kept accounts of their history through the telling of poems. They're not afraid to speak of those far-off days, nor ashamed of what their forefathers had to do to survive. Just as your own kinsmen recall myths and legends about killing dragons and such, my people tell our children where we started from, how we followed the lines of metal-bearing rocks, smelting them, selling the jewellery they made and giving thanks for their good fortune. Once we settled on this island, we found it unnecessary to appease the gods with sacrifice, but we remain grateful for what we have, therefore we give our prayers of thanks on special days reserved for that purpose.' He led her to a grassed area where two horses grazed. 'Now that you know what sort of family you belong to, you can tell me where you saw these sacrificial altars, but before then, I will introduce you to our means of transport.'

Towards the rear of the armada, an eagle circled three times before it landed on a crossbeam that spanned the ship's section where warhorses were tethered. A groom—cautious of any omen where circling eagles might affect his beasts, alerted the blacksmith who, being a non-believer, flung a horseshoe sending it spinning upwards towards the beam. The missile didn't reach its intended target but was caught instead, by a knot in a rope tied to the beam. To the groom's horror, the horseshoe spun round, flung free of the knot and returned to where the blacksmith stood, hitting him full in face and knocking the man unconscious. Screaming in terror, he ran to tell one of the priests, pointing towards the eagle as it rose into the air. It circled three times again before flying off to survey the contents of another loaded ship.

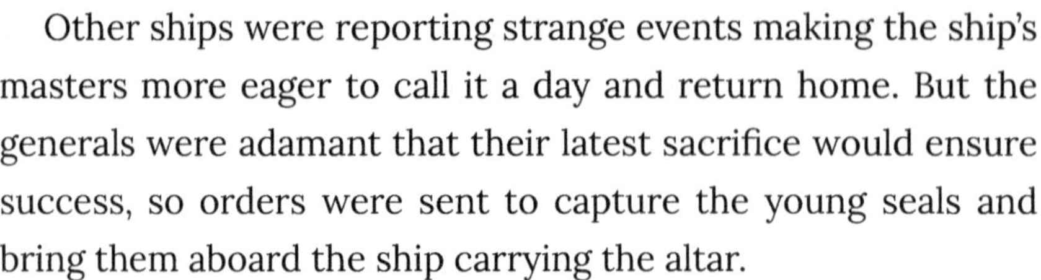

Other ships were reporting strange events making the ship's masters more eager to call it a day and return home. But the generals were adamant that their latest sacrifice would ensure success, so orders were sent to capture the young seals and bring them aboard the ship carrying the altar.

A raven was taking particular interest in the sacred regalia spread across an upper deck. It eyed the temple fashioned to represent an elaborate cage constructed of the tiny bones and skulls of thousands of birds. The raven flew closer to inspect the cage's roof where multiple layers of tassels fluttered in the sea breezes—this way they fluttered blue, that way black. The raven's yellow eye was distracted by the sound of a bark—a honking bark made by a seal. It flew up to a higher lever where an aerial view gave grim sightings.

'We have to stop these people!' Fiedra cried as the horse she rode came to an immediate stop.

Yorevyn circled his mount to return to Fiedra's side. 'What is it?'

'They're dragging seal pups onto their decks.' Her words brought a horror into his eyes—a look she'd not seen before. 'They're going to *sacrifice* them.'

'But you said they were superstitious,' He questioned as he drew near, 'is it possible they don't know about the seal-women?'

As Fiedra ingested Yorevyn's words, her psyche struggled to comprehend the strength of abhorrence building up inside her. She swayed in a sea of anger unable to breathe—refusing to believe people could be so cruel. She felt swamped, out of her depth—futile in her efforts to resist filling her lungs with air that boiled with ire. But, before the rage engulfed Fiedra's heart, Mira's voice came into her head and whispered, *Fiedra, don't give into it... use the power of the seal-women to punish them... they will wreak revenge and go to the pups' plight. Keep focused on the main battle... I am on my way to you.*

'Fiedra—come back to me.' Yorevyn was reaching across his horse, shaking her by the shoulders. His relief trembling through them both, when she focused her eyes again and smiled.

'My grandmother's on her way to us.'

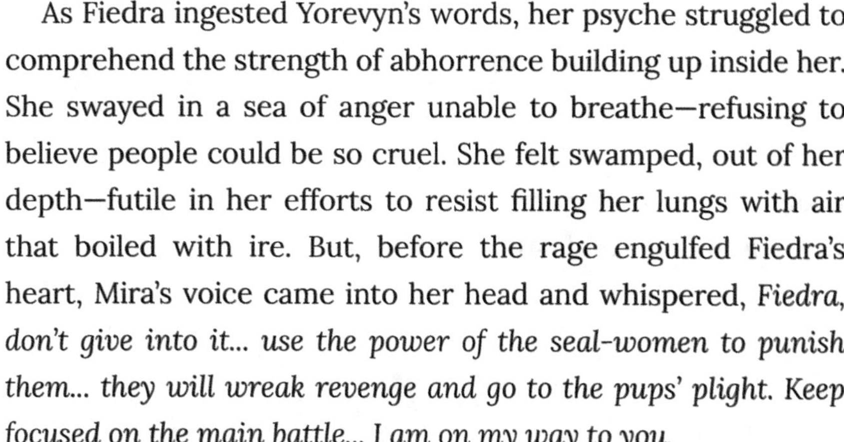

From the depths of the sea, bubbles began to pop under the hulks of the ships. These were not playful childish bubbles but huge and menacing, striking the ships' underbellies like cannonballs, sending deafening sounds to boom across the decks.

The seals caught and trussed ready for sacrifice called out, sending their pitiful cries across the waves. They were answered by a mournful wind that churned the waters surrounding the auger's vessel, sending the deck high on one side before dropping it suddenly to dip, almost to the water's

edge on the other. The priests were sent running down the slope to hang onto whatever came to hand before being flung away when the ship rolled back. Picked up in wind's song was the rubbing of the cage-like frame of the temple, where bone could be heard grinding against bone—like the gnashing of teeth in the jaws of death.

Fiedra urged the horse on, Yorevyn by her side keeping vigil ready to grab her if she swayed again. But she didn't. She was energised with news that her grandmother had sensed her distress and responded.

The horses slowed to a trot upon entering the town where Yorevyn's men were billeted—women and children stopped what they were doing to line the streets, waving and cheering to greet them. Fiedra noted how many of their features shared likeness to those of Yorevyn. And here and there, an odd giant of a woman with flame-coloured hair stood out in the crowd.

'I see you've got families related to Bryn's kinsmen,' Fiedra said as she waved back.

He nodded. 'They join us in battle. As do Methiu's men.' She turned to face him, her eyes growing darker, a sign telling Yorevyn to heed what she was about to say. 'Did my mention of the king of the West trigger a deep thought?'

'My grandmother travels with a man called Methiu.' Yorevyn's raised eyebrow caused her to laugh, 'she is a very desirable lady.'

'And the king is a likeable fellow. When will they reach us?'

'Her companion has secured a passage on a ship—it has a name—er, allow me to think—it's called—"Blushing..."'

'Rose?'

'Yes—Blushing Rose, that's it.'

His shock was transferred to the horse, taking several heartbeats for Yorevyn to settle it. He shook his head. 'You are telling me your grandmother is travelling towards us on one of *my* ships?'

Her eyes grew wide, 'I didn't know it was one of your ships, she, my grandmother put the name into my head. That's all.'

'So your granny's companion is Methiu, King of the Westlands? Well, well the crafty old goat. By the gods, the way things are turning out, we'll have only Elvad left to wed.'

They arrived at the garrison, where Fiedra picked up a more regimented, less celebratory atmosphere. Men clashed swords, their sweated muscular arms glistening in the dusk pink of the setting sun. Further back others wrestled, throwing their opponents in unarmed combat onto sand-filled practice fields. Fiedra scanned the garrison's rooftops searching for signs of a raven, but found none. Warriors came to greet Yorevyn placing a clenched fist on their hearts as he rode by—he, in return did the same. She felt their loyalty and his to them, they would be comrades in battle, but this was rehearsal for the real thing, they practiced their fighting skills against kinfolk, friends and

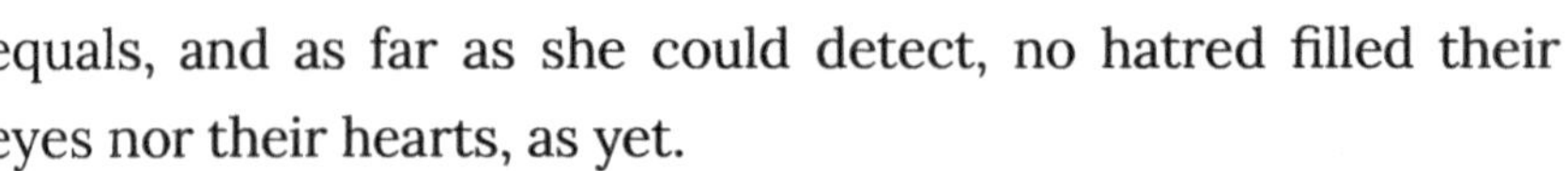

equals, and as far as she could detect, no hatred filled their eyes nor their hearts, as yet.

The last shipload of supplies was rowed ashore and dragged onto carts to be transported to the assigned base-camp. Having lost their luxurious tents in the stricken ship, the generals took the next best accommodation, with each rank taking the next until the lowest ranks were squashed together into what tents were left.

Shadows fell across the shore as the sun dipped towards the rim of the sea, sending ripples of darkness to lurk under every swollen wave. All the ships rolled and strained against their anchors, with the exception of one. The sky streaked pink and orange telling the masters of the ships that the following day would be cloudless—a good sign to sail home.

On the deck of the ship, where the priests and their acolytes prepared their ritual, a column of smoke rose up sending the scent of sacred leaves to the heavens. The temple's personnel knelt to sing out the responses to the priests' incantation. The smoke rose steadily, its uniform column telling those gathered it was a sure sign the gods were listening, and prepared to grant them good fortune for the oncoming battle.

The high priest raised his sacrificial knife to the sky, its blade picking up the orange of the sky, turning it blood red. All eyes were on the crucial moment when the soul of the animal

would be taken by the smoke to the gods. Transfixed by the raised arm of high priest, nobody thought to look down at the dark red sea or see the transformation taking place below: the turning of the dark shadows moving toward the ship. No one saw the seals moving silently in the water, their shape shifting from aquatic creatures to seal-women sprouting arms and legs enabling them to climb aboard, and when they snarled at the sight before them, their upper lips pushed back their needle sharp whiskers to reveal rows of deadly pointed teeth.

In one fluid movement they pounced upon the gathered ceremony, ripping the throats of the minor priests—turning the sacred songs into blood-curdling gargles. In a blur of red, the high priest was taken by two of the seal-women—his knife forced to turn upon his own throat and thrust in by his own hand. The seal pups were untied, lifted from the ship and returned to the waters where they swam fast, diving through the sleek black waves heading for their home—to be reunited with their colony.

Unaware of the bad omens heading their way, the generals had their mind on tactics. They stood with the last rays of sun behind them, long shadows spread across a chart drawn in the deep red soil at their feet. One of the scouts was showing them aspects of the terrain ahead.

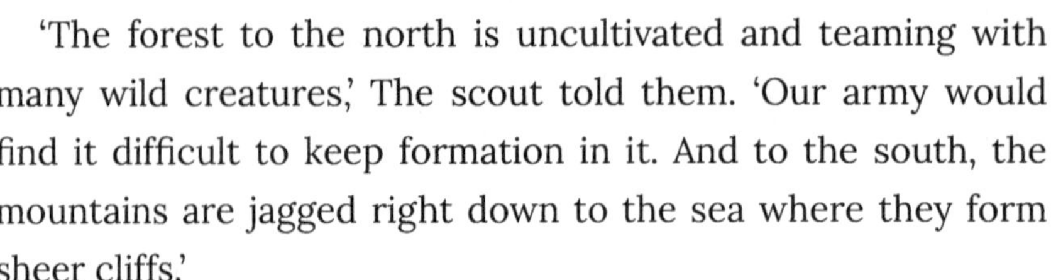

'The forest to the north is uncultivated and teaming with many wild creatures,' The scout told them. 'Our army would find it difficult to keep formation in it. And to the south, the mountains are jagged right down to the sea where they form sheer cliffs.'

'We've experienced them already,' The General snapped. 'Which is the best way for our troops?'

'To the east,' The lead scout stepped in, 'our survey shows the ore is mined here,' he indicated by cutting an arrow-shaped line in the rich dirt, 'it's plentiful, and beyond the mines is a city of immense wealth and,' he looked somewhat scathing at those around him, 'exquisite beauty.'

One of the generals spat, 'Not for long—eh men, not for long.'

'Quite,' The leader scout continued, 'that—is where the alchemists have their consulting chambers - the seat of learning where their experiments take place. The safest passage to this citadel is through those hillocks.' He pointed to a ridge of low-lying hills, fading now as the sun began to dip below the sea behind them. 'The ridge forms a natural barrier to the mines—and are not as gentle as they appear. Between the dunes are treacherous deep ravines barely a soldier's shoe length wide, yet hidden.'

'What do you mean—hidden?'

'The ground is red like this, but hard as rock and rippled to look like a sandy beach. We found to our dismay that until the sun reaches a certain height, the deep crevices can be mistaken for shadows—step in one, and break a leg.'

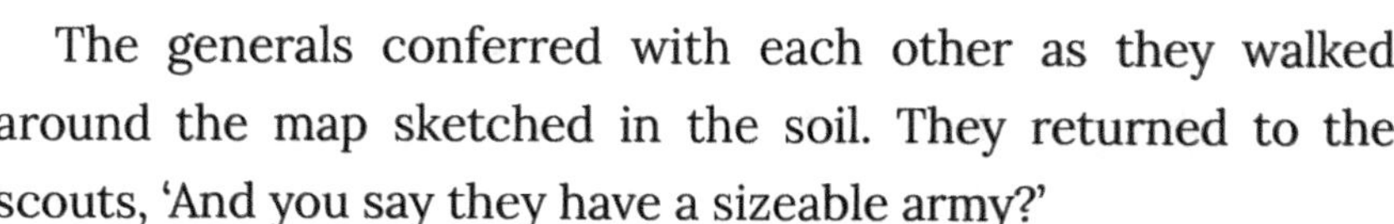

The generals conferred with each other as they walked around the map sketched in the soil. They returned to the scouts, 'And you say they have a sizeable army?'

'Yes sir, our spies have watched them practice throughout their winter—they improve their skills but they are no match for our men.'

'Good. Then we march at first light.' He caught the look of warning in the eyes of the lead scout. 'Rest easy—we will do as you advise and wait for the rising of the sun.'

That evening as the camp settled into groups squatting around their fires, the sound of oars hitting the water turned the soldiers' attention back to sea. Those camped nearest to the beach took up their swords and ran to investigate.

'Where's the general?' One of the ship's masters shouted, 'We need to speak on an urgent matter.'

The soldiers, still with their swords drawn, escorted the group of masters to the officers' tent, watched them enter and waited outside.

What they overheard was unbelievable.

The masters told the generals they had witnessed strange creatures boarding the temple ship. These pale green-grey females attacked the priests and killed everyone on deck save for the two seals tied to the sacrificial table—those they set free.

The roar of abuse given by the chief general could be heard further afield, with others taking up arms to join the guards. 'What's going on?' They asked the soldiers and were told exactly what they had overheard. Soon the camp was abuzz with lurid stories of strange creatures sent by the evil one.

Inside the tent the voices rose to fever pitch with the ships' masters storming out, threatening to take their ships and leave the army behind. The leading general gave the order to place the masters under armed guard.

To the north of the island, a fleet of boats glided silently south, their oarsmen pulling the boats loaded with extra personnel. They reached the ships and boarded them one by one, pulling up their anchors, manning the oars and taking them back north under the cover of darkness. They obeyed Yorevyn's orders exactly—taking only the ships loaded with goods and leaving the empty vessels for the retreating army.

Dawn lit the sky a pale yellow, casting the hills beyond the plateau into dark relief. Across the rippled landscape where the ridge met the horizon, a line of brightness appeared—

brilliant and startling white; it etched the horizon against the sky, heralding the rise of what would be a cloudless day.

As the dew began to evaporate underfoot, the soldiers formed into their battle positions and stood ready for the command to march. They were trained *not to show* the fear they felt, yet even so, they found it difficult to ignore the skittering of the horses' hooves sliding on the hardened ground—a sign that told seasoned soldiers the animals smelled the fear their riders suppressed.

One of the generals took position in front—behind him other mounted officers held banners sewn with threads of gold that glinted, picked up by the sun's corona as it peeped above the hilly horizon.

To the left of the gathered army, the forest was coming to life with birds stretching their wings and filling the air with their individual choruses—it felt like spring had arrived. And behind the large formation of men, sea birds screeched and dived, adding to the cacophony surrounding them. The sun edged above the ridge—throwing their generals into silhouette —blurring their outlines with orange-red halos, which caused a stir among the ranks.

The chief of the generals held up his hand to still them, bringing the men before him to attention.

'I know the stories reaching you about last night's horror are a concern—but you must set them aside.'

His horse's involuntary shiver was reined back. The moment it was brought under control, he continued. 'What happened aboard the auger's vessel was nothing but wilful damage wrought by the ship's masters.' He spat into the red earth at his

horse's feet. 'My men have dealt with the culprits—so now, we can move on.' He turned his head so as to face each unit of soldiers, making as much eye contract as he could. 'We don't need greedy seamen who want to steal our spoils of war for themselves; we can sail the ships without them. We haven't come this far just to yield to mariners—we're trained soldiers—it has been our strategy that has won the battles—found the treasures and taken it. It's what we do best. We are invincible. And, when we return home—with ships bursting with rare treasure and a brig full of alchemists—our Emperor will grant us favours beyond everything we've ever dreamt for.'

It was what the men wanted to hear.

The cheer that rose in the air broke the fear hidden in the psyche of the men. The general's rousing speech had done the trick, and the sun rising above the hills ahead of them brought warm air wafting across, dispelling unease and lifting their spirits.

'Roll the drums,' shouted the chief general, 'time to march.'

He turned his horse to face the hills, pulled the banner of his helmet against the glare and signalled for his army to follow. From the south, a flock of swans flying in formation cut across the scene. At their head, the leading birds formed the shape of a spear that crossed the morning sky - they were followed by a skein of geese forming similar arrows and ducks took up the rear until they flew across the sun and began to circle, their pointed dart-shape flight paths leading the way for other birds to follow.

A breeze came from nowhere causing the forest trees to sway making noises like waves crashing over a pebble shore.

The men started to march, though their eyes focussed on the sky as more flocks joined the circle spreading it wider, making it denser—turning the soldier's side of the divide from daytime into night—*from warmth into sudden cold.*

Starlings and fieldfares joined in to spread the blanket of darkness across the campsite, leaving only the beach, where the rowing boats were stacked, bathed in a pool of sunlight. Soldiers towards the rear of the battalion slowed down, holding back their forward march, readying themselves to turn and run for the boats.

The deepening darkness, caused panic among the horses; they began to rear and buck, throwing their riders off and galloping, wild-eyed into the straight lines of the marching soldiers. The disarray was made worse when the herding instinct of the animals sent them into a circular course, similar to that of the birds, where they trampled the campsite before eventually falling into line, and heading for the protective canopy of the trees and the natural shelter of the forest.

'It's taking all my strength.' Fiedra held her hands to her head, grasping bunches of hair between her fingers, pulling it out by the roots. Yorevyn tried to get close to her but was knocked away with a force he had never known—a mighty surge radiating from his new bride.

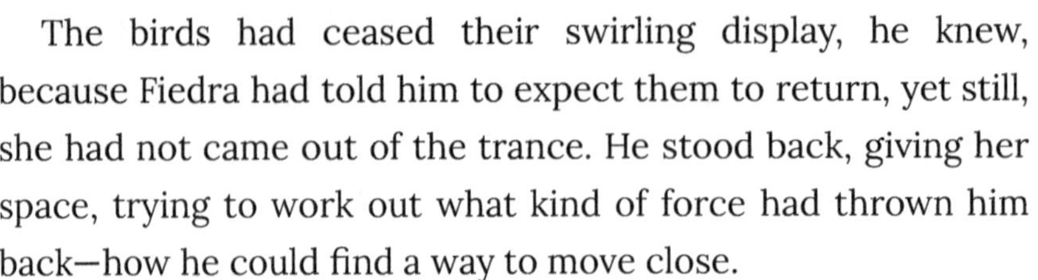

The birds had ceased their swirling display, he knew, because Fiedra had told him to expect them to return, yet still, she had not came out of the trance. He stood back, giving her space, trying to work out what kind of force had thrown him back—how he could find a way to move close.

'Fiedra!' he shouted, 'Fiedra come back to me.'

Above the hissing in her ears, Fiedra could hear him calling her name. Her name, spoken by Yorevyn, held music—like a serenade written only for her. She tried to concentrate on his voice—tried to cut through the buzz fuzzing her mind but the hatred of the generals against the men fleeing the island was interfering with her brain patterns, blocking her normal process of thinking.

As though they picked up her distress, gulls flew into her mind's eye and began to swoop onto the chasing men, pulling at the insignias of rank, tearing the straps on their helmets, each peck loosening the headgear, causing it to slide with every jolt of the generals' feet. Fiedra could see it all—feel the hatred burning her up, wanting to break free, yet unable to leave the scene.

This is no longer your battle.

Grandma? Fiedra opened her eyes and at once the fizzing in her ears was gone. Before her was Yorevyn - his worried brow knitted into knots across his forehead. He searched her eyes, looking for what was ailing her, then when he picked up that she was all right, she caught a glimpse, a hint of his twisted smile. 'I'm sorry,' She whispered, 'did I frighten you?' She untangled her fingers from her hair and fell into his outstretched arms.

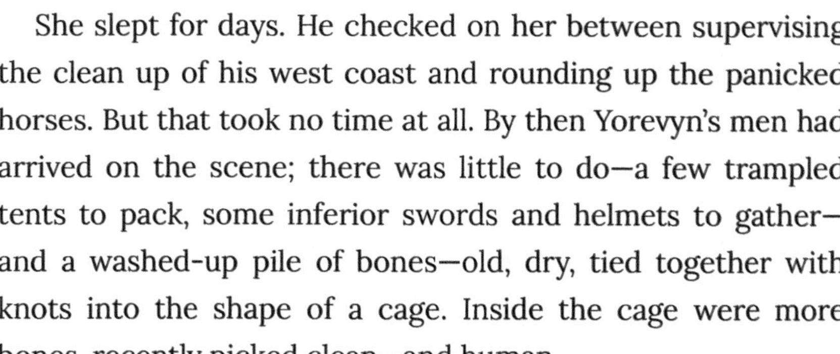

She slept for days. He checked on her between supervising the clean up of his west coast and rounding up the panicked horses. But that took no time at all. By then Yorevyn's men had arrived on the scene; there was little to do—a few trampled tents to pack, some inferior swords and helmets to gather— and a washed-up pile of bones—old, dry, tied together with knots into the shape of a cage. Inside the cage were more bones, recently picked clean—and human.

His men told him they buried the cage-shaped thing on the water's edge but after the tide had been in and gone out, there was nothing but an empty hole left in the sand.

Chapter Forty-One

A raven walked across the balcony of Yorevyn and Fiedra's private part of the house. It tapped the metal shutter with its beak, alerting the sleeping occupant in the bed to his presence. She rose and allowed him entry. She knelt, held out her hand and watched him climb in a dignified, though awkward manner onto her outstretched palm.

She examined his feet with care, saw the missing scales, the healed but still tender-looking flesh beneath and stroked his neck with her free hand.

He's done well, her mind told his.

'There is no need to relay through Dandijack,' The voice of Mira said—not in her head, but from below the balcony.

Still holding the bird, she ran to the balustrade and looked over. 'Grandma—where are you?'

Yorevyn's voice came from the room, 'Come,' He urged, 'time for you to bathe and dress—we have guests.' He wedged open the shutter, allowing a fresh breeze to blow through. He took the bird from her, placing it onto a marbled table. 'Your grandmother wishes to attend you.' He said throwing a handful of titbits for the bird to peck. 'She insists she does your hair— says she has much catching up to do. I will leave you to it, but when you are done, there is someone you should meet.'

Fiedra was stunned, hardly taking in her husband's words. She scanned the doorway. 'But where is she—where is grandma?'

'Oh she's made herself at home. She's rifling through my mother's old rooms—searching wardrobes—looking for something suitable.' He rolled his eyes before taking hold of her shoulders. 'Apparently, you have to look your best this evening. She's already scolded me for not giving you a maid, not bringing dressmakers to fit you out.' He kissed her, turned and left.

'But....'

'But nothing.' He looked over his shoulder, his twisted smile mimicking a grimace, making her want to curl up and laugh, 'I thought you'd find it all amusing—she's got my household in a real tizzy—can't you hear their laughter?' he mocked, 'their sides are splitting as we speak.' He turned, gave her a wave and disappeared down the wide staircase.

Fiedra ran to where the sound of doors opening and closing could be heard. She found Mira pulling arms full of petticoats from a chest and placing them onto an oversized bed. She flew into the arms of the older lady, feeling the power that belied her age—the strength her grandmother possessed pour into her. Mira held the young woman tight against her breast, rocking her as though she were a baby—feeling the wet tears stream down her granddaughter's face—knowing they were tears from long, long ago—tears that should have been shed then, but instead, were held back.

They bathed in the pool warmed by the thermal flow that rose from deep in the earth. Mira sprinkled more dried

lavender onto the surface—watched them dissolve and breathed in their perfume. 'So,' Fiedra said when she emerged from rinsing her hair, 'you gave the Shaman a good send off?'

Mira's smile went far away, 'Yes.'

'Will you return to the forest?'

Mira swished water over the residue of dried lavender and watched the tiny fragments swirl to the bottom of the pool. 'It would appear that I am needed here—with you.' Fiedra's eyes lit up—their lavender glow reflecting in the purple of her grandmother's eyes. Mira held up a hand, preventing Fiedra from speaking. 'Your power overwhelms you, and I am sorry to say it will only grow stronger as you mature. But you will learn to tame it—learn to keep it under control.'

'You make me sound like one of Yorevyn's hounds.'

They laughed but Mira got back to the subject. 'We think it may be you who will be the new Shaman.'

Fiedra mulled over the words. 'An honour indeed but one I know I'm unable to fulfil.'

'It isn't given with a choice—it is ordained.'

'I cannot be a spirit leader.'

'Why?'

'I am married—I am to become a mother to countless children, to walk forever by my husband's side, to be his right hand and love his people. I cannot guide the spirits of the northern people as well.

'You can and you will. If it is you who must be Shaman, then you will learn to fill the people's hearts with your spirit—they will be guided by your wisdom. And you will do all this whilst

you are being a good wife and mother. Do you think the last Shaman put aside his life for the spirits?'

'I never considered he had to.'

'Nor did he—nor should you.'

'I've always known there is something strange about me. Was that the reason I was placed in the care of the Marsh Wives?'

'Partly—but there were other reasons. It is suffice to say, they protected you for as long as was necessary—then your mother's spirit began to cause mischief, so it was deemed necessary for you to have as much a normal upbringing as possible.' Mira reached for the paved side of the pool, placed both hands on the top and leapt out like a woman of twenty summers instead of sixty. 'Come,' She said as she wrapped a drying robe around her. 'We must make haste. We have an eternity to discuss your destiny. First you must meet Yorevyn's guests. You chose well—I sense he is a good man, and handsome—must've inherited his fine looks from his mother. She must have had elegance; her clothes are like nothing I've ever seen. Now, you and I have work to do. We have to do justice to these magnificent gowns.'

That evening, Yorevyn's house dazzled with bright light and down on the harbour, ships poured in carrying those wishing to share in the celebrations of peace. In the square up the rise

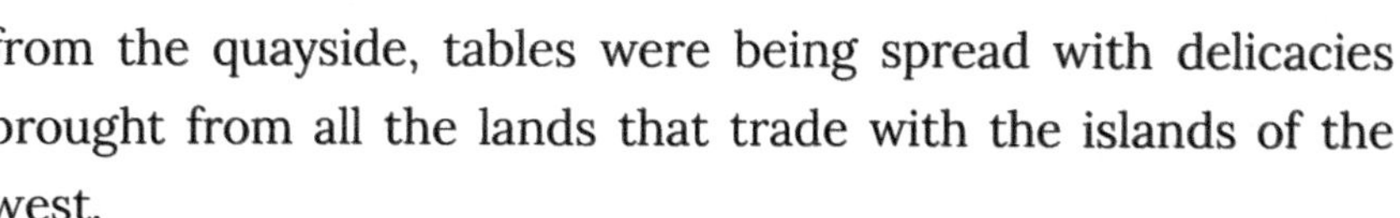

from the quayside, tables were being spread with delicacies brought from all the lands that trade with the islands of the west.

Children played hide and seek in the labyrinth of Yorevyn's garden where lanterns hung from branches to light up the many twists and turns of the winding paths. Music played all around them, with some people dancing a jig, whilst others preferred a gentle stroll with a loved one, or one they hoped would become a loved one. All in all—there was plenty to rejoice in. And there was nothing the people of the islands loved more than a party—with lots of food, large jugs of ale, and plenty of laughter.

Guests filled Yorevyn's house too. They came to catch a glimpse of his new bride but were told to be patient as she was catching up with her grandmother and would appear when she was ready. Seated by the artificial lake were the harbour master and his wife who chatted and laughed with people from Bryn's island, now free from learning the skills of war.

Yorevyn stood with Methiu in the grand hall. They were dressed in smart attire and clean-shaven—a custom in the west meant to herald the passing of winter. They spoke in hushed tones, each bringing the other up to date with events since they last met.

'I don't think she knows,' Yorevyn whispered to Methiu. 'She was injured and aboard Bryn's ship when we left the wharf.'

'Mira has thoughts transferred by birds—but none have picked up evidence that pestilence afflicted the lakeside folk.'

'Fiedra also converses with birds, but never once has she mentioned any sickness—perhaps this fellow Zak was alone in

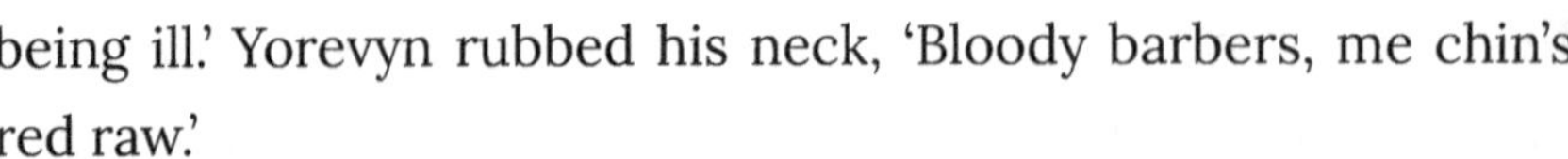

being ill.' Yorevyn rubbed his neck, 'Bloody barbers, me chin's red raw.'

Methiu did the same, 'Aye, so is mine. Maybe Zak drank too much mead, wasn't pestilence after all.'

Yorevyn shook his head, 'No, Elvad confirmed it.'

'Yes, unfortunately, my son knows only too well the symptoms—if he said it was plague—then it was.'

'What was plague?'

They spun round—admiration and love filling their eyes. Methiu took Mira's hand, kissed it and bowed. Yorevyn looked on in awe, 'Bless the gods,' his eyes roamed over her, 'what've they done?'

'You're not supposed to say it like that,' Fiedra slapped the back of Yorevyn's offered hand, 'you're supposed to say, "my darling, how stunningly beautiful you look tonight" or something like that.'

'My darl...'

'Oh, shut up.' She held her hand to his cheek. 'I liked the beard, but smooth might grow on me.' He laughed at the witty comment, hooked his arm inviting her to slide hers through. She sparkled beside him, leaned close and lowered her voice, 'I've got something wonderful to tell you—grandma is going to marry Methiu and that means she will be living in the west—like me. Isn't that wonderful?' She gripped tight his arm, smiled at the people entering the hall, their faces glowing with happiness—she sensed the love they had for her, helping to heal the effects left by the eclipse. 'Do you know, my darling, this is the first party I've ever been to—I love it, but you will remember that I can't dance won't you?'

'I will—this once—but when we attend the great ball on the night of the Midsummer Solstice—you will dance because between now and then, I will teach you.'

Suddenly losing her sparkle. 'Please don't jest—have you not forgotten my clumsiness when we met.' But he wasn't listening and when he kissed her, those in the hall sighed. 'Now see what you've done.' She said, her cheeks flushing with embarrassment.

'I will kiss you whenever I want—and I will always want to kiss you. You are my wife, and trust me, we will dance the night away at the Midsummer ball.' Something behind her caught his eye, 'Ah,' he chimed, 'time for you to meet our guests, darling, this is my cousin Kaylak, and his betrothed Perak.'

Perak curtsied with grace, her head bowed to Yorevyn and his bride.

Fiedra hid her smile. 'Have you forgotten me so soon?'

The child-like heart-shaped face lit up as Perak linked the voice to the elegant lady stood before her. 'It can't be—it is—but how?' Tears filled her eyes, 'Oh, I have so missed you.' She broke protocol to grab Fiedra and pull her close. 'You travelled so fast?' She let go and turned to Kaylak, 'Oh thank you—how did you do it and so quickly?'

Kaylak raised an eyebrow, looked from Yorevyn then to his father, Methiu. 'Is somebody going to tell me what's going on here?'

Chapter Forty-Two

When Elvad kicked snow onto the embers of the fire, they hissed as though to show resentment at being dowsed.

Dion dismantled the bivouacs, shaking snow from the furs and packing them onto the sledge. The camp fell silent after Elvad was forced to tell the group about the sickness down by the wharf.

'It is true—I don't know whether those in the Roundhouse have the sickness. But if they do, then you too will fall down with it.' That was what he had told them. Still, they wanted to press on.

Their reluctant leader Volta, couldn't be sure his decision to move on was right. He stared across the lake and to the valley where his village had once stood. The wind had dropped leaving an eerie silence in its absence and flakes big as beechnut leaves began to fall—their downward journey spiralling straight down and heavy. Whilst he stood there, his mind drifted back to summer months, happier times, and his herd of goats that gave the settlement cheese—a rare, new food for the people of the lake.

By his side, the child Dion stood. He too stared across the lake and to the purple rocky crag that lay along the bank. Something caught his eye. First it was there, and then it

shimmered out of view. Dion had seen the creature before, knew that if he kept control of the sighting, it would come back to focus. The creature's colour blended in the background changing purple like the rocks it perched on. 'You can see me?' It asked. Dion nodded. 'And you understand my tongue?' Dion nodded. 'You have seen me before?' Again the solemn nod. 'Yet you fear me not.' When Dion shook his head the creature grinned showing his pale green needle-sharp teeth. Dion watched as the creature shimmered in and out of vision—watched it disappear behind a veil of snowflakes before turning his attention to Volta.

Volta's gaze was also on the purple rocks.

'Can you see it?' Dion whispered, placing his hand in Volta's. Volta gave it a gentle squeeze.

'Can I see what?'

'Oh nothing.'

In his reverie, Volta had been thinking of those left in his care and of the animals crushed under the avalanche. 'I hope I'm not driving my people into another disaster.' Volta whispered, 'I am a bad leader.'

The boy thought for a while then shook his head.

'Sickness gone,' He said, his voice deeper than Volta expected it to be.

'Do you know, Dion, I think that inside that child's body of yours, there lives a man with a big, big heart?' Dion looked towards the craggy rocks and nodded. He pulled at Volta's hand leading him towards those waiting to leave. He gave Volta's hand another squeeze and nodded his head towards

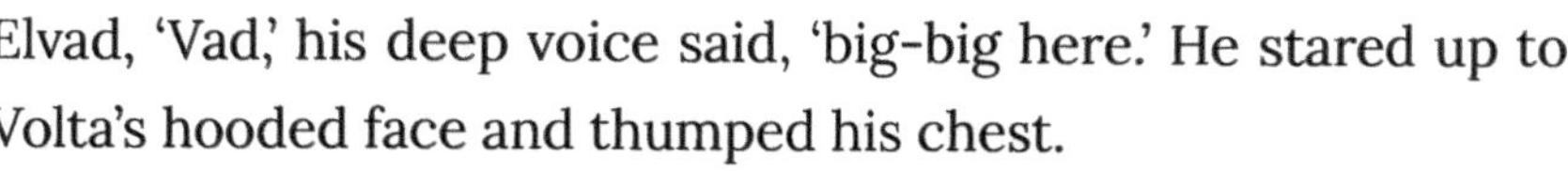

Elvad, 'Vad,' his deep voice said, 'big-big here.' He stared up to Volta's hooded face and thumped his chest.

'I believe he does have a big heart, my little friend—though because of my insistence to move on, it lies heavy at the moment.'

The survivors in the lodging house slept past their normal waking hour, even Zak's baby snoozed on, his belly full of barley given to him late, the night before. A banging to the heavy door roused them and voices they recognised as fishermen yelling for them to open up.

'Must come quickly,' the man said as he stepped back the moment the door inched open. 'Roun'ouse,' He yelled, moving further back. 'Burnt t'groun.'

Skaldric was the first to gather his wits. Zak grabbed his hooded fleece and ran to catch up with him.

'Best thing that can happen,' Zak said as he caught up. 'Fire kills the spirit of the sickness—stops it jumping from folk to folk.'

Without slowing his pace, Skaldric hissed, 'My wife's body is in there. Have you no feeling? You know we must honour our dead—otherwise we are nothing but savages—no better than boars roaming wild in the forest.'

Zak pulled on Skaldric's arm, slowing the clan's chief. 'You are letting your heart cloud your mind. You are supposed to be

our leader, those in the Roundhouse are dead—we can do no more for them. And when our people regain their strength, we will build a memorial and give them a burial fit for kings.'

Inside Skaldric's head came the voice he was now getting used to hearing. It told him that Zak spoke with wisdom. He stopped and looked into the young man's eyes. 'I just had a vision of that memorial. You are right, Zak, son of Sarash, we can build a splendid place to bury our loved ones—it will be the first thing ships will see when they enter the lake.'

'Yes—I see it too. And above the rocky slopes where the water runs over black slabs is another kind of rock. One that is white. I can see a great monument built of white rock.'

Skaldric slapped Zak's back, 'Okay,' he said, 'but first I need to spend a moment with our dead people—see what damage the fire has done—will you join me in the grim task?'

The journey towards the wharf took time, Elvad delaying as much as he could by insisting they caught fresh meat on the way—enough to see them through several weeks.

'But you said you had stored provisions,' said Volta.

'I do—but there is no saying the fishermen haven't had need of them, or perhaps the lovely ladies who bring pleasure to the seafarers are hungry.'

'I worry our delay will worsen our people's plight — I am not cut out for leadership.'

'You doubt your own capabilities too much—you are doing very well. You have brought your people so far—and safeguarded an heir for your chief.' Elvad looked across to the women, the mother suckling her baby acknowledged his kind words with a shy smile. He coughed, smiled with equal shyness and turned his attention back to Volta. 'The woodlands over yonder has good game. Dion can teach the two boys to hunt. The women can teach the girls to cure the meat—it will keep their minds off what lies ahead.'

'And delay us further.'

'With luck, yes.'

Volta looked across to the women, they nodded their agreement with Elvad's words. 'Alright,' he said at length, 'I will help you make camp for another few nights.'

"Good.' Elvad gave the women a sly wink, 'there is a sheltered cove ahead, Dion and I used it on our journey up, it has a stream and where the water trickles into the lake, undercurrents are full of fish. All we have to do is break the surface ice and drop in a line or two.'

They stood on the top of the hill and looked down. Smoke curled around the debris that was once the largest building Zak and Skaldric had ever seen. Standing on the shore, surviving members of the clan, stood side by side with the fishing community. Zak turned away allowing the chief a moment of reflection before urging him on.

'They're following us,' Skaldric was saying, 'they too wish to mourn their dead in the correct way.'

Zak pulled on Skaldric's sleeve. 'Perhaps they do, but come,' he urged, 'I will show you what caused the water to be fouled.'

'You said it was the latrines.'

'Yeah, and it was—but other times, I think the hovels up here have brought the fever from those inhabiting them to jump to those by the lake.'

Skaldric hesitated. 'Why are you so sure it won't jump into us again?'

'Because Elvad said so.'

'I thought you disliked the views of foreigners.'

'I do.'

'Then why are you quoting them now?'

'Because when we rebuild this place, I don't want us to make the same mistakes. Whether I like him or not has nothing to do with anything, he spoke wisdom, and that I have to acknowledge.'

'You have grown, Zak, my man.'

Zak nodded, 'I prayed for the gods to give me wisdom, and when it came, it was from a foreigner's tongue, the last place I looked to hear it.'

Skaldric's arm across Zak's broad shoulders showed real fatherly tenderness. Zak allowed it to rest there, waiting for the chief to speak. 'If we rebuild the wharf, what then of your dreams for our settlement?'

'I don't know—but this...' Zak unhooked himself from the embrace and stepped up to the rim of the hill where below, the

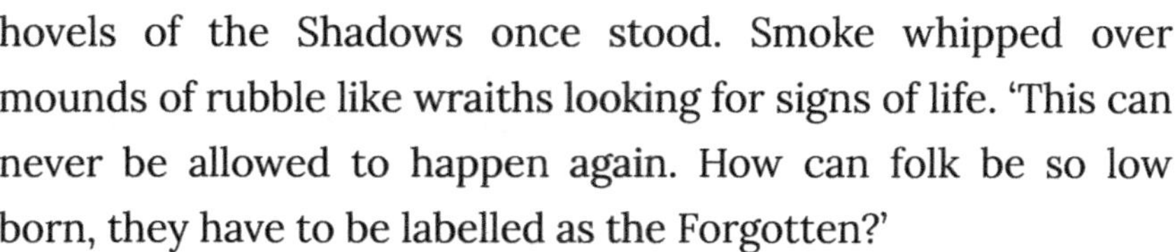

hovels of the Shadows once stood. Smoke whipped over mounds of rubble like wraiths looking for signs of life. 'This can never be allowed to happen again. How can folk be so low born, they have to be labelled as the Forgotten?'

Skaldric came to his side. 'What was it?'

'Something of the past.' Zak took Skaldric's shoulders. 'Will you help me build my dream?'

'Here?'

Zak's eyes shone. 'Why not?'

Skaldric rubbed his chin. Inside his head the voice whispered, *why not!* 'We don't have enough people left to return to the settlement. Yes Zak, son of Sarash, I will help you build your dream. I will help you build a strong citadel that will withstand prowling wolves, but first, we honour our dead.'

Chapter Forty-Three

It was the Equinox and as promised, the youngest sons of Skaldric were making their journey back to reunite with their clan.

Three ships had departed from their separate islands, each bearing gifts and loved ones. Not knowing what to expect, the captains of each ship agreed to enter the lake at different times. They agreed to slow the oarsmen's strokes so as to scan the area for life before disembarking.

Bryn's ship was the first to arrive in the lake. Immediately, he noted that the previous landmark was no longer there. Instead of the dominant Roundhouse, a row of gleaming foundation stones stood on the site, dazzling white in the mid-day sunshine.

Animals grazed on the hills beyond the white stone building and here and there, a lone figure tended some crop or other. No living person stood on the wharf and the air had a strange eeriness to it. Birds swooped and dived as was usual, bees buzzed over spring flowers, and here and there, goats bleated. Another sound echoed from the craggy hills to the south. Bryn recognised it—quarrying—but somehow it didn't fit the tranquil lakeside landscape.

Skaldric looked up from his work, wiped the sweat from his brow and straightened his back. He glanced across the lake and blinked. 'Zak?' His whisper barely heard, his voice coated with dust, 'is that the fire headed giant's boat?'

Both men walked around the new edifice to watch the brightly painted ship manoeuvre through the lake, oars cutting arrow-shaped wakes across the surface before turning to bring her gently into dock

Both men had an immediate thought of a heart-shaped face with violet coloured eyes.

'I wonder if he has news of Perak?'

'And your boys, Skaldric, don't forget your boys.'

'Yes—of course, I meant my boys too. And Cadic, your brother.'

Putting aside their tools, they ran down the hill, shaking off dust, sending clouds of white powder billowing behind them. Others too had noticed the ship. Volta, for one, was tending his goats when he looked up and saw the ship pull alongside the wharf. He carried the pails of fresh milk to the new dairy and called by the kitchen to announce the arrival of a ship.

In tiny groups, the survivors edged to the rickety old wharf —afraid to go near the visitors, lest they carried sickness. Yet

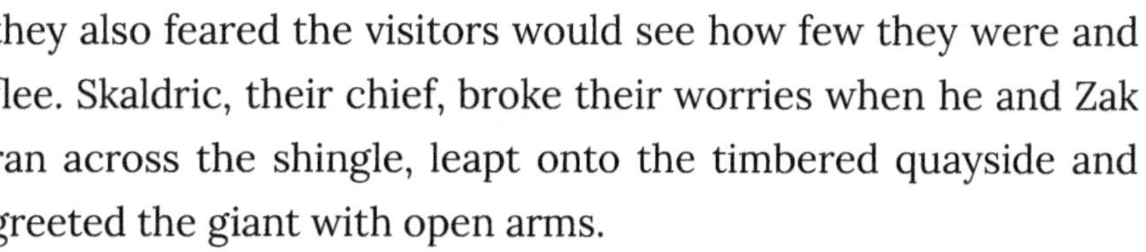

they also feared the visitors would see how few they were and flee. Skaldric, their chief, broke their worries when he and Zak ran across the shingle, leapt onto the timbered quayside and greeted the giant with open arms.

Whilst the tiny welcome committee gathered around their leaders, the ship's crew began to unload crates. Skaldric suddenly aged, he gestured towards the huge stack. 'I am sorry captain, but we are in no position to do trade with you.'

Bryn whispered, 'Not trade my friend, spoils of war, sent from your daughter, also some from Yorevyn's lady, and some from my wife.'

'But I don't understand?'

'You will, my friend, but the telling will have to wait. My ship came ahead to help you prepare to receive more visitors.' Bryn turned to Zak. 'You look well, my friend, better than last I saw you.' The giant gave a quick glance up and down the wharf. 'Tell me, have you news of our king's son? And that little mite?'

'They are well.'

'Good,' Bryn leaned his head down, bringing it to Zak's level, 'then where are they?'

'Hunting.' Skaldric interrupted, 'They will return before sundown, meanwhile, there are two lodging houses still empty, that is the only accommodation I can offer.'

'No need—we will sleep on the ship.' Bryn beamed. 'We have brought food, and enough braziers and coals to light up the shore,' he slapped Skaldric's back, coughed when a cloud of white dust hit his face, 'and a couple of casks to take that chalky dust away from our throats, eh my friend?'

As the sun began to dip, Kaylak's ship neared the wharf. He held onto the neck of his ship's prow guiding his men to dock by the side of the giant's. His bride-to-be leaned over the rail, straining her eyes to find the faces of her parents. She took in a sharp breath when she spotted her father stood by Zak.

'Dada!' she yelled as the ship rocked and jostled against the wharf. Kaylak ran to steady her, taking her hand as though she were a child, patting it with care. 'Where's mama?' She asked, her eyes flicking across the almost deserted wharf.

'Perhaps, beloved, she wishes to beautify herself before greeting you.'

Perak nodded, 'Yes, that will be it. I feared dada would have taken our people back to the settlement. Normally, he's so keen to leave before the thaw.'

Suddenly Kaylak swallowed. She was right—the clan should've returned to their home in the purple mountains. His eyes searched the area—but the sun was setting and the braziers lighting the shore threw more darkness on the landscape behind. He looked to where the Roundhouse once stood and saw another building under construction in its place —pale yet solid.

'Beloved?' Kaylak asked softly, not wishing to alarm her. 'Those gathered to welcome us, are some missing?'

She scanned the meagre crowd and nodded, 'Lots and lots— perhaps they too are beautifying themselves.'

Sensing foreboding she did not, Kaylak squeezed her hand. 'It is—I think, the time you shed your girlish tendencies. I fear there may be a reason other than beautification that keeps the numbers down.' When she turned her lovely eyes on him, he felt his heart ready to break. 'Come, my angel, we must ready ourselves to meet with your dada.'

The sun was setting by the time the third ship docked. Yorevyn and Methiu had already assessed the numbers of those gathering on the shore.

'It's as you feared, I think.'

'Aye,' Yorevyn let out a ragged breath, 'I must grab hold of Cadic and Perak's young brothers. They need to prepare themselves for bad news.'

Methiu watched him move among the crew, lean forward to speak to Zak's brother, then on to where the two boys were. He glanced back to where Mira and Fiedra were stood, gave them a sideways nod, his eyes informing them of Yorevyn's mission.

Mira turned to the gathering on the shore. Perak was wrapped in her father's arms. Kaylak spotted Cadic leaving the ship and moving towards him, ready to meet up. The two boys ran past them, engulfed in Skaldric's fatherly embrace, leaving Perak alone for Zak to comfort.

Mira turned to Fiedra, 'Why didn't we see this sickness?'

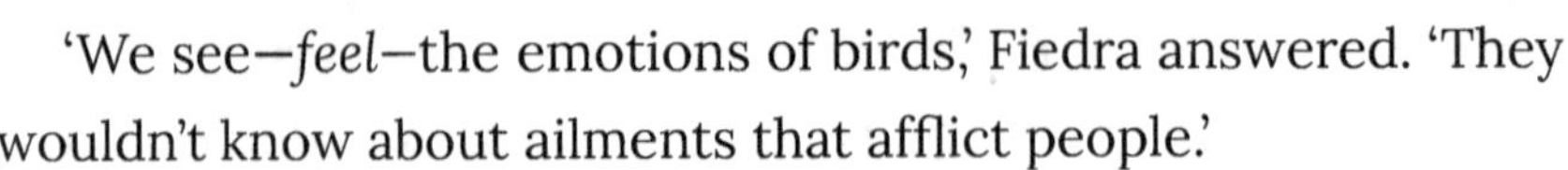

'We see—*feel*—the emotions of birds,' Fiedra answered. 'They wouldn't know about ailments that afflict people.'

'No, they wouldn't. Like poor Dandijack—I'll never know how his feet got burnt.'

'I'll bet my mother's spirit does.'

'Aye—I'll wager you are right. I wonder where she is?'

They waited whilst the ship's crew tied her up. Both women were deep in thought, watching the seafaring men go about their tasks, making their work look easy. A sparrow fluttered by and landed on the capstan. Mira narrowed her eyes, 'Do you see what I see Fiedra?'

'I see her grandma, I see her.'

When Yorevyn and Methiu helped their ladies disembark, most of the people had gathered by the braziers. All of them stood in little groups, huddled together in low conversation. Fiedra saw Kira crying happy tears with Cadic, as he lifted Zak's baby high and threw him, the baby's chuckle carrying across the shale when he was caught and thrown up again. For a moment the sadness evaporated, filling Fiedra with hope that given time, they would heal.

A cry of joy broke the spell, taking her eyes to where the noise came from. Yorevyn focused uphill and saw Elvad running down towards them. Before him was the little boy Meg

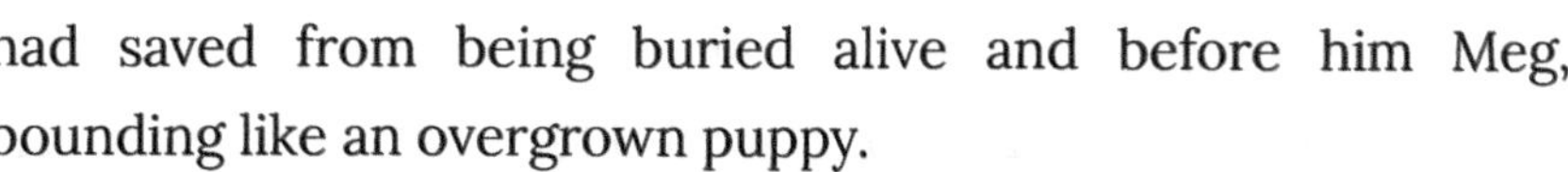

had saved from being buried alive and before him Meg, bounding like an overgrown puppy.

Fiedra heard Yorevyn's voice yelling to warn her—but too late. The hound's bulk and enthusiasm came upon them knocking the two females to the ground sending them sprawling across the wooden planking of the walkway.

Yorevyn took a deep breath, reached to help his ladies to their feet and emptied his lungs with gratitude when he saw no harm had been done. He turned to Methiu, who was being mauled with canine affection, then to Elvad whose arms were outstretched pulling him into manly embrace and whispered in his ear, 'What's that foreign saying that means, "I think this has happened before"?'

Later, after the sun had set and people had begun to relax from the heavy emotions of reunion and recounting horrors, Fiedra wandered to where Perak was stood, took her hand and whispered, 'Come, walk with me. Tell me your thoughts.'

'I have no thoughts. I feel numb.'

'Yes, I can see, but it should help you to share your thoughts with me. I am your friend still. Don't ever forget that.'

Perak turned her pale eyes onto Fiedra. 'Mama told me that the bond between daughter and mother could never be broken. Not through distance, nor time, not even death. She was wrong.'

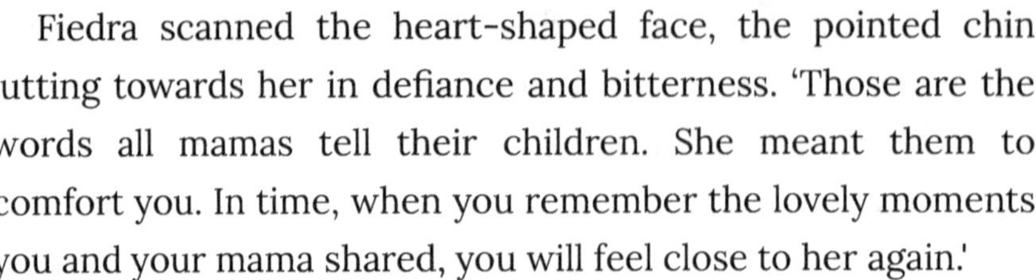

Fiedra scanned the heart-shaped face, the pointed chin jutting towards her in defiance and bitterness. 'Those are the words all mamas tell their children. She meant them to comfort you. In time, when you remember the lovely moments you and your mama shared, you will feel close to her again.'

'I should have *felt* she was dying.'

'Why?'

'Because mama and I always felt each other's emotions.'

Fiedra raised an eyebrow. 'And your dada, did you feel his emotions too?'

'Of course not,' snapped Perak, 'dada is a man. Only mamas and daughters share thoughts. Honestly, Fiedra, don't you know anything?'

'I am a witch of the Plain's bastard, I'm not allowed to know such things.'

Perak gave Fiedra a strange look. Her eyes suddenly cold in the faint light, 'There is a voice that speaks to me. I mistook her for mama and she did not correct me. Do you know who she might be?'

Involuntarily, Fiedra's eyes moved to where Skaldric was sitting with the menfolk, and to the little bird asleep in a bush nearby. It was a sparrow very similar to the one that hovered by the chief after the boat docked on the wharf.

Before she could answer, Perak walked past. Her face caught in the light of the braziers, her lips tight and peevish. Fiedra watched Perak return to her group. She saw Zak was ready to escort her to where Skaldric was sitting. She took a deep breath. She was saddened by the mood Perak had taken.

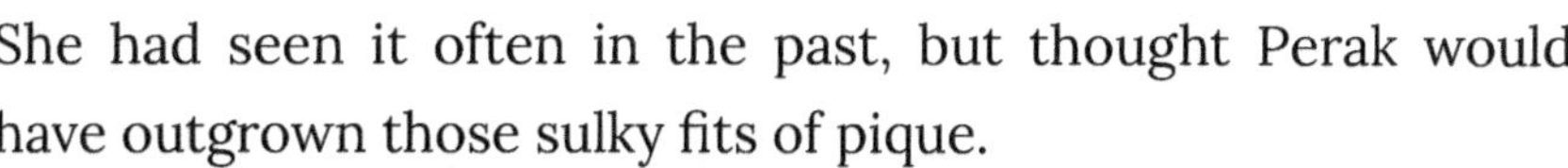

She had seen it often in the past, but thought Perak would have outgrown those sulky fits of pique.

Picking up the hem of her gown, she walked as carefully as she could over the rough shale to join with her husband Yorevyn. He came towards her, slid his hand under her elbow and steadied her across the pebbly surface. She stretched her hand toward his smile, traced a finger over his twisted lips, and whispered, 'Have I ever told you that I love you?'

'Not for at least an hour.'

'Well I do.'

THE Journey Continues...

The echoes of fate do not fade so easily. As one chapter closes, another begins—woven with threads of betrayal, survival, and the relentless pull of destiny.

In *The Gluemaker's Demise*, the past resurfaces with a vengeance. A man who thought himself forgotten is found. The trade that once masked his presence now betrays him, and the ghosts of his youth stir in the shadows. Across the darkened waters, something watches—bearing needle-sharp teeth and a patient hunger. Elsewhere, power shifts, alliances tremble, and a young woman's path twists toward a throne she never sought.

Old debts are coming due—and not all who flee will escape.

ANTICIPATED PUBLICATION AUTUMN 2026

Glossary

Anteroom	A private area in the Roundhouse reserved for women's grooming and preparation.
Apprentice	A young person learning a trade or skill, referenced in ship crews and craftsmen.
Boudoir	Humorous reference to Bryn's makeshift luxurious bath space for Fiedra.
Bryn	Captain of a western ship, known for his fiery red hair, practicality, deep care for family.
Cadic	Zak's brother, more cautious and traditional, often opposing Zak's schemes.
Cairn	A mound of stones built as a grave marker, part of funerary customs.
Chief/Chieftain	Leader of a clan, responsible for governance, protection, and trade.
Clan	An extended family or tribal group, essential to identity and social structure.
Dandijack	A raven, spirit-vehicle for Fiedra's grandmother, watching over family.
Dion	Young boy rescued by Elvad, grows into a companion and learner.
Elder(s)	Senior clan members respected for wisdom and decision-making.
Elvad	Kaylak's brother, skilled healer, becomes guardian to Dion and mentor figure.
Fiedra	Lame girl guided by Marsh Guide, Perak's closest friend, with special spiritual sensitivity.

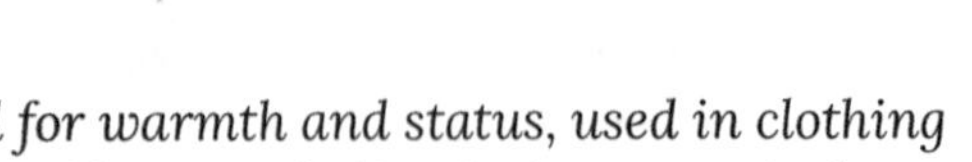

Furs/Fleeces	Vital for warmth and status, used in clothing and bedding, symbolic of winter survival.
Glue-maker	Fiedra's uncle, whose glue is traded with the western ships for weapons and tools.
Kaylak	Suitor and betrothed to Perak, son of Methiu, strong leader from across the Salt Sea.
Kira	Handmaid and confidante to Perak, later shifts loyalty to Zak's family out of necessity.
Krill-eater	Large aquatic creature trapped in the lake, ultimately guided to freedom by Fiedra.
Marsh Guide	Wise woman from the marshes who brings Fiedra to the clan for care.
Marsh Wives	Mysterious, possibly magical women tied to fertility rituals and clan superstitions.
Mead	Fermented honey drink central to feasting and social life.
Methiu	Father of Kaylak and Elvad, king-like figure among westerners.
Midwinter Feast / Solstice	The clan's major ritual festival marked by blessings, songs, and the Shaman's visit.
Mooncap	Fertility plant used in erotic rites and cautionary tales among the clan.
Mowdah	Elder of Skaldric's clan, dies during the sickness that befalls the Roundhouse.
Perak	Daughter of Skaldric and Urdeth, with violet eyes, destined to wed Kaylak.
Roundhouse	Large communal dwelling for clan gatherings, feasts, and protection from winter.
Salted Fish	Preserved staple food, significant in trade with westerners.
Shaman	Revered spiritual leader, brings blessings, guidance, prophetic insight.
Skaldric	Chief of the clan by the lake, father to Perak, married to Urdeth.
Sleigh	Shaman's winter transport pulled by reindeer, its bells herald his arrival.

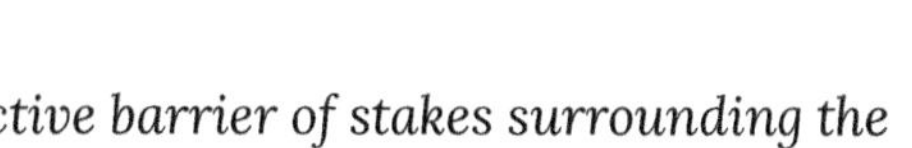
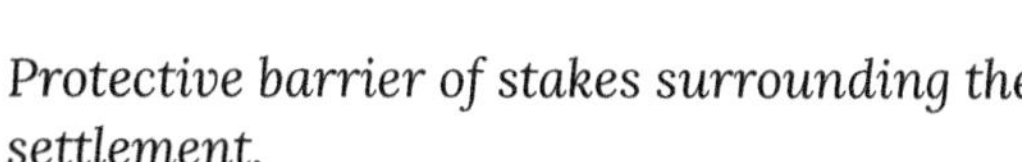

Stockade	Protective barrier of stakes surrounding the settlement.
The Forgotten	The poorest people living on the edge of clan society, ignored and neglected.
The Salt Sea	Great western ocean separating the clan's land from Kaylak's people.
The Shadows	Squalid district where the Forgotten live, marked by disease and poverty.
Urdeth	Wife of Skaldric, mother to Perak, known for her deep empathy and hidden burdens.
Wolfhound/Meg	Loyal large hound belonging to Methiu, protective and sensitive, companion to Elvad.
Yorevyn	Trader from the west, connected with glue trade, facilitator of alliances.
Zak	Ambitious young man seeking change, disrupts tradition, faces tragic consequences.

ABOUT Pat Barnett

Pat Barnett is a storyteller at heart, weaving rich narratives that blur the line between reality and folklore. Now settled in North Yorkshire, where she has lived for fifteen years, her path led her from the hills of North Wales to the sunlit streets of Pomona, Queensland, before finally returning to England's rugged northern landscapes.

Before embracing the writer's life, Pat worked as a nursery nurse in inner-city Manchester, an experience that deepened her understanding of people, relation-ships, and the quiet moments that shape our lives. Though she calls herself a hermit and cherishes the solitude that feeds her creativity, she finds genuine joy in the company of her writing group, *The Wordbotherers*. There, stories and laughter are shared in equal measure.

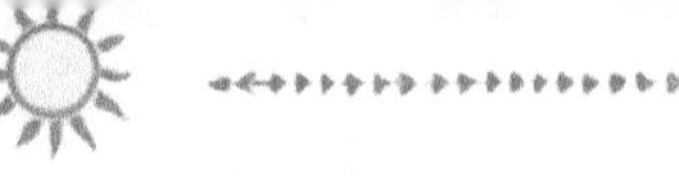
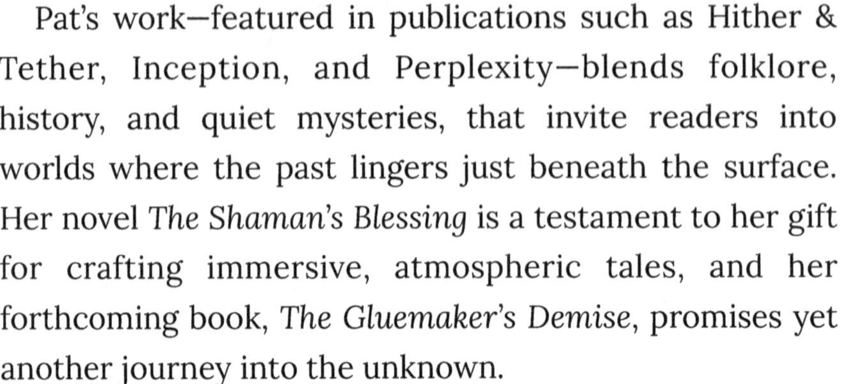

Pat's work—featured in publications such as Hither & Tether, Inception, and Perplexity—blends folklore, history, and quiet mysteries, that invite readers into worlds where the past lingers just beneath the surface. Her novel *The Shaman's Blessing* is a testament to her gift for crafting immersive, atmospheric tales, and her forthcoming book, *The Gluemaker's Demise*, promises yet another journey into the unknown.

When she's not writing, Pat can often be found tackling puzzle books, lost in thought, or deep in conversation with her fellow *Wordbotherers*—always ready for the next tale to be told.

Find out more about Pat and her stories at

www.wordbotherers.com

9 781068 431029